MY FRIEND
THE ENEMY

DAN SMITH

Chicken House

SCHOLASTIC INC. | NEW YORK

Text copyright © 2014 by Dan Smith

All rights reserved. Published by Chicken House, an imprint of Scholastic Inc., *Publishers since 1920*. CHICKEN HOUSE, SCHOLASTIC, and associated logos are trademarks and/or registered trademarks of Scholastic Inc.
www.scholastic.com

First published in the United Kingdom in 2013
by Chicken House, 2 Palmer Street, Frome, Somerset BA11 1DS.
www.doublecluck.com

ISBN 978-0-545-78948-6

10 9 8 7 6 5 4 3 2 1   14 15 16 17 18

Printed in the U.S.A.   40
First printing, September 2014

The text type was set in Adobe Caslon.
The display type was set in Bank Gothic.
Book design by Yaffa Jaskoll

FOR ANISHA AND ASHWIN

SEPTEMBER 1939
Nazi Germany invades Poland. France and Great Britain
declare war on Germany. The British Expeditionary Force
is deployed to Belgium.

JANUARY 1940
Rationing begins in Great Britain.

MAY 1940
Winston Churchill becomes Prime Minister of Great
Britain. Nazi forces invade the countries of Belgium,
Luxembourg, the Netherlands, Denmark, Norway, and France.
Operation Dynamo begins and the British Expeditionary
Force evacuates at Dunkirk in Northern France,
retreating to the south coast of England under heavy
Nazi bombardment. More than 80,000 people from both sides
are killed or injured during the evacuation.

JUNE 1940
Nazi forces occupy France.

JULY 1940
The Battle of Britain begins. London is bombed intensively
during a period known as the Blitz. Nazi bombers also
attack other major cities in Great Britain. Civilians and
industry are targeted.

By OCTOBER 1941 the Battle of Britain was over and the
concentrated bombing of Britain had ended, but sporadic
raids continued throughout the war. Only in 1945 did the
bombs stop falling.

SUMMER 1941

North-East England

"When war came and then the fall of Dunkirk, that narrow belt of land across northern England was a danger point of invasion. Then it was we saw the stuff of the people."

JACK LAWSON, A MAN'S LIFE

CRASH

I was in the far corner of the woods, setting snares, when the siren started.

I stopped.

Crouched low with my arms out, my fingers laying the wire in the right position, I stopped *dead*.

I was quite far from the village — over the fields and deep in the trees — but that terrible noise reached right across to me. As if it were looking for me. Just me. It started as a single tone, a sound so frightening it almost made my heart freeze. Then it grew louder as it warmed up, the tone falling and rising. Falling and rising. A second siren joined it a few moments later, then a third, so all the village sirens were screaming at the sky.

This was the signal for us to run for our shelters.

To run for our lives.

I'd never been caught out in the open like this before. The warning had never sounded during the afternoon. The Germans liked to come on clear nights, filling the air with the buzz and groan of their planes, like angry monsters coming to turn everything to dust. And then it was a fast and scary rush to the

Anderson shelter, to sit in the half dark, waiting for a bomb to land on top of you and blow you into a million pieces.

All the way out here, though, I wasn't sure what to do. I didn't know if I could make it home across the fields to Hawthorn Lodge, to the tin shelter at the bottom of our garden. Or maybe I didn't need to. Maybe I was *already* in the safest place, right there in the trees.

But I didn't want to be on my own. I wanted to be with Mam. I wanted to know she was safe, and she'd want to know I was safe. I imagined her sick with worry, wondering where I was. She wouldn't know whether to run out and call for me or take cover in the shelter. Her heart would be thumping just like mine was. *Thump, thump, thump.* Her mouth would be dry. Her muscles tingling and shaking. She'd be standing in the garden as the planes came over: wave after wave of them, raining their bombs on her, all because she was out looking for me.

I shook my head once and squeezed my eyes shut, straining to get rid of the images. Then I stood and began to run.

Sprinting past the pheasant pens, I hardly noticed the stinging brush of the nettles that caught my bare knees. The twigs crunched and snapped under my feet. The tops of my wellies paddled against my bruised shins. I jumped fallen logs and scraped my legs against brambles. I splashed through the burn and weaved around the trees bordering the cold creek, throwing myself to the ground when I came to the barbed-wire fence and scrambling through the low gap that was made just for me. The skin tore on my knees as I crawled on the dry soil, but I ignored the pain.

I was moving as quickly as I could, clambering from all fours back onto my feet, rushing through the final line of the woods before I burst out into the field. I ran out into the early evening just as another sound broke from behind the terrible cry of the sirens. It was as if this noise smashed through the solid wall, cutting through and drowning it out. And this sound was worse. Much worse.

It was the angry buzz of German bombers filling the sky.

Panic swelled in my chest. I had to get home. I had to find Mam.

I sprinted farther out into the field, wishing I could make one great big jump and be there. I wished my feet would move faster. I wished our house were closer. I wished there were no war. I wished . . . I wished so many things.

But for that moment, it felt like there was nothing else in the world except for me, my need to get home, and the planes. That noise. The sound of engines was so loud, as if the planes were following me, chasing me, whining and coughing like dirty giants. My head was filled with their growling, my whole body shook. I could feel their breath on my neck. Smell their darkness.

But then they stuttered.

Once.

Twice.

Three times.

The engine caught and died, caught and died, and then cut out completely. No more droning, no more coughing, no more stuttering. All I could hear was the scream of the siren in the village and the rush of air behind me, as if an enormous bird of prey were arcing down to take me. In those seconds I knew how a rabbit must feel at that last moment by the hedgerow, when the hawk swoops down to carry it away.

And that's when I risked a look back. Stumbling on the loose soil of the furrowed field, I turned to look over my shoulder and saw the plane coming toward me.

Not a mob of hungry giants, but a single plane. Just one.

A giant metal beast falling, gliding, faster and faster, coming right at me.

I saw the gunner sitting in the glazed front section. He was staring dead ahead, seeing nothing. His eyes were so wide I could see the whites. Both hands were gripped around the machine gun's handle as if it would save him. The gun barrel was sticking out from the plane's glass nose cap, pointing to the exact place where the plane was going to crash.

Behind and above him, I could just about make out the top of the pilot's head, and then I ducked as it went over, no more than thirty feet above me, the wind in its wake ruffling my hair.

I heard the metallic rattle of its parts as it went. I saw the pale gray underbelly of the monster. And then I turned to watch it smash into Mr. Bennett's field.

The ground shook when the German bomber hit the soil. It went down nose first, the glazed nose cap shattering into a thousand pieces, filling the air with splinters of glass. The gunner was crushed in his seat as the nose crumpled, forcing him up and back into the pilot, squashing the two bodies together, mashing them into a mess of blood and bone.

With a deafening screech of metal, both propellers were ripped from the wings. They spun off to either side, slamming into the field several feet from the plane, bouncing away at different angles. Twirling blades of destruction, they tore through the potato plants, throwing thick clouds of dry dirt into the air as they went. If anybody had been in their way, they would have been shredded.

The plane gouged an ugly furrow through the field, plowing the soil in front of it, lifting into the air so it was standing on its nose for a moment. It hung like that for a split second, and I saw the size of the monster, raised up, the tail section painted with the symbol we'd been taught to fear and hate. The Nazi swastika.

Then the plane twisted, its whole weight moving to one side, shearing the right wing with a horrible squeal of tearing metal that was followed by an instant of silence — barely the blink of an eye — and then a tremendous explosion as the first of the fuel tanks erupted with deafening fury.

An orangey-yellow fireball burst from the right side of the plane, belching outward and upward. It spat across the field, reached up to the sky, ripped the wing away, and blew the fuselage in two. Shards of glowing metal spewed into the air, pattering on the soil like heavy raindrops, and then a second explosion broke the larger pieces apart and hurled them aside as if they weighed nothing.

The blast raced at me over the field as a solid wall of sound and heat and stink. It hit me like a demonic fist, forcing me backward, slamming me down into the soil and knocking my breath away. Oven-hot air raced around me, thick with the smell of burning fuel and rubber.

And then everything went dark.

I had an odd light-headed feeling, like I sometimes had when I stood up too quickly. My head spun, my thoughts were muddled. Then it was as if someone reached down, dragged me out of my body, and threw me up into the air. Everything felt numb and I wondered if I was dead. I was far above myself, looking down at my small twelve-year-old body lying in the dirt among the dark green leaves of the potato plants. I was bathed in thick smoke and surrounded by a hundred tiny fires in the places where shrapnel and splashes of fuel burned. But then sounds began to creep in and the smell filled my nostrils. My mouth was thick with the bitter taste of burning. The orange light behind my eyelids darkened and brightened.

When I opened my eyes, I stayed as I was, lying on my back. The smoke circled overhead like a living thing, and I stared at it, but I didn't watch it, because my mind could hardly concentrate as things slowly came back into focus.

I don't know how long I was unconscious, but when I sat up, coughing and shaking my head to rid it of the awful sound that rang in my ears, I saw the plane, a hundred feet away, swallowed by an angry fireball. Black smoke was streaming into the sky, blocking the evening sun, and all around me, small fires flickered among the furrows.

For a moment I thought I heard cries of pain, maybe the death throes of the crew as they burned inside the wreckage, but the explosion was still singing in my ears and the sounds were drowned by the crackling of flames. I tried to stand, but was disoriented, and I looked around, seeing movement from somewhere to the right of the main crash site.

Something caught my eye, making me look up and back toward the trees. The breeze shifted and black smoke swirled, but somewhere through the foul-smelling clouds, I saw the bright white of a silk parachute beyond the woods. A long way off, it looked so small — no bigger than the size of a marble. Then the smoke thickened as it rose and circled over the tree-tops, blocking everything from sight.

It was the summer of 1941 and the weather was good over Northumberland, England, but it felt as if the world were dying. So many things were coming to an end. That day, though, something was just beginning.

AFTERMATH

For what seemed like a long time, I sat in the soil and stared at the burning plane, trying to clear my head. And as some sense came back to me, I looked down and saw how dirty I was. There were streaks of muck all down my shirt, and that was almost worse than being nearly blown up; it had been clean this morning and Mam would be fuming, because I wasn't supposed to get dirty. Soap powder was rationed and we had to wear things for as long as we could before washing them. And, she always told me, the more we washed our clothes, the quicker they would wear out.

"Hell's bells, there you are!" The voice sounded as if it was coming from a long way off. "I was so — Oh, Lord, are you all right? Peter? Peter? Say something!"

I turned to look up at the hill, seeing Mam coming down toward me. She was still wearing her apron and the old slippers she wore in the house. The look on her face was a mixture of terror and relief.

She rushed down, falling to her knees and putting her hands on my cheeks. "What's the matter?" she said as she turned my face this way and that. "Are you hurt? Did you get hurt, Peter?"

"I'm sorry," I said, still dazed. "Sorry, Mam. I'm dirty."

"What?"

"Dirty."

"Never mind about that. Are you hurt?" She didn't even look at the burning plane.

"No."

"You sure?" She continued to inspect me, checking my head and neck. "I was so worried." Her breath was coming in great gasps between each word and her eyes were almost as wide as the German gunner's had been. "Where were you?" Her hands were shaking as she lifted my arms, ran her fingers over my legs. "Your knees," she said. "You're bleedin'."

"Just grazes."

"Can you stand up?"

"I'm fine."

She sat back and stared at me. "I was scared witless." Then she leaned forward again and put her arms around me, pulling me right against her chest and squeezing me tight. "I thought something had happened to you. When I saw you sittin' there, I . . ."

"I'm all right, Mam." I hugged her back. "I'm all right."

"Where were you?"

"In the woods."

"The woods? I thought I told you not to go that far this late in the day. How many times have I told you to stay close to home? Imagine if somethin' happened to you. What would I do if . . ." And then she did something that took me by surprise.

Her hand darted out and she slapped my left cheek. "Don't ever do that again," she said. "And look at the state of you."

"I'm sorry, Mam." I fought back the tears. It hadn't hurt, but I knew I'd done something terrible. "I'm sorry."

Mam nodded. "I know." She put her arms round me again. "I'm sorry 'n' all. Come on, let's get you home."

But before we could stand, we heard voices, and when we looked back, there were children reaching the crest of the hill behind us.

Our house wasn't in the main part of the village, it was just on the other side of the hill, so it hadn't taken Mam long to get here. She probably started running just after she heard the sirens and realized she couldn't find me. But now everyone else was coming. The all clear would have been sounded and everyone would have come out from their shelters and seen the smoke over the field. Now the whole village was rushing to see it.

Standing silhouetted at the top of the hill, they stopped and watched the flames, the black smoke, afraid to come closer. Then the adults came, passing the children, their pace slowing as they descended the hill. There were men carrying sticks and shovels and pitchforks. There were men from the Home Guard, too. They weren't in uniform, but they'd brought their Ross rifles and were holding them to their shoulders, training their sights on the burning aircraft.

And then there were the soldiers who had taken over Bennett Hall and the farm close to the beach. A whole truck-load of them was arriving now, following a jeep that drove out into the field and skidded to a halt close by.

A soldier jumped out from the vehicle shouting, "What the

hell are you doing here?" He was a short, stocky man with a thin nose and a mouth that opened more on one side than the other when he shouted. The three stripes on his left arm told me he was a sergeant.

"Get them away from here," he yelled, and two other soldiers leaped from the back of the jeep and hurried past the sergeant toward us.

One of them dragged me to my feet while the other grabbed Mam and, as the sergeant continued to bark orders, the soldiers took us back to where the crowd had gathered, and the people parted as they took us through.

"Need a medic over here," the soldier said, leading me up the hill. His grip was firm on my wrist.

When we reached the top, he told me to sit down, and within a few seconds Mam was crouching beside me. A few of the children circled around us to see what was going on, but it didn't take them long to realize that watching the burning plane was more exciting.

Doctor Jacobs came over, wearing a jacket with patched elbows, taking a white medical bag from over his shoulder. "I'll see to him," he said. "I know Peter."

The soldier looked him up and down.

"I'm Doctor Jacobs," the older man said, holding up his medical bag, displaying the red cross on it. "I picked this up on the way over, just in case . . ." Then he seemed to remember he wasn't in uniform and that the soldier wouldn't know who he was, so he stood to attention and saluted. "*Private* Jacobs," he said. "Home Guard."

The soldier considered him for a moment longer, looking back at the wreck as if he couldn't make up his mind what to do.

The real soldiers didn't take the Home Guard very seriously because some of them were quite old and, at first, they didn't have any supplies so they had to pretend they had rifles when they practiced on the green. People used to watch them and laugh, but the soldier who had pulled me up the hill probably just wanted to get back to where the excitement was, so he sighed and waved a hand at Doctor Jacobs. "All right, then. Get on with it." And, with that, he went back down the hill.

Doctor Jacobs crouched beside me and put his bag on the ground. "You feeling all right, Peter?"

"I think so," I said.

"Well, you've got a few cuts and scrapes. Let's clean those up, shall we?" He unfastened the bag and rummaged through the bandages and dressings before pulling out a bottle of disinfectant and some cotton balls.

"So how did you do this?" he asked, dabbing the Dettol onto my knee, wiping away the blood. "In too much of a hurry to see the crash?"

"He was right there," Mam said. "Right there when it happened."

Doctor Jacobs looked up from what he was doing. "You saw it happen?"

I nodded.

"Must have been quite something," he said.

"Quite somethin'?" Mam said. "He could've been killed. Stupid lad. I've told him so many times not to —"

"Well, he seems fine to me," he said. "Just scraped knees, that's all."

I looked at my knee, seeing how small the graze was now

that Doctor Jacobs had cleaned away the blood. It looked like nothing at all.

"Doesn't even need a bandage," he said.

"Did I hear that right?" a voice said behind me. "You saw the plane crash?" I recognized the voice straightaway, because Mr. Bennett was the only person I knew who didn't have an accent like mine. His was much posher.

Mam got to her feet beside me. "Mr. Bennett," she said, smoothing down her apron. "I didn't see you there."

"Mrs. Dixon." He nodded once at Mam, then looked down at me. "Peter. Glad to see you're not too badly hurt," he said. "Always good to have a small wound so people know you were there, though, eh?"

Maybe he said that because he had a big scar of his own. It was on the right side of his face and ran from just beside his eye to about the middle of his cheek. I heard he got it at Dunkirk, but no one seemed to know what really happened.

"I got this climbin' under a fence," I said. "Not from any crash."

"Well, you don't need to tell people that, do you?" He looked out at the plane. "Bloody Germans ruining all my potatoes. Don't they have anything better to do?"

"Well, I don't s'pose it was the tatties they were after," Mam said.

"Maybe it *was*," I answered.

I knew that the bombers came from their base in Norway to attack the shipyards in Newcastle where aircraft carriers and submarines were being built. But sometimes they bombed farms, using the Farne Islands or Dunstanburgh Castle as landmarks.

One night we saw them bombing farther down the coast, and it looked as if the whole place was on fire. Incendiaries had showered one of the villages, burning churches and farm buildings and homes.

Mr. Bennett nodded and pursed his lips. "Maybe," he said. "Maybe they *are* after the crops."

He was about Dad's age, but he wasn't anything like Dad. My dad worked hard for everything. Before he went away to win the war, he worked all day and all night on the estate. Gamekeeping, Dad said, was a full-time job. Mr. Bennett, though, he *owned* the estate. In fact, he owned most of the land around the village. It used to be his dad's, but he died of pneumonia just before the war and Mr. Bennett got everything. The fields were his. The ground we were standing on was his. The woods where I'd been playing were his. Even the house we lived in was his.

Dad said it must be nice to be born with a silver spoon in your mouth, but whatever Mr. Bennett's spoon was made of, it didn't keep him in his own house. It seemed like Mr. Bennett was always coming to ours, bringing us things, being nice to Mam. It would have probably been all right, except that some of the other boys had noticed and started to rib me about it.

"Or maybe they were looking for the air force station at Acklington," said Mr. Bennett.

"Do you really think so?" Mam asked.

"It wouldn't be the first time they've tried it," Doctor Jacobs agreed.

Mr. Bennett was watching Mam with a serious expression. "I shouldn't worry," he said to her. "They probably just lost their way. We're quite safe here." I think he was just trying to make

Mam feel better, though. I didn't think any of us were safe, wherever we were. It seemed like the Germans didn't care who they killed. Sometimes the planes just emptied their bays for the return flight home, dropping unused bombs right on top of whatever lay under the flight path. It made the planes use less fuel. That's what our lives were worth to them: a few gallons of fuel.

"I reckon they got shot," I said, standing up. "That's why it was on its own. It was comin' from Bamburgh way, and they've got anti-aircraft guns up there. I heard the engines just before it crashed, I did. Sounded like it got shot and needed somewhere to land."

"Good thinking, Peter." Mr. Bennett pointed a finger at me. "You might just be right."

"Well, whatever the reason," Mam said, "it's time to go home. Come on, pet, we need to get you cleaned up."

I looked over at the spot where the other boys and girls had gathered to watch the burning wreck. The sergeant had organized soldiers to stand in front of them, keeping them from going any closer, and was telling them to stay back, but I could see he didn't want to be there. Like everyone else, he wanted to be a part of it. He was facing the children but kept looking over his shoulder to see what was happening.

There were four groups on the hill now. The children, the adults from the village, the soldiers, and the men from the Home Guard. The soldiers were mostly at the bottom of the hill, taking orders, deciding how they were going to deal with the crash site. The Home Guardsmen were watching closely, trying to get involved, and Doctor Jacobs excused himself from us as soon as he could, hurrying down to be in the thick of it. Everyone wanted to be there, to be part of the action — me included. Everyone, that is, apart from Mam.

"Come on," she said. "Home."

"Aww, Mam . . ." I hesitated and looked down at the wreckage of the plane lying in the middle of the field. Here, on the hill, the ground was too awkward for the tractor, so the grass was kept for the small flock of sheep that now roamed it. I glanced to my left, where the hill dropped down to another field of vegetables planted in regimented lines like leafy soldiers. Beyond that, on the other side of a narrow track, was Hawthorn Lodge, where I lived with Mam. Our house was a gray stone building and Mam always kept the window boxes bonny with orange nasturtiums, but the rest of the garden was turned over to growing vegetables. The Germans kept blowing up our supply ships, so Mam said it was our duty to dig for victory even if we were already surrounded by potatoes and sheep.

In the far corner of the garden there was a small henhouse encircled by chicken wire. Close by was the netty — the outside toilet — and, next to that, our Anderson shelter, all covered with dirt so we could grow peas over the top of it. The shelter doubled up as a garden shed, and we kept all our tools in there — tidied at the back, of course, otherwise Mr. Charlton, the Air Raid Precautions warden, would have something to say about it. I don't know why it was called an Anderson shelter, but when they were delivered to the village, Mrs. Armstrong said they could call them whatever they liked — if she was going to meet her maker then she wanted to do it from the comfort of her own bed, not in a hacky tube at the bottom of her garden. It was only when a rumor went around that a low-flying German plane had machine-gunned a man on Bracken Hill that people started to run for the shelters when the warning came.

"Can't we stay a bit longer?" I asked, looking back at the burning wreck.

"No."

"Aww, but —"

"No buts, Peter. Home."

Mr. Bennett came a little closer to Mam. "Why don't you let him stay?" he said, gesturing at the other boys. "All his friends are here. You don't want him to be the only one."

Mam narrowed her eyes.

"Look," Mr. Bennett carried on. "Everything's safe now. The soldiers are here, the raid's over. Let him go and sit with his friends."

"I don't think —"

"Tell you what," he said. "I'll take you home, and Peter can stay here a while longer. Then I'll come back and chase him home myself —"

"You don't have to do that."

"Why not give him a few minutes?"

Mam's face relaxed.

"Please?" I begged.

"What do you say?" Mr. Bennett asked.

And then Mam caved in. Not to me, but to Mr. Bennett. "A few minutes," she said.

Mr. Bennett winked at me. "Go on, then, quick. Before she changes her mind."

KIM

The other boys spotted me coming over, and a few of them started asking questions before I'd even got to them.

"Is it true you saw it come down?" asked Jonathan. "Did you see it blow up?"

"How close were you?" asked someone else.

"What was it like?"

"Did you get hurt?"

I answered their questions, half enjoying the attention, half hating it. The plane continued to burn as I told them what happened, and the air was still heavy with the smell of fuel and burning rubber. But they were distracted by the sound of a motor, and everyone turned to watch an army fire engine making its way across the field. The driver was careful to keep the green tanker off the crops, but once he came to the scar left by the crash, he drove right out into the field and stopped not far from the wreck. The lieutenant in charge started shouting orders and then they were all rushing about, busying themselves trying to put out the fire.

Everyone was quiet for a while, watching the flames die

back, until Tom Chambers, one of the boys from my class at school, said, "What about the parachute? I saw a parachute."

"Me too," Alan Parson added, but all eyes were on Tom because he was the first to say it.

In all the excitement, I'd forgotten about it. I'd seen it just after the crash, disappearing behind the thick smoke.

"Parachute?" asked the sergeant who was there to stop us from trying to get closer to the plane. "There was a parachute?" He was wearing a uniform that looked to be made of itchy wool, with puttees above his gleaming boots and a rifle over his shoulder. The three stripes on his arm looked clean and new, as if they'd just been stitched on.

"Aye," Tom Chambers stepped forward, pleased for the attention. "Aye. Maybe even two, like. Three. I don't know."

"Three?"

"There was only one," said Alan.

"Where?" asked the sergeant.

"Over there." Tom pointed back across the tops of the trees, in the direction the plane had come from. "I saw it, I did. A long way off. Maybe over Armstrong's place."

"You're sure about this?"

"Aye."

And then all the children were nodding, even the ones who hadn't seen it. I wondered how it was that none of the soldiers had seen the parachute, but the sky *was* full of black smoke, and everybody would have been watching that, not looking for a parachute.

The sergeant told us to stay right where we were, and hurried down the hill, going straight to the man in charge. The lieutenant was tall and strong-looking, with a cap on his head and a mustache on his lip.

They spoke for a moment, the sergeant turning to point up at us, then both men climbed the hill to where we were waiting.

"Who saw this parachute, then?" said the lieutenant when he reached the top. He stood with his hands behind his back, his right wrist resting on the flap of his holster, and he was slightly out of breath.

"This one, Lieutenant." The sergeant pointed at Tom Chambers.

"Is this some kind of joke? Because if it is —"

"It's no joke, mister. I really saw it."

"Aye, it's true," said Alan Parson.

The lieutenant looked around at each one of us. "Did anyone else see this parachute?"

I put up my hand, along with most of the other children.

"You're sure?" asked the sergeant. "Because there'll be trouble if you're lying." He leaned forward and looked at each of us in turn, furrowing his brow and staring as if he could see right into our heads and pick out the lies.

After a moment, almost everyone dropped their hand so that only three of us were still holding them up.

"That's what I thought," said the sergeant. "I know how to deal with this lot, Lieutenant. It's all games to them."

"Thank you, Sergeant," the lieutenant said without looking at him. "And you boys saw it over that way?" He pointed across at the place in the sky where I'd seen the parachute.

The three of us nodded.

"Right, then." He turned to the sergeant. "Well done, Sergeant Wilkes. As you were." And with that, he turned and marched away.

When he reached the bottom of the hill, the lieutenant shouted an order and all the men stopped what they were doing and ran over to stand in front of him. He issued instructions to the full-time soldiers and to the Home Guard, and then they started leaving the crash site, moving away in small groups until only the lieutenant remained, along with a handful of men who stayed to douse what was left of the fire.

"Don't you worry," said Sergeant Wilkes. "We'll find that Jerry in no time. We've got good men looking for him now." He puffed himself up a bit. "Good men like me. It's all under control."

"You really think you'll catch a German, mister?" Tom Chambers asked.

"You just watch." The sergeant came closer to us and crouched to our level. "We'll get 'im, you can bet on it."

"What you gonna do when you get 'im, like?"

"What do you think?" He tapped one hand on the stock of his rifle and grinned like a wolf. "If I see him, he doesn't stand a chance. I can put a bullet through a rabbit's eye at five hundred yards, you know."

"Really? That far?" Tom Chambers couldn't hide his wonder, but he probably didn't even know how far five hundred yards was.

"Maybe even farther," said the sergeant. "So don't you worry, we'll give 'im what every sackless Jerry deserves. Just like we got that plane."

Some of the boys laughed and punched fists in the air. "We showed 'em!"

"We didn't show them anything," someone mumbled beside me. "It crashed."

"What's that you said?" Sergeant Wilkes stood up quickly and looked about with a flash of anger, but everyone fell silent, some of the boys shaking their heads. The soldier waited a few seconds, scanning our faces, then he scowled and stepped back, turning to watch the men dampening the fire.

But I knew who had said it. Beside me there was a girl I didn't recognize. I hadn't noticed her before because she was sitting so quietly, just watching what was going on. She was a little taller than I was, and her hair was the blackest I'd ever seen. The only other person I knew with hair as black as that was Mrs. Robertson, but she was old and everyone knew hers was dyed. The girl beside me didn't have dyed hair, though. Hers was natural, and when the evening sun caught it just right, as it did now, it looked as if it had bits of blue in it.

I didn't speak to her, I just looked at her, but she didn't seem to notice me looking. She was concentrating on what the soldiers were doing at the foot of the hill. And as she watched them, she tightened her lips, chewing the inside of her pale cheek.

"It's a Heinkel," she said. "I wonder why it was flying here."

I glanced around, wondering if she was talking to herself or someone else.

"I'm talking to you." She looked sideways at me.

"Hm? Me?"

"Yeah, you." She turned so her brown eyes were looking into mine. "You saw it crash, didn't you?"

"Aye. Came right over the top of me. Knocked me off me feet when it blew up, it did."

"Lucky beggar." Then she looked away and continued watching the soldiers as some of the villagers grew bored and started heading home, taking their children with them. A few of us stayed, though, ten or eleven of us waiting at the top of the hill on the warm grass.

I sat with my legs crossed and my elbows on my knees, casting my eyes sideways from time to time, snatching glimpses of the girl, but she didn't speak again. She just stared ahead, fascinated by the crash site, taking in every detail, not missing a thing. She even seemed to sit up a little straighter when the fire started to die down and one of the soldiers was ordered to inspect the plane.

The young soldier approached slowly, leaning his body away from the smoldering beast as if that would make any difference at all. He called back to the lieutenant that it was too hot to get any closer, and he walked around the area, looking for anything of interest.

"You think they're looking for bodies?" the girl asked when the soldier disappeared behind the twisted metal.

She hadn't said anything for some time and I turned to her, studying her features for a moment before she looked at me.

"D'you think that's what they're doing?" she asked, raising her eyebrows at me.

"I s'pose," I said. "Aye. Maybe." But really I hadn't even thought much about the people in the plane. Not until right then, when I remembered the gunner, terrified as the ground came at him.

"As many as a five-man crew, that thing, you know. You think they all died? Apart from the parachutist, that is."

"How do you know about that, like?"

"I saw him, too."

"No, I mean how d'you know how many people are in a plane like that?"

She shrugged. "Everyone knows, don't they?"

"I don't."

She made a noise as if she were laughing through her nose. A quick rush of air accompanied by a half smile. "My dad told me. *And* my brother's a pilot."

"Is he?"

"Yeah. And anyway, I've seen a hundred of those planes."

"Honest?"

"Yeah."

Down below, the soldier had completed his walk around the wreck and was speaking to the one in charge, but I couldn't hear what he was saying. Behind me, some of the remaining children were growing restless, chattering and starting to mess about.

"How come?" I asked. "Where've you seen hundreds?"

"Well, maybe not *seen* hundreds," she said. "But I've *heard* hundreds."

I looked at her again, wondering why I'd never seen her before. She wasn't dressed like most of the girls I knew. Most of *them* wore dresses or shirts and pinafores, but this girl was dressed more like I was. As if she were a boy. She was wearing a pair of shorts that came to her knees and a blue shirt, open at the neck. She had gray socks, one pulled up and the other ruffled close to her ankle. The only real difference between the way we were dressed was that I was wearing a pair of old wellies and she was wearing shoes. I had some shoes at home, but I wasn't allowed to wear them. Mam was saving them for best, even though they had holes in them. She got them from Mrs. Drake because her son, Matthew, was a few years older than me and had grown out of them. Mam swapped some old dress material for them, then she cut out some stiff card and pushed it into the bottom of the shoes to cover the holes. It wouldn't keep the water out if it rained, she said, but they'd be good enough for best. In the meantime I could wear my wellies, and when they got holes in them, we'd mend them. I'd given my bike up for the collection, to be turned into bullets or guns or something, but we'd kept the inner tubes and they were perfect for repairing Wellington boots.

Mind you, she might have been dressed like me, but she definitely didn't sound like me. She didn't have the same accent — the same one nearly everyone I knew had. She sounded more like the voices I heard on the wireless, or maybe like Mr. Bennett. She made the words seem bigger somehow. More important. The way she said them made her sound clever, and I liked that a lot. It made me think she was special.

"I used to lie in bed and hear them go over," she said. "Last year, it was like they were coming every night. And then Big Bertha would start up. That's the gun. At least, my mum and dad always call it Big Bertha."

No one I knew said "mum."

"Isn't your da' fightin' the war?" I asked. "Mine is."

"My brother is — he's in the RAF — but my dad's a doctor at the hospital in Newcastle. He wasn't allowed to go to war because he's too important."

"Oh."

"And, of course, then I'd hear the bombs. After the planes, I mean. It's much quieter here. This is the most excitement I've seen since I got here."

I stared at her, the activity at the foot of the hill almost forgotten.

"I'm from Newcastle," she said, "in case you hadn't guessed."

"An evacuee?"

"Kind of. I came here to stay with my aunt because Dad thought I'd be safer, but really I'm just bored. Nothing ever happens here at all, does it? Until now, anyway." She brushed a wisp of hair from her face and looked at me. "Well? Are you going to say something?"

"Er. Aye. I'm Peter."

"I'm Kim." She put out her hand and I thought that was very strange. No girl had ever done that before. Even so, I put out my own and we shook. Her hand was very soft and warm and a little bit sweaty in the palm.

I watched her face, seeing the way her nose turned up slightly at the end. It made her look a bit like a drawing I'd seen in a book about Peter Pan.

She seemed to be studying me, too, then she raised her eyebrows and looked down at our hands joined together. It was as if something clicked into place, reminding us where we were, and I took my hand back, looking around to see if anyone was watching.

"This is pretty exciting, don't you think?" Kim said.

"Aye."

"I bet you don't get many crashes here."

"No. Not many."

"So what's the most exciting thing you've seen? Apart from this?"

I thought for a moment. "Prob'ly when the soldiers first came."

"Doesn't *sound* very exciting."

"Well, it was. They took over Bennett Hall and put up these giant tents and an assault course. They built pillboxes out on the links, too. They're like these little concrete houses with slits in 'em for machine guns and —"

"I know what a pillbox is."

"Oh. Well. They put mines on the beach," I said. "And in the sea. There's tank traps an' these big poles stuck right into the sand to stop gliders from landing."

Kim nodded her approval. "I've seen them."

"There's mines on the links, too," I went on. "We used to play down there all the time, but we're not allowed anymore, in case we get blown up." Then I remembered about Mr. Bennett's young collie that went missing. Everyone said she'd gone onto the links and tripped a mine. *Blown into a cloud of blood and meat,* was what the boys said at school.

"A dog got through the fence on the beach an' exploded," I said.

"Wow. You saw that? What did it look like?" She turned so she was facing me. All her attention was on me.

I shook my head. "I didn't actually see it, but —"

"Doesn't count, then."

"Well, there was the time a mine came ashore. One of them big 'uns with the spikes sticking out all over the place. They had to evacuate half the village."

"Did it explode?" Her eyes sparkled and her face lit up. She was more alive than anything I'd ever seen, and I thought I could look at her all day.

"No." I wanted to make her happy — she seemed so keen for it to have blown up — but I was a terrible liar and was sure that if I tried to make up a story, she'd know it.

"Oh well." She shrugged.

"What about you, like? What's the most excitin' thing you ever saw?"

She puffed out her cheeks and looked up at the sky, as if there were just too many exciting moments to choose from. "I saw a barrage balloon get loose once. It floated all over the place causing all sorts of trouble." She lifted her hand and pretended it was a loose balloon. "And there was the time I saw a parachute caught up on the tail of a plane."

"Was there a man on it?"

Her face took on a grim expression and she nodded. "One of ours."

"Oh."

"Another time a bomb landed just down the street. We were in the shelter when it happened, but it felt like the whole world was coming down around us, and when the raid was over we went out to see half the street gone. Some of the houses were nothing but dust and bricks."

"That must have been *terrifyin'*."

"I suppose so. Anyway, we went out to see who could collect the best souvenirs. I found a piece of the bomb."

"How do you know?"

"That it's a piece of bomb?" She shrugged. "You can just tell. I'll show it to you sometime."

"Maybe I can get a souvenir from this," I said, liking the idea of having a memento of the occasion. Then something occurred to me. "Was anyone in them houses that got bombed?"

"I think so."

And for a second we looked at each other, half understanding what she had just said. There was a touch of embarrassment and we looked back down the hill. We were young enough for the war to bring excitement, but we were also just old enough to feel there was something deeper. Something darker. Lives were being lost.

But the thought was snatched away when someone spoke behind me.

"Hey, did you scrape your knee, puny lad? Did you have to get your mammy to kiss it better?"

Trevor Ridley was fifteen and big for his age. His hands were thick and grubby, his dark hair cut close to his scalp, his face twisted in a permanent scowl. His dad was a farmer and wasn't allowed to fight because his job was too important, but that made Trevor feel left out. While his friends talked about their brave dads, he could only stay quiet. He didn't see it as good luck that his family was unbroken, while other people's had been split. He only saw that he couldn't boast about his soldiering dad, and that made him ashamed.

My dad, on the other hand, had gone away with a uniform and a rifle to battle the Germans, and somehow that didn't seem fair. While my dad was fighting for his life, Trevor Ridley's was tending his animals and growing vegetables that were taken away to be split into rations. And while I desperately wanted my dad to come home, Trevor Ridley wished his would go away. To me, just twelve years old, it seemed as if the whole world had been turned on its head, and I couldn't wait for the war to be over so that everything would be back to normal.

I didn't know how long Trevor and his two friends had been standing there; I hadn't noticed them earlier, but he must have been behind some of the others. Either way, it didn't really make any difference — he was here, which meant I was going to have to leave. I didn't want to. I wanted to stay and talk to Kim, to watch the way her upturned nose wrinkled, to see her chewing at the inside of her cheek. I wanted to see the way the low evening sun turned her hair blue. But, instead, I stood up and turned around, seeing that all the other boys and girls were looking at me, waiting for my reaction.

"You goin' to run away to Mammy?" said Trevor.

"She won't be interested," Bob Cummings said with a laugh. "I saw her goin' home with her fancy man, Mr. Bennett."

I hated it when people said things like that. It made my blood boil.

"Me da' reckons your mam gets whatever she wants from his lordship since your da's not around," said Trevor. "Wouldn't surprise me if you end up livin' with him."

Adam Thornhill snickered like an animal, raising his upper lip to show oversized teeth that made me think of horses. "That's right, isn't it? Mr. Bennett gives your mam what . . . ever . . . she . . . needs."

I couldn't think of anything to say. All those other people watching me like that as Trevor Ridley and his two friends stood there like thugs, the three of them in a line, looking down at me.

The others laughed nervously and I stared at the three boys, feeling my anger rising. Anger mixed with fear, that is. Trevor was bigger than me, older than me, and stronger than me. There wasn't much I could do.

"Why don't you pick on someone your own size?" a voice said, taking me by surprise. In fact, it took everyone by surprise, because no one ever faced up to Ridley and his gang.

Kim stood up beside me, close enough for our shoulders to be touching.

Ridley looked taken aback. "Who the hell are you?"

"Just leave him alone," Kim said.

"You s'posed to be a lad or a lass?" Ridley asked.

"A girl, of course. Which are you supposed to be?"

Ridley opened his mouth to speak, but couldn't think of anything clever to say, so he closed it again.

"Or maybe you're supposed to be a fish," Kim said, opening and closing her own mouth a few times. The insult was followed by a wave of silence. There was the gentle sigh of the evening breeze and the sound of the soldiers working on the wreck, but that was all. The others who were sitting on the crest of the hill had all focused their attention on Kim.

And then the first of them laughed. A girl, no older than seven or eight.

"Shut your gob," Ridley spat, pointing a finger.

The little girl stopped, but Kim carried on taunting him.

"Or maybe you're just a chicken," she said. "Picking on people smaller than you."

And then another child snickered, followed by another, until almost all of them were looking up at Ridley, taking his power away from him.

"Stop it," he said, turning about, glaring at each of them. "Stop it or I'll —"

"Or you'll what?" Kim asked. "Bully them in front of all these grown-ups and soldiers?"

Now Trevor looked over at the adults grouped not far away, the sergeant close by, and the soldiers at the foot of the hill, then he turned back to Kim, red-faced and fuming. He looked as if he was about to say something, but he didn't get the chance, because just then there was a loud crack, a sharp gunshot, and everything erupted into chaos.

"Incoming!" one of the soldiers yelled at his comrades, and they all dived to the ground. "Get down!" he shouted up at the rest of us, waving his arms. "Get down!"

There was a moment of confusion, none of us quite sure what was happening as the adults began screaming and waving at us as they dropped to the grass. It was as if we were frozen to the spot by the sudden madness. Sergeant Wilkes yelled, his face contorting as he hurried over and pulled the first of us to the ground. He threw Tom Chambers down, grabbing other girls and boys, toppling them like trees and shouting like a lunatic before we all began to take cover. More loud cracks split the evening as the machine-gun ammunition, heated by the fire inside the plane, began to go off. The air was filled with the crackle of gunfire. Bullets were whizzing into the sky, zipping overhead, battering the inside of the plane and smacking into the soil around the base of the hill.

One of the soldiers screamed out in pain and doubled up, clutching his thigh.

"He's hit!" another shouted, and began crawling toward the wounded man as blood blossomed on the leg of his uniform trousers, spreading out until they were dark red.

All around, bullets hammered into the field, sending up spurts of loose soil as the soldiers dragged their comrade away. They pulled him backward up the hill until they were at the top, close to us and away from the center of the confusion.

Doctor Jacobs was already waiting for him, down on his knees. He didn't seem to care about the bullets as he went to the wounded man, using blunt-ended scissors to slit open the trouser leg.

It was impossible to see where the bullet had gone in, because it was bleeding so much. I'd never seen anything like it — the most blood I'd ever seen in one go was the time one of the younger boys fell off the wall at school and split his head open. This was much worse, though. The blood was thick and red and kept on flowing, draining out of him and onto the grass. Doctor Jacobs pulled bandages and pads and swabs from his bag and began wiping it away so he could get to the wound. I could hardly take my eyes off it.

When the gunfire settled down, the lieutenant crawled up the hill to the rest of us. "We need to clear this whole area," he said to the sergeant. "Get everybody to move back. Everyone away. No one's to come round here."

For a moment, no one moved. At the bottom of the hill, the plane was becoming quiet. The crackle and spit of the bullets had almost stopped. We tore our eyes from the wounded man and looked at the man in charge.

"Well, go on, then," the sergeant said. "You heard the lieutenant. Clear off. All of you."

Still we watched him.

"Go! Get out of here!"

Now people began to get to their knees and crawl back, moving beyond the top of the hill, where they stood and milled around for a while before the sergeant shooed us away for good.

"And there's a curfew tonight," the lieutenant told us as we left. "No one out after dark. There might be a German on the loose. Keep your eyes peeled."

I was still shaking when Kim and I crossed the field on the other side of the hill and headed toward my house. So much had happened. Seeing the plane crash had been incredible, all the fire and bullets and blood, but it wasn't the best thing that had happened to me that day. Meeting Kim was far more important, and I knew something special had happened. So when we reached the other end of the field and it was time for me to turn home, I wished I had farther to go, that I could walk with her for the rest of the evening.

"Do you really think there's a German on the loose?" I said.

"You saw the parachute, didn't you?"

"Aye."

"Well, then. What do *you* think?"

"Don't know." I thought about the posters of Germans they put up on the village notice board. They always looked so dangerous. "You think we're safe? I mean, if there really is a German wandering about, what d'you think he'd do? You think he'd look for people to kill, or . . ." I shrugged.

"One German?" Kim said. "I don't think there's much he *could* do. There's soldiers everywhere. Anyway, they've probably found him already."

"Aye." I nodded. "Hey, d'you want to come to mine, like?" I asked when we reached the track. "You could have tea. Mam wouldn't mind."

"Can't," she said. "I'd better go back, otherwise . . . well, my aunt doesn't like it when I'm not there on time. I'm already late as it is and she'll be batty with worry, probably. I'm surprised she hasn't come after me."

"Oh. All right." I kicked at a loose stone.

"Can you get out tonight, though?" she asked.

"What?"

"Can you get out? Sneak out, I mean."

"Why?"

"Meet me on the top of the hill at ten o'clock."

"What for?"

"We're going souvenir hunting."

"With that German out there? And the soldier said there's a curfew."

"What's the matter?" Kim said. "You scared?"

"Course not."

"Well, then," she said, starting to run. "I'll see you later."

LETTERS

Mam was standing at the kitchen window, staring out as if she'd been watching for me.

Mr. Bennett was there, too, right beside her, so close they were almost touching.

"Did we miss anything exciting?" he asked when I came in.

I shrugged.

"Don't keep us in suspense." He moved away from Mam and went to the strong wooden table that was right in the middle of the kitchen. It had been there as long as I could remember. And when Mr. Bennett sat down, I thought about how Dad would sit there to clean his shotgun, and Mam would get mad with him for making a mess. Dad would tell her not to get so het up and he'd look across at me and wink as if we were sharing a joke.

There wasn't a gun there now, though. Instead, there were two cups, side by side.

"Well, I don't think much of it at all," said Mam. "It might be excitin' for you young'uns, but all that racket nearly frightened the life out of me. And then all that smoke coming this way, ruinin' my washing? Now everythin' smells and we're on the last of the soap powder and —"

"I might be able to get you some more of that," Mr. Bennett said.

"Oh, I don't want you to go to no bother."

"No trouble at all," he said, lifting his cup and taking a sip. He screwed up his face as if he'd drunk something nasty, then looked into the cup and swallowed hard before putting it back down again. His tea must have gone cold. "Maybe I can get a few bits and pieces for you, too, Peter. I don't suppose you'd say no to a few sweets, eh?"

Just about everything was rationed — clothes, sweets, sugar, meat, tea — but some things were easier for us to get because we lived in the countryside. We had a few hens, so we could get eggs, and we had a bit of a garden, so we could grow vegetables. We kept all the scraps and slops in a bin outside, and Trevor Ridley's dad came on a pony and trap once a week to collect them for the pigs. Sometimes he'd slip us a chop or a couple of slices of bacon as a way of saying thank you, but no one could get the things that Mr. Bennett could.

"That would be nice, wouldn't it?" Mam said. "Mr. Bennett's very kind, isn't he?"

"Mm."

"Well, I won't stay any longer," he said, getting to his feet. "I suppose I should go and find out what's going on with the crash. See if the lieutenant needs anything."

He came close to Mam again, the two of them just a few inches apart.

Mam smiled like she was embarrassed about something, and glanced at me. "Aye. All right. Bye, then."

Mr. Bennett nodded, paused for a moment, then came to ruffle my hair before he turned and let himself out.

When he was gone, I flattened my hair back down with one hand.

"So who was that lad I just saw you with?" Mam said. "Someone new?"

"She's not a lad."

"Really?" Mam went to the window again and looked out, as if Kim might still be there. She stood for a while, just staring out. "Hm, well," she said. "Looked like a lad to me."

"Well, she's not. She's a lass and she's called Kim."

"Excuse me," Mam said in a sarcastic voice as she came back to me. "And how are you feeling, pet? Your knees all right?"

"Fine."

"You feel dizzy at all?" she asked. "Sick? Does anything hurt?"

"No." I sat down at the table.

She nodded gently. "Good."

"Someone got out of the plane," I said. "Jumped. There was a parachute."

"Did they catch 'im?" She looked worried.

"Not yet. But the soldiers said they will."

"Well, let's hope they do. We can't have Germans runnin' around all over the country now, can we?" She went through into the scullery as she spoke.

From my pocket, I took the penknife Dad had given me. It had two blades — one large and one small — and the handle was made of fake pearl that had a yellowy tinge to it. I opened the small blade and used the tip to scrape dirt from under my fingernails. "What will they do if they catch 'im?"

"What's that?" she asked, coming back into the kitchen carrying a small package wrapped in paper.

"What will they do to 'im?" I said again. "If they catch 'im?

"Haven't a clue."

"Will they shoot 'im?"

"They might. And you can stop doing that," she said. "We're not animals."

I closed the knife and squeezed it in my fist.

"Now, let's get some tea on, shall we?"

"What is it?"

For a moment she looked at the package as if she wasn't going to tell me. "Tripe."

I made a face. "Isn't there anythin' else?"

"Don't go gettin' all persnickety, young lad, there's lots of people who'd be happy to eat your tripe. This is all we've got left until we can collect the rations from Mr. Shaw. Maybe, if we're very lucky, Mr. Bennett will bring us somethin' tomorrow." She looked at me with a hopeful smile.

"Tell 'im to keep it. I'd rather have tripe."

"What?"

I thought about Trevor and his father over at the Ridley farm. I thought about Dad fighting a war in Africa — in a country I'd hardly even heard of. And I thought about what Ridley had said about Mr. Bennett: about him coming here, trying to take Dad's place.

"I don't like 'im," I said. "And I don't like 'im comin' here."

Mam swallowed hard and put a hand on the fireplace. The surrounding mantel was deep black and shining because Mam had scrubbed it with a shoe brush just yesterday.

"Whyever not?" she asked.

"He's always coming since me da' left."

"He's looking after us. Your da' worked hard for him and now he's repaying us. He's looking after us until your da' gets back."

"People are sayin' he's your fancy man."

"Are they really?" She looked indignant, but there was something else there, too. An expression the children at school had when they'd been caught doing something they shouldn't have. "Well, he's been very kind, and people can say whatever they like. You'd do well to rem —"

"I don't want him givin' us stuff and I don't like him comin' here all the time."

"It's not up to you, young man."

"I'm the man of the house now."

Something like a smile came to her lips and her expression softened. "Aye, I s'pose you are, pet, but you're not an adult, and there's a lot of things you don't understand. We all do what we have to."

I looked at my penknife and opened the blade. Opened and shut it. Opened and shut it.

"It's hard for us both, looking after you on me own."

I looked over at her and sighed. "I wish me da' was here."

Mam came over and put her arms around me so my head was on her stomach. She was warm and smelled of soap.

"I wish he was here, too," she said. "I wish it more than anythin'."

Mam cooked the tripe and put it furry side down on the plate so it didn't look too nasty. There were boiled potatoes and carrots from the garden, too, so I ate the vegetables, avoiding the rubbery blob, pushing it around the plate for a while. I knew I'd go hungry if I didn't eat it, though, because there was nothing else, and if I left it, Mam would only give it to me for my breakfast. Nothing was wasted. Not a thing. So, eventually, I forced it down, cutting it into small pieces so I didn't have to chew it.

When it was gone, and my stomach was as full as it was going to be, Mam went through to the scullery and put the kettle on to boil.

"I think we deserve a treat, don't you?" she said, taking a teapot from the sideboard and putting a small amount of tea into it. "Somethin' sweet."

She made weak tea and poured it into her cup, adding a tiny amount of milk. When that was done, she opened the sugar pot in front of us on the table and we both looked in at the last two sugar cubes.

"One lump or two, vicar?" Mam said in a posh voice, just like she always did when she opened the sugar pot.

"Just the one for me," I said with a grin.

Mam dropped her cube into the cup and stirred it gently. I popped mine straight into my mouth and savored the sweetness as the lump dissolved in my spit. I waited until it had melted into almost nothing, then I ran my tongue around my mouth to find the last taste of it. A few undissolved grains crunched between my teeth.

"Delicious," I said.

"Agreed." Mam took a sip from her cup and stood. She did a little curtsy and said, "I think I'll take this on the settee. Would you care to listen to the wireless?"

Beside the fireplace in the kitchen, there was a huge sideboard. It looked like it was a hundred years old. On top of it was a wireless that Dad bought before he went away to win the war. We didn't have electric in the house so it ran off three big glass-sided accumulator batteries that had handles over the top to make them easy to carry. And when they ran out, it was my job to take them down to the garage to get them recharged for a few pence.

We listened to *Children's Hour*, sitting on the settee, not talking, just listening. We always did that together — Mam called it our ritual — but she only sometimes brought her cup of tea with her.

I looked up at the shotgun on the wall above the sideboard, and then at the small collection of letters that leaned against the wireless. There were only five, all of them from Dad. Mam had read them out when they arrived, her hands shaking with each letter, her mouth tightening as she carefully opened them. Then she had taken out the folded paper, opened it up, and breathed out as if she'd been holding her breath the whole time. After that she had smiled at me, a kind of forced smile, and read out what Dad had written.

The letters were all about how much he was missing us and how he couldn't wait till it was all over and he could come home. Each time, Mam had a tear in her eye when she read the words, but I always pretended not to notice.

Mam had tied them together with an old piece of string and put them beside the wireless so we'd think about Dad whenever we sat on the settee and listened to it. We hadn't had a letter for a long time now, but I always looked at his gun and his letters and imagined he was beside us on the settee, with his arm around Mam's shoulder. She would draw her knees up so that her feet were tucked under her, and I would do the same. Dad would smell of fresh air and gunpowder and mud and he would laugh at the names and copy the voices that came out of the wireless. And when it was over, he'd listen a while longer, hearing the news, before going back out to check the estate.

I always thought the news was boring, all those voices droning on, and I used to sit on the hooky mat and read a comic instead. But since the war started and Dad went away I listened every night. Without fail.

There'd been something on one time last year, about Operation Dynamo, and British soldiers retreating from a place called Dunkirk in France. They'd said there might be an invasion after that, and when I looked over at Mam, she'd had one hand on her mouth and she'd gone white. I thought it was because she was frightened of a German invasion, and when I told her it was going to be all right, she hugged me tight. Back then, last year, I hadn't realized why Mam had looked so scared, but I knew now. It's because Dad had been in Dunkirk, and Mam was afraid for him. Afraid for his life.

But I had something else to think about now, and while we listened to the voices, my mind turned to the crash and to the girl I had met out there at the top of the hill. I thought about what she'd said before we parted. And so, for that moment, I forgot about Trevor Ridley and his promise to find a way to deal with me. I forgot about my father fighting a distant war, and I forgot about Mam's struggle to raise me alone. Instead, I thought about Kim, and about going out in the night to collect souvenirs from the crashed plane.

SHAPES IN THE MOONLIGHT

Later, I lay in bed staring at the ceiling, thinking about what Kim had said. I thought about looking for souvenirs, and what Mam would do if she caught me sneaking out in the night. I told myself I shouldn't go, but when I was sure Mam was asleep, I dressed and stood at my bedroom window. I opened the blackout curtains enough to put my nose to the glass and look out at the fields and the moon. There were no lights anywhere because it wasn't allowed. Mr. Charlton and his Air Raid Precautions men patrolled the village every night, even as far out as our cottage, shouting at anyone with even a chink in their curtains. So much darkness made the sky brilliant with stars on a cloudless night. Some of the people in the village said they couldn't ever remember seeing so many stars, but they'd always been there; the lights on the ground just stopped us from seeing them so well.

Condensation misted the glass and I wiped it away, staring over in the direction of the hill. I wondered if Kim would be there; if she'd really meet me like she'd said. And even then, I wasn't sure if I was going to go. Somehow, I couldn't picture myself doing it.

I pulled back into my room and closed the curtains before checking my watch with the flashlight Dad gave me a couple of years ago. It was an old one of his that hadn't worked for a long time, but Dad had managed to get it going again and had given it to me for my tenth birthday. It meant I could go out with him when he was doing his rounds in the dark, but when he left he told me never to point it up in case it let the Germans know where we were. When he told me that, he clicked the shotgun shut and pointed it at the clouds saying, "We'll blow the buggers out of the sky, eh?" and it made me laugh because Mam would never use a word like that.

At quarter to ten, I made up my mind and crept from my bedroom. I avoided all the steps that squeaked and tiptoed down the stairs, along the hall, and across the kitchen floor. I slipped on my boots and let myself out into the night.

I stood on the front step and, for a last moment, I thought about going back inside. I shouldn't be here. I shouldn't be doing this. But there was a brilliant excitement about it that seemed to make my whole body tingle and push the doubt away, so I jumped down and started to run. Through the garden, past the gate, over the path, and on to the field. The cool wind rushed around me. The air smelled so fresh and I felt so free. It was like I was running wild, the only person in the world. Nothing could stop me.

I ran through the bare furrows, kicking the soil, jumping and hopping over the plants, careful not to damage the potatoes. There was a near-full moon and enough stars for me to see where I was going, so I ran until I could hardly breathe. When I eventually had to slow to a walk, I enjoyed the feeling of the cold air when I drew it into me, and I took deep breaths over and over again as I trudged through the soft soil. I leaned forward and put my head down as I climbed the hill, arriving at the top to find Kim already waiting.

She was sitting on the grass behind a scrubby bush that was half eaten by sheep. She had a satchel beside her on the ground, and I realized I should have brought mine, too. I'd need something to carry all my souvenirs in.

"What kept you?" she whispered.

"It's only just ten. You said ten o'clock."

"Shh. Not so loud." She grabbed my shoulder and pulled me low. "Someone's down there."

I strained to look down at the crashed plane. There were a few places where pieces glowed hot in the wreckage, and while the air had been fresh closer to home, the smell that now drifted up the hill was still thick with the stink of the fire.

"I can't see anyone," I whispered.

"There's soldiers guarding it."

"You sure?"

"Well of course I'm sure," she said. "You think they'd just leave this plane out here with no one watching it?"

I nodded to myself and couldn't help feeling disappointed. I'd been looking forward to finding something. "Then how are we —"

"Shh." She nudged me hard. "Look."

Two dark figures came around the broken nose of the aircraft, walking side by side. I could hear the low tones of their voices. For a second, they stopped, and then a match flared as one of them lit a cigarette.

"Shouldn't be doing that," Kim said. "Germans might spot it."

"That looks like Mr. Shaw," I said, recognizing the big frame of one of the men. "The butcher."

"*The butcher?*" she said. "Why do they call him that?"

"'Cause it's his job."

"Oh. I thought it was a nickname or something."

"He's in the Home Guard," I said, trying not to laugh. "Most of the men are."

"Home Guard? Shouldn't the real soldiers be guarding it?"

"Maybe they're all out lookin' for that other one. The parachute, remember? There's a German wanderin' around some —"

"Who's that?" Kim's voice was quiet but urgent. I felt her whole body tense beside me.

"Where?" Even before I saw the figure, I began to feel afraid. It was something about the way Kim had said it.

"There." She hardly moved at all as she pointed to the base of the hill and over to the right.

Settled low among the potato plants, I could see a dark shape that made me feel very cold. It looked as if something was hiding down there, and my head was flooded with the poster images of evil Nazi soldiers peering from underneath their dark helmets, eyes glowing red.

I stared at it for a long time without speaking.

"Is that a person?" I said eventually.

She didn't reply. She just shook her head.

We waited a while longer, both of us lying on our stomachs and looking down at the shadow, watching for movement, but we saw nothing. By the plane, the two men from the Home

Guard finished their cigarettes and continued their patrol. The wreckage was spread all over the field, but they walked the length of the main crash site, coming within just a few yards of the lurking shadow. They rounded the tail end of the plane and disappeared from sight.

And then it moved.

The dark shape shrank and then lengthened. It was like some kind of ghost, shape-shifting in the moonlight. Twisting and growing until it was the outline of a person. And then two more shapes rose from the furrows. They had been too well hidden for us to notice them before, but now we could see them clearly. All three began to slink forward.

"Who *is* that?" I said. "Germans?"

"More souvenir hunters, probably."

We watched as the three figures came together, creeping toward the wreck, but they'd only taken a few steps when there was a groaning of metal and a long creaking sound, followed by a sharp bang.

The noise came so suddenly, and was so loud and strange in the darkness, that it made me jump and sent my heart racing faster than it had been when I ran across the field. I could feel it thumping in my chest and, when I opened my mouth, I thought I could actually hear it. Beside me, Kim was breathing hard, too, and I was sure that if I dared put my hand on her chest, I'd feel her heart beating just as hard as mine was.

Below, on the field, the three figures froze. They stayed as they were for a fraction of a second, then dropped low to the ground, no more than a few feet away from the left wing. They were well disguised by the shadow it cast.

"What was *that*?" I managed to whisper, even though my mouth was dry and my throat was tight.

"The plane settling."

"I thought it was goin' to blow up again."

"Look," she said as the two Home Guardsmen came around the nose of the plane once more. I could hear them chuckling, a kind of nervous laughter, as if they were pretending not to have been frightened by the noise. I watched them coming closer, continuing their patrol, and I looked over at the place where the three figures had dropped into the shadows.

"They're going to bump straight into them," Kim whispered. "That's right in the place where they went round."

I glanced back at the two men, walking slowly, then I flicked my eyes across to those shadows, back and forth, watching them come closer.

Closer.

I wondered if the figures would try to run, like the rabbits that hid in the long grass and bolted for their burrows just at the last minute, when you were about to stand right on top of them.

Closer.

Then the men stopped dead in their tracks. They fumbled their rifles from their shoulders and aimed them down into the shadows.

"WHO GOES THERE?"

I heard the words as clearly as if they'd been spoken to me across the counter in his shop. That thick Northumberland accent. It was Mr. Shaw, all right, just as I'd thought.

"Stand up." His voice was loud and firm. I hoped he wasn't

in any danger. He was one of Dad's friends, and I'd always liked him. It would be awful if something bad happened to him.

"Stand up," he said again.

Then, very slowly, the three figures rose from the darkness of the scattered debris.

"Identify yourselves."

The voice that spoke next was too quiet for me to hear, but I saw Mr. Shaw and the other man step forward, still pointing their rifles.

"There's a curfew on tonight 'cause of this plane," said Mr. Shaw. "You lads shouldn't be out here."

They approached the three figures, seeming to relax. The two men from the Home Guard slung their rifles over their shoulders and spoke to the three figures, their voices quieter now so we couldn't make out what they were saying. They talked for a while, and then the threesome was coming in our direction, straight up the hill.

"Stay quiet," Kim whispered as we shuffled right in among the shrubs. "Don't move."

We couldn't see them anymore, but we heard their footsteps approaching. The heavy footfalls of three people climbing the hill, coming straight at us.

I tightened my lips, biting them together, terrified I'd let out a sound. I stopped breathing as the footsteps came closer.

"Me da's gonna kill me for this if he finds out," said a voice I recognized immediately. "You think he'll tell on us?" It was Trevor Ridley. The boy who'd given me a hard time this afternoon, right here on the hill. The other two were probably his friends Bob Cummings and Adam Thornhill.

Wherever there was one of them, the others were sure to be close behind.

"What about me mam?" said Cummings, his breath coming heavy from the effort of climbing the hill. I could tell he was frightened, and I didn't blame him. I knew who his mam was — a big woman with a loud voice. If Mrs. Cummings was in the greengrocer's, my own mam would hesitate at the door and go to the butcher's instead.

Kim and I stayed as still as we could, keeping our faces hidden in our folded arms as we waited for the boys to go past. Even when they were long gone, the sound of their boots just an echoing memory in our ears, we stayed perfectly still.

I was the first to speak.

"Well, that's it, then," I said. "We should go home."

Kim didn't reply.

"I mean, there's no chance of gettin' any souvenirs now, is there?"

"I suppose not." She sounded annoyed.

I was lying on my tummy with my arms crossed in front of me, so I put my chin on my forearms and turned to look at her. "So what's a canny good souvenir?" I asked, trying to brighten her mood. I didn't want her to be disappointed.

Kim did the same, our noses just a few inches away from each other. She sighed. "Anything, really. But it's best if it's got something written on it. Or a swastika would be even better."

I thought about the tail piece I'd seen with the symbol painted on it, and that made me remember the way the plane had rattled over me that afternoon, the gunner waiting to be smashed into the ground.

"Do you think they're still in there?" I asked. "In the plane?"

"I don't know. Probably too hot to get them out. And then too dark. They can't use lights, can they?"

"No."

"So, yeah, they're probably still in there."

I looked at Kim, seeing the way her eyes sparkled in the moonlight.

"That would be something, wouldn't it?" she said. "Seeing inside the plane."

"Aye."

Kim stared at me and grinned. "We should go in. Have a look."

"What?"

"Right now."

"But they're guardin' it." I looked down at the dark shapes of the Home Guardsmen beginning another patrol around the plane.

"It takes them a few minutes to go round each time," she said. "If we time it just right, we can get in while they're on the other side. They won't see us."

"They caught Trevor Ridley."

The Home Guardsmen had reached the place where they first saw the three boys hiding behind the wing.

"We're smaller," she said. "Quicker. And we're better."

"I don't know."

"It'll be fun."

"It'll be *dangerous*." I watched Mr. Shaw and the other man come to the tail end of the plane.

"Of course it will," she said. "That's the fun of it."

"But —"

"And what's the worst they'll do?" she asked. "Tell your mam?"

"That's bad enough."

"Then we have to make sure we don't get caught."

"What about the plane, though? Is it safe?"

"Safe?" she asked with a wicked smile. "Where would be the fun in that?"

The Home Guardsmen disappeared from sight.

"Come on." Kim got to her feet. "Follow me."

And, with those words, she dashed away down the hill.

I hesitated for a second, a million thoughts in my head. So many tiny details to influence my decision, but one thing overpowered all the others. I wanted to be with Kim, and I wanted to do what she did.

So I ran, too. Straight down the hill, toward the wreck.

BODIES

I was both terrified and excited as I followed Kim. The breeze that rushed around me was cold on my face and arms. The tops of my wellies battered against my shins and calves, smacking back and forth. It was like the sound of thunder in my ears — surely the Home Guardsmen would hear me running. Surely the noises would reach them and they would come to investigate.

But no one came.

They were on the other side of the crash site, probably almost half a field away from where I was.

I chased Kim down to where the plane was lying flat on its belly, the fuselage ripped into two pieces. The tail section was at least twenty yards away, crooked and bent, as if twisted away by giant hands. It was blackened by flames, but the swastika was visible in the moonlight. The main body was also charred by the fire and riddled with holes from the exploding ammunition, but it was more or less a broken tube, crushed at one end, open at the other. The open end was ragged with uneven fingers of ripped and twisted metal.

I slowed down as I came close to it, seeing Kim stop, glance around, and then climb inside. When I reached the same spot, I took a deep breath and followed.

The smell was awful. The acrid stench of burnt rubber and oil and fuel mixed together to make something I thought would be unbearable for any longer than a few seconds. It filled my head with a thick blackness. I could taste it in my throat, feel it burning my nostrils. And there was the hint of another smell, too — something not quite so unpleasant, but horrible all the same. Sickening. A kind of sweetness, like the smell of bacon on the grill, but it was almost completely drowned by the stink of the fire.

I lifted my shirt and put it across my nose, but it did nothing to take the smell away, so I let it drop back to my chest.

Kim was crouching in what would have been the inside of the airplane, bending over to examine a handful of ash and broken pieces. She held it up and showed it to me before gently putting it back on the ground with a quiet tinkling of metal against metal, the ash clouding about her knees. "Cartridges," she whispered. "From the machine gun. They're still warm."

I put one finger to my lips and she nodded agreement. Talking was too much of a risk. The Home Guard would hear us.

Kim reached out and took my hand in hers. Her skin was soft and a little damp, like it had been earlier that day. She turned my hand over and picked up a cartridge from the floor, placing it on my palm.

I liked her holding my hand like that, and I didn't take the brass casing until Kim closed my fingers around it so my fist was inside hers. The metal cartridge was, indeed, warm, but I could hardly concentrate on it at all.

I looked up at Kim, seeing her watching me with those sparkling eyes and, for a moment, we stayed like that. Then she smiled and took her hand away, patting my pocket. She leaned close to my ear.

"Souvenir," she whispered.

I nodded and put the bullet casing in my pocket, just as she tapped me and pointed into the darkness at the nose of the plane. She put her fingers to her eyes and pointed again. *Let's look deeper inside.*

I gave her a thumbs-up and tried not to look scared.

Kim kept low and went farther in. She moved slowly, careful with her footing. Once she was a little way ahead, I began to follow, trying to be quiet, but my wellies were a little too big and I misjudged my footing. I stepped on a loose pile of bullet casings, and the whole lot gave way under me, sliding out in all directions.

The sound of metal on metal was loud in the confines of the crashed plane. It was like hard rain pelting a tin roof. The ping and clatter of the casings echoed as if the noise would never stop. And, like stepping on a pile of marbles, the spent cartridges moved against each other like little rollers, and I stumbled backward, my feet slipping out from beneath me.

I tried to stay upright. I put my arms out and tried to keep my balance, but I knew I was going to fall. And I knew that anyone close to the plane would have heard the racket from inside.

As I fell, my fingers grasped something soft and held tight, but whatever I had grabbed wasn't fixed to anything and I continued to go down, pulling it with me. With the tinkle of spent bullet casings raining around me, I hit the floor of the plane with a loud crash.

"What the hell was that?" Mr. Shaw's voice sounded as if it were right beside me. Loud and deep and thick with accent. "You heard that, right?"

I looked over at the place where I'd last seen Kim, but she was gone. I imagined she'd found a dark corner to squeeze into and was keeping as quiet as possible.

"Probably just the plane settling again," said the other voice, and I identified the soft tones of Doctor Jacobs.

As quietly as possible, I shuffled back, pulling myself under some debris.

"You hear that? Somethin' movin'? Think them lads is back?" Mr. Shaw said. "They're trouble, they are, all three of 'em."

"Well, yes, but I don't think they'd come back."

"Still. Better check, eh?" It sounded as if Mr. Shaw was taking his job very seriously. Either that, or he was hoping for some action. "Might be that German come back."

There was a moment of quiet, then I heard Doctor Jacobs sigh. "All right. Come on."

The next few moments passed in slow motion, as if they were a dream. I stayed where I was, hardly breathing, blood whooshing in my ears as the footsteps came nearer. I pressed my lips together, biting them between my front teeth as the two men came so close that I could hear their heavy breathing. I heard them step over pieces of the wreckage and come right to the open end of the fuselage.

"Who's in there?" Mr. Shaw said, and I knew he'd be pointing his rifle right into the darkness. "Who is it?"

Even the night didn't dare make a sound.

"WHO GOES THERE?"

Not a whisper.

"Give me the flashlight," said Mr. Shaw.

"That's not a good idea," the doctor replied. "You know, with the blackout and everything."

"I'll be quick. We have to check. This could be important."

"I don't think —"

"Just give me the flashlight, Simon."

There was a long pause, the sound of fumbling, then a beam of light cut into the darkness of the plane. It swept from side to side.

"Nothing there," said the doctor.

Then the light came close to where I was hiding. It passed just inches from my face, and I squeezed my eyes shut and wished I could shrink to the size of an insect.

"It's 'im," said Mr. Shaw, and I knew I'd been found. "Look."

Thinking I was caught, that there was no point in hiding anymore, I was about to move, but when I opened my eyes, I saw they weren't talking about me. I was well covered by the shadow of what I'd hidden under, but a few inches away, the circle of orange light illuminated the face of a dead German.

"He's slipped to one side," said Mr. Shaw.

He was lying on his back, right next to me, but his legs were twisted too far around to the side, as if they had been put on backward. His arms, ragged with charred flesh and fabric that had become part of him, were bent underneath, like an old rag doll, and there were places where he'd been scorched right down to the bone. Turned toward me, his face was a craggy mess, his mouth open in a silent scream, his eye sockets nothing more than burnt-out blackened holes. It was hard to believe that what I was looking at had once been a person.

I must have pulled him when I'd slipped back. That's what I'd grabbed hold of. The dead German had been close enough for me to reach out and drag down with me as I fell.

And now I realized what the sweet smell was. It was the smell of cooked human flesh.

I only looked at the body for a fraction of a second before I squeezed my eyes shut again, but it was enough to take in all that information. It was in my head like a photograph. An image I would remember for the rest of my life. I bit my lips harder, desperate to shout out, but determined not to.

"What the bloody hell's going on here?" said a voice I'd heard before but couldn't quite put a face to.

The light snapped off and I was in darkness once again. I put my hand to my mouth to stop myself from making a noise. That horrible burnt body was so close to me. That face with the flesh missing. I tried to not to think about it; tried not to keep seeing it in my mind.

"What do you two think you're doin'? You tryin' to bring the whole of the Luftwaffe down on us?"

"We —"

"Get over here. *Now*."

There was the sound of stumbling, then the footsteps of Mr. Shaw and Doctor Jacobs walking a few yards away from the plane. When they stopped, the voice was speaking again, saying the words with authority. "Why aren't you patrolling? We just walked right up behind you without you even noticing."

"Sergeant. We thought we heard somethin'," said Mr. Shaw, and I knew immediately who he was talking to. Sergeant Wilkes. The one who had been on the hill earlier that day; the one with the mouth that opened more on one side than the other, and the eyes that looked right through you. The one who had grinned like a wolf when he talked about shooting Germans. It made me even more afraid, knowing he was out there, too.

"So you thought you'd turn on the flashlight?" he was saying. "Invite the Germans to come and bomb us, eh? Is that what you thought?"

"No."

"And no one's supposed to get that close. You might damage vital intelligence, you daft old granddads. No sign of any intelligence right here, is there?"

"You can't talk to us like that," said Mr. Shaw. "Just because your lieutenant isn't here, doesn't mean you can —"

"I can talk to you however I want, *Private*. I have stripes on my shoulder that tell you I'm a sergeant. You got any stripes, *Private*? No. I didn't think so. And you call yourselves soldiers? Can't even guard a plane wreck."

"I think we're doing rather well," said Doctor Jacobs.

"Rather well?" said Sergeant Wilkes. "Beaming your flashlight about, bumbling about like idiots? You call that '*rather well*'?"

"I —"

"A parachute was spotted, you know," the sergeant went on. "There might be a Jerry running about, and here you are, standing out like sore thumbs. We've got men looking for 'im but what if he came here and crept up on you and *criiick* —" He made the kind of noise people make when they draw a finger across their throat like it's a knife. "How about that, *Private*? Two dead old men and a Jerry still on the loose. Either that or someone'll drop a bomb on your head. Lucky you've got the likes of me around to keep you right. You lot runnin' around on the village green with broom shanks for rifles, banging dustbin lids to make gunfire, doesn't make you soldiers, you know. I've never seen anything so ridiculous."

Someone laughed.

"We do what we can," said Mr. Shaw. It sounded like he was gritting his teeth.

"Well, it's not much good from what I can see," the sergeant scoffed.

"And we have rifles now," said Doctor Jacobs. "Not broom shanks."

"Aye. Ross rifles from the last war," said Wilkes. "With five rounds of ammunition apiece. Hardly gonna stop the invasion with that, are you?"

"All I have to do is shoot one Jerry," Mr. Shaw said. "And there's sixty thousand of us Home Guardsmen, you know. If we all shoot just one Jerry, I reckon that's a canny start. And you never know — I might even get two. I'm a good shot."

After that there was a long silence, then someone cleared their throat loudly.

"Aye, well, we're here to relieve you, anyway," said the sergeant. "There's not a lot of searching we can do at night, and we need to keep this place *well guarded*." He stressed those last two words as an accusation.

"One of the bodies slipped," said Doctor Jacobs. "We thought there was someone inside."

"Well, they won't be there much longer," he replied. "We're gettin' them out as soon as it's light enough to see what we're doing."

All the time they were talking, I'd been lying still with my eyes squeezed shut, so it came as a shock when I felt Kim tap me gently on the foot. I flinched and looked up, seeing her crouched by my feet. She beckoned with one hand and I sat up slowly.

She pointed at me, then at herself, then at the open end of the plane. She wasn't pointing in the direction of the hill, though, but away at the woods, where I'd been earlier that day. I understood, straightaway, what she meant. There was no way we could make a run for it in the direction of the hill, but if we were quiet, we might be able to get out while the men were arguing, and make our way to the woods. Once inside, we'd be well hidden, and we could double back around.

I nodded and got up into a kneeling position, feeling something hard and angular digging into my knee. I tried not to think about the body lying close by, and reached down to pick up the object. Then Kim tugged gently on my sleeve and beckoned.

I took a deep breath and together we crept from the plane.

Once outside, I glanced back to see if the soldiers were in sight, but they were hidden behind part of the fuselage. I could still hear them talking, but they were too far away for me to hear what they were saying.

"Come on," Kim whispered, and together we made a run for it.

I kept low, bent at the waist, as I pumped my legs as fast as they would go. They were still shaking from the fright, and they trembled as I ran, but I gritted my teeth and kept going. I sprinted alongside Kim, not looking at her, keeping my eyes fixed firmly on the darkness of the woods at the edge of the field. Once or twice, I kicked the tops of the furrows, showering soil, but I managed to stay up and keep on.

When we reached the treeline, we dropped into the shadows, puffing and panting, exhilarated by the run. "They're still in there," I said between breaths. "His face was . . ." I stopped without finishing my sentence. "It was horrible. He was all burnt up. It hardly even looked like a person. I was so scared."

"I saw it, too."

"He had no eyes."

"Are you all right?"

"Aye," I said, shaking myself. "Aye, I'm fine. It's just . . . it was . . . you know."

"We shouldn't have gone in there."

"Maybe," I said. "I mean, it was bad an' I was scared, but . . . well, it was fun, too. In a scary way."

"Yeah. Hey, you find something?"

"What?"

"In your hand."

"Oh, aye." I'd almost forgotten I'd picked it up, but now I held out my hand and looked at the metal object in my fingers. "I *have* found something," I said. "I really have."

GUN

We sat in the undergrowth just inside the line of trees and looked at the object I'd found. There wasn't much light, so it was hard to see, but we knew exactly what it was.

"It's a gun," Kim said. Her voice was quiet, less than a whisper. There was no one close enough to hear us, but something about the darkness and the plane and the dead airman made us speak in hushed tones like we were in church.

"Aye," I said, turning it over in my hands before gripping the handle and aiming it out into the night.

"You think it still works?"

I lowered it and shrugged. "Don't know."

"Do you even know how to work it?"

"Not really."

She took it from me and felt its weight. "Good souvenir. Best I've seen."

"You should have it," I said without thinking. "It was your idea to come."

"No way, you have to keep it. You found it; it's the rule. Finders, Keepers." She put it down between us and we said nothing for a while. I could hear Kim breathing in and out.

"That smell in there," I said. "I half wished I had me gas mask. I'd always thought the inside of *that* smelled bad, but . . ." I looked at Kim. "We got 'em fitted at the school hall last year."

"Us too," Kim said.

"Some of the bairns got masks with a kind of Donald Duck beak that made a fartin' noise when they breathed out, then the teachers made us parade around the playground wearin' 'em, and it was so funny."

"Poor kids! Those masks smell awful," Kim said. "Makes me feel . . . trapped. I hate mine."

"It's nothing compared to the smell back there."

Kim nodded, but she didn't say anything.

After a few minutes, she crawled away from the cover of the trees and lay down on her back in the soil. "There are so many stars," she said. "Have you ever really looked at them?"

"All the time." I picked up the gun and went to sit beside her. "Me da' knows all their names. Well, maybe not *all* of them, like, but a lot of them." I put the weapon down beside me and looked out at the dark shape of the plane, but we were too far away to see the guards now.

"Seems as if there's loads more now. More than before," she said. "With all the lights in town, you could hardly see them, but now . . ."

"Me da' said in Newcastle it's like daylight when all the streetlamps are switched on."

Kim laughed quietly. "It was never *that* light."

"Don't laugh."

"Why not? It's funny."

"It's what me da' told me."

Kim turned her head so she could see me sitting beside her. "Sorry. I didn't mean to . . ."

"That's all right," I said.

"You miss him a lot."

"Aye."

"I miss my brother."

"Is he really a pilot?"

"Flying Wellingtons," she said. "And I don't mean the boots."

"I know what a Wellington bomber is," I told her, and for a moment I tried to imagine what it would be like to fly one, but after the crash, I wasn't so sure I'd ever want to. And that made me think about how Kim must feel, having seen what was inside the smashed-up Heinkel. I wanted to say something to her, about her brother being a pilot and about the crash, but I couldn't think of the right thing. "How old are you?" I said, changing the subject instead.

"Twelve."

"Same as me. What month?"

"April."

"Mine's May."

"You ever seen a dead body before?" she asked.

"No."

"Me neither." She took a deep breath. "I didn't think it would be like that. It was the worst thing ever."

"Aye."

And we were quiet again, so I lay back and stared at the stars, too, trying to remember some of the ones Dad had pointed out to me. He'd said that people could use them to find their way at night, and I wondered if he was doing that right now, somewhere else in the world.

"That's Orion up there." I pointed. "See the three stars in a row?"

Kim shuffled closer, putting her head against mine so she could follow the line of my finger. Her hair was soft and it tickled my cheek. She smelled clean.

"Those three are Orion's Belt," I said. "And at the corners you can see the rest of him." I traced the tip of my finger around the stars, drawing the outline of the hunter Orion.

"Which ones?" Kim asked, but I didn't get the chance to tell her again, because we heard someone cough. It was unmistakable. A quiet cough, as if someone was trying not to be heard.

Kim grabbed my hand, pulling it down so I was no longer pointing. She put her finger on her lips, telling me to be quiet.

"Someone's there," she whispered.

The cough again.

"It's behind us," I said, turning around. "In the woods."

"Maybe the soldiers came after us," Kim said. "That Sergeant Wilkes."

"Can't be. We'd have seen them comin'."

"Others, then," Kim suggested. "The ones who're looking for the German."

"We'd have heard them in the woods." And then a thought came to me. "Unless they've been there all along. From when we got here."

"Maybe it's the German."

"I want to see."

"What?"

"I want to see who it is." I didn't know why I said it. Perhaps it was to prove to myself that I could be brave just like Kim, but whatever it was, something made me want to see.

I picked up the pistol and started to crawl toward the trees.

Kim grabbed my shirt. "Don't."

I pulled her hand away and pushed to a crouch, creeping right into the edge of the woods. Once I'd passed the first trunks of hazel and oak, I stood up and took a soft step forward. Dad had shown me how to walk quietly in the woods. He said he had to do it all the time at night, be as quiet as possible when he was hunting poachers.

I put down my right heel and rolled onto the ball of my foot, feeling for anything that might snap and make a noise. I took extra care to remember I was wearing wellies — something I'd forgotten earlier — and, moving like that, I crept deeper into the trees, coming closer to the barbed-wire fence.

And then I saw him.

Highlighted by a sliver of moonlight that cut through the leaves above, I saw a man, sitting back against one of the fence posts.

I stopped dead in my tracks and stared at him.

A stick snapped, making me spin around to find Kim standing just behind me.

"Who is it?" she asked.

"I don't know," I said, turning back to look at the immobile figure.

"Is he asleep? Or dead?"

I was mesmerized by him. My whole body had gone cold with fear. My stomach tingled, my hands trembled, my muscles tightened.

And then he spoke — *"Bitter"* — and he put his arm up as if to protect his face. *"Bitter."*

I stayed as I was, my breath going right out of me.

"*Bitter.*" He said it over and over again. "*Bitter.*" His voice quiet, his arms across his face.

Kim grabbed my arm and tried to pull me back. "Let's go," she said.

When she broke the spell like that, I turned to run; my instinct was to do as Kim said, but before I took a step, I had second thoughts. Something made me stop.

I resisted her, tugging my arm away, inching closer so I could look down at the man half sitting, half lying on the ground. My breathing was shallow, my throat was dry.

"*Bitter,*" he said again.

"What's wrong with 'im?" I said, swallowing my fear and surprising myself that I hadn't run away. My curiosity was growing, drowning my fear. "Is he drunk?" I took a step closer.

"Drunk?" she asked, trying to pull me away once more. "What d'you mean?"

"Why's he keep sayin' 'bitter'? What's 'bitter'?"

Kim pulled me harder. "What are you talking about, you idiot? He's saying 'please.' *Bitte* is German for 'please.'"

And then I understood why she was pulling me away. We had found the missing German. And if I knew anything about Germans, it was that they were brutal killers. They were animals raging for the blood of Englishmen. I had been told enough times what they were capable of, and I knew that if I stayed here any longer, he would kill us both.

But this man didn't seem as if he was trying to kill anyone.

"Is it 'im?" I said. "The one on the parachute?"

"Must be."

I stared down at him. "Why's he saying '*please*'? Why's he scared of us?"

"I don't know. Maybe . . ." She stopped.

"What?" I said. "Maybe what?"

"Look at what you're holding."

I lifted my hand and looked at the pistol. "He's frightened of me."

"Come on, let's get help." Kim turned. "We'll get the soldiers."

But I put out a hand and stopped her.

"What?" she said. "We'll be heroes. Everyone'll be talking about us 'cause we found him. We need to get someone."

"We're not s'posed to be out here. Remember the curfew?"

"Forget that," Kim said. "They'll be too proud of us to tell us off."

"Then maybe we should capture him ourselves," I said, feeling brave. "We've got the gun."

"No way."

"Imagine it. You and me."

"I don't think —"

"*We* capture the German. How about that?"

Kim was silent. I could almost hear her thinking about it, but when she eventually spoke, it was to say, "You're mad."

"Maybe," I replied. "But look how frightened he is. More frightened than us."

"You really think we should?"

"Definitely."

She sighed. Turned away. Took a few steps and then stopped. Kim stood still for a moment, then came back to me and nodded once. "All right, then," she said. "We'll do it. We'll take him to the soldiers."

THE SOUVENIR

The man didn't do anything at all. He just sat there as if he'd given up and decided enough was enough. There was no point in running anymore, so he was sitting with his back against the fence post, his legs stretched out and his arms by his sides.

I raised my arm and pointed the gun.

"*Bitte,*" he said. He said other words, too, but I couldn't understand them, and it sounded as if he was having trouble talking at all. The light wasn't that good, but we could see enough to know his face was streaked and the left arm of his flight suit was torn from shoulder to cuff. It glistened wet with what I imagined to be blood.

"Get up," I said in my strictest voice. "You're coming with us."

"He doesn't know what you're saying," Kim said.

"You tell 'im, then."

"How am *I* going to tell him?"

"You speak German."

"I know how to say 'please'; it doesn't mean I can speak German."

"All right, well . . . get up!" I made a lifting motion with my hands, flicking the pistol up and down, but that only alarmed the airman even more and he flinched away from us. He looked the way I'd felt when Trevor Ridley had picked on me earlier that evening, and seeing him react that way made me feel sorry for him. I started to feel bad for frightening him.

"I'm not going to hurt you," I said. "I just want you to stand up."

"*Wasser,*" he said.

"Vasa?"

"He wants water," Kim said.

"We haven't got any."

"I have. I brought it in case we got thirsty."

I stared at him. "Maybe we should give 'im some, then."

"Really?"

"I don't think he's dangerous. I mean, he doesn't *look* dangerous. What do you reckon? A bit of water should be all right."

Kim thought for a moment, then agreed, and took the water bottle from her satchel. It was made of metal, like a soldier's water bottle, and she threw it toward the man. It landed in the undergrowth beside him with a dull thump and he picked it up in his right hand. He tried to open it, putting the bottle between his thighs to hold it while he twisted the cap, but it was too tight. Then he tried unscrewing it with his teeth, but still couldn't do it. Eventually, he dropped the bottle and began to sob.

"He's crying," Kim said.

"Why?"

"He's thirsty, I suppose."

"And scared."

"Yeah. Probably sad that he's lost his friends, too." She stepped closer to him, picking up the bottle. "Keep pointing that gun at him." She half crouched beside him, ready to escape at any moment, and unscrewed the cap of the water bottle and offered it to him. She waited, watching, but he didn't move. He just looked at her, afraid, so Kim stretched out her hand and lifted it to the man's mouth.

He drank a long, deep drink and moved his head away from the bottle, whispering, *"Danke."*

"He's hurt," Kim said, relaxing a little. "Not breathing much."

The airman coughed.

"I think he might be dying."

"Dyin'?"

"Maybe. I don't know. I'm not a doctor."

She stayed where she was, suddenly unafraid of the man now that she could see he was hurt, and I found myself losing my resolve to keep pointing the gun at him.

"He looks young," Kim said.

"He looks old enough to me."

"Maybe to you, but I've got a brother," she said. "He's nineteen — eighteen when I last saw him — and *he* looks about the same age."

"You sure? He looks older to me."

"No, he's no older than Josh, and that makes him just a teenager."

"Who's Josh?"

"My brother, you clot."

"Oh."

Kim sat down and continued to look at the man. I kept my

distance, held the gun up, but it was beginning to feel heavy now. I couldn't keep pointing it all night.

"We should take him now," I said. "To the soldiers."

"What do you think they'll do to him?"

"I . . ." I shook my head. I hadn't really thought any further than taking him prisoner and becoming a hero. I'd imagined Trevor Ridley's jealousy and I'd seen Kim boasting about the capture, but I hadn't thought about what the soldiers would do with this man.

"D'you think they'll kill him?" Kim asked. "It's what that soldier said today, isn't it? That sergeant. He said they'd shoot him."

"He didn't say that. Not exactly."

"No, but that's what he meant."

"They wouldn't kill him, would they? That would be . . . I don't know. It wouldn't be right. Put him in a camp, maybe, but not kill him."

"You heard what they said."

Kim opened the water bottle again and put it to the man's lips. When he had drunk, he made a low moaning noise and closed his eyes as if he was fighting to stay awake.

Kim crouched on her haunches and studied him as she might have studied a wounded hedgehog curled beneath a hedge. "We can't capture him," she said, coming to a decision.

"What?"

"Not if they're going to kill him. It wouldn't be right. You said so yourself."

"What do we do, then? Leave him here? We can't have Germans runnin' around the country, can we?" I thought about how much my words sounded like Mam's.

74

"I don't think he's in much of a state to go running around anywhere," Kim said.

"Maybe he's a spy, tryin' to trick us."

Kim shook her head. "I don't think so. I think he needs help. He's wounded."

"We could go to Doctor Jacobs. He's really nice and —"

"He'd tell the soldiers," Kim said. "He's a grown-up; they always do things like that. What we need is somewhere for him to hide."

"Hide? We can't —"

"Yeah. We can help him get better, and then he can escape over the sea. Go back to Norway, where their base is."

"I don't think he'd get that far," I said. "It's a canny long way, isn't it? Anyway, we can't just free 'im to go off and fight the English again. He's German. We have to turn him over to the sergeant. It's our duty."

"So he can shoot him?"

"D'you really think he will?"

"I do." Kim turned to look at me and I wasn't sure what to say. This man was a German. He was *the enemy*. I shouldn't even think about helping him. But, at the same time, he didn't look very dangerous. He was crying, for goodness' sake. I didn't think he deserved to be shot, so maybe we *should* help him. And then there was Kim — brave Kim — and how much I wanted to show her how brave *I* could be.

"I was thinking," Kim said with a shrug. "About my brother."

"What about 'im?" I asked.

"Well, he's a pilot, isn't he?"

"So?" The word came out before I really thought about it. *Of course* it mattered that her brother was a pilot. I looked back in the direction of the crashed plane and knew Kim had seen what I had seen. The difference was that when I saw those bodies, they were German airmen, but when Kim saw them, it would have made her think of her brother, Josh.

"Well, we haven't heard from him for such a long time."

"We haven't heard from me da' either. That doesn't mean —"

"No, but . . . you know . . . what if it *did* mean something? What if my brother got shot down?"

"He hasn't."

"But what if something *does* happen to him? Or to your dad? What if . . . I mean, wouldn't you want someone to help him? If someone found him — someone like us — wouldn't you want them to help him?"

"You mean, like, if we help him, maybe someone would help my da' and your brother?"

"Yes."

I knew what she meant. I sometimes played games in my head, thinking that if I could run to the end of the road in less than ten seconds, then it would mean we'd get a letter from Dad. Or if I could get to the top of the hill before Mam could take in the washing, then it would mean there'd be a rabbit in the snare that day. Only this was more serious. More important.

I looked down at the German lying there, silent now, and imagined it was Dad in some far-off place, hurt and afraid. It was hard to imagine him being afraid. He was always so strong.

"They're all right," I said. "Me da' and your brother. They're all right, I just know it. And anyway, they're not German, are they?" I remembered the posters on the village notice board, and the ones they put up in the shops. The pictures were scary, letting us know how bad the Germans were, telling us that all they wanted to do was kill us. "They don't bomb us and —"

"Stop making it all so complicated, Peter. He's wounded and he needs help. The sergeant will shoot him if they find him, so it's up to us. *We* have to help him. *We* have to look after him." She began to sound excited. "Hey, *that* will be our souvenir. The best souvenir ever."

"What d'you mean?"

"I mean *him*. The German. *He'll* be our souvenir."

"A person? I thought we were looking for metal stuff. Small things."

"This will be even better."

"I don't know. I don't think it's a good idea. What if someone finds out?"

"Come on, you started this. Don't go all gutless on me now."

"I'm not, it's just —"

"Where can we take him? Are there some outbuildings or something? A barn, maybe?"

"They'll search all of *them*."

"Somewhere no one'll find him, then."

"I don't think we should," I said.

"We have to," Kim said. "What if it was Josh? Or your dad?"

"It isn't, though, is it?"

"Please," she said. "Maybe if we look after him, someone will look after Josh. Or your dad. We *have* to."

And there was something about the way she said those last three words that made me feel very sad. Doing something to help the German had become important to Kim, as if it would make a difference to what happened to her brother. She thought if we were kind to him, then someone would be kind to Josh. None of us talked much about how much we missed our dads and brothers and uncles and cousins who were away fighting. No one ever wanted to look scared or weak or upset. But we were all of those things all of the time, and Kim had decided that doing this would make her feel better.

"Please," she said again, and I found myself thinking of all the places we might hide a German. It didn't seem right that we were going to try to keep him, but it also didn't seem quite real. It felt as if, any minute now, an adult would step out from around the wreckage of the plane and take charge of everything, and the adventure would be over. I was excited and scared and confused and sad all at the same time. Excited because we had found him, but scared because he was a German and he might try to kill us. I was also afraid of how much trouble we'd be in if we were caught, but Kim was right — he seemed just as frightened as we were — and I couldn't stand the thought that he might be killed if we turned him over. I couldn't bear to think something like that might happen to Dad.

So it was all of those things that made me tell her about my den. I'd never told anyone else except Dad. Not even Mam.

"There is a place," I said. "A good place. The best hidin' place ever."

THE BEST HIDING
PLACE EVER

"How are we going to get him over the fence?" Kim said. "Isn't there a gate or something?"

Dad had put it up years ago, three lines of barbed wire attached to wooden fence posts, just a few trees deep into the woods. Most of the fences around there were old and rusted and falling apart, but Dad kept this one in good condition. He always repaired it if it started to sag, and he always coated the posts to keep them protected from the weather. The wire was taut and even, right along its length, except for one spot.

"No gate," I said. "But there's a place. It's over here." I pointed along the fence, showing her a space between two posts where I had snipped away the lower two pieces of barbed wire. Dad had let me do the cutting, saying it could be my special way in and out. He always stepped over the wire. I'd watched him do it so many times, over and over, but his legs were long and his hands were hard, so he never snagged his clothes or cut himself. I, though, was always cutting my fingers, scraping my legs, tearing my clothes, and ending up getting told off by Mam, so, one day, Dad took me to the fence and pulled a pair of wire cutters from his bag. He told me where to snip the wire so it would make a place for me to get through and, after that, I never ripped my clothes on the barbs again.

"You sure you want to do this?" I said to Kim as we came to the gap.

"Yeah. I think so."

"You *think* so?"

"I mean, yes. I'm sure."

I took a deep breath. "All right, then."

Kim and I could crawl though the gap easy enough, but getting the airman through was a different matter. It was hard pushing and pulling him through a gap made for a child, trying to do it without hurting him. His flight suit snagged on the wire a few times, and it ripped in places along the back. It might have even cut his skin once or twice, but that didn't seem to bother him. He just went where we made him go, as if he were under our spell.

When he was through, we rested a few minutes. Kim gave him some water and I stood by, holding the pistol.

"We should get a move on," I said. "It's gettin' late."

"Are you tired?" Kim asked.

I hadn't had time to think about being tired. "Not really." There were too many other things for me to think about. "But we can't take too long. Come on, let's get movin'."

I stuck the gun into the front of my trousers and we went to stand on either side of him. He was shaking and kept muttering words we didn't understand, but he was weak — too weak to fight us, anyway. He could hardly stand on his own, so we draped his arms around our shoulders, like the soldiers had done earlier with their wounded friend, and we made our way through the trees. He wasn't big, but he was heavy for us and we struggled with his weight, moving slowly.

I supported the airman with my left shoulder and kept the flashlight in my right hand, shining it ahead of us from time to time, but only in short bursts when needed. There were no paths in the wood, so we had to be careful where we were walking. There were thick brambles and areas where the nettles grew at least as high as my chin, so I had to make sure I didn't lead us the wrong way.

The woods were almost silent. It was a long time since I'd been in there at night, and it was strange for it to be so quiet. All I could hear now was the tinkling of the burn and the rustle of the wind in the treetops. When I used to come in with Dad, though, there was always plenty of noise. The birds made a racket sometimes, and they gave you a right scare if you disturbed them and they exploded from the undergrowth with a rush of beating wings.

We waded across the burn at the shallowest point, the cold water coming over Kim's shoes and soaking the leather, and carried on. The airman grew heavier and heavier as he grew weaker and weaker, until we felt as if we were carrying his whole weight.

"What are those for?" Kim said, pointing at one of the pens, picked out in the beam of the flashlight. It was waist-high and about twelve feet long, one of a few that stood in a row, like miniature barracks.

"Rearin' pheasants," I said.

"Pheasants?"

"Aye. The birds."

"I know what pheasants are," she said, "but why put them in cages like that?"

"Me da's the gamekeeper here," I said. "Well, when he gets back, like. He rears the pheasants for shootin'."

"He helps them grow so he can shoot them?"

"*He* doesn't shoot 'em; it's the posh lot that do that."

"What for?"

"For fun, I s'pose. There's no birds here now, though."

"I can see that."

The pens were all overgrown with weeds and nettles pushing through the wire mesh, and there was no movement in them at all. Before the war, Dad used to come out here at night, "do his rounds," he used to say, looking for poachers and foxes. I wished he were here now. He'd know exactly what to do with the man we'd found. And I was sure he wouldn't have just shot him. He would have done the right thing, just like we were trying to.

"How much farther?" Kim asked.

"Not much." It seemed like we'd come a long way, but I knew it was because we were carrying the man. If we'd been on our own, we would have made it there in just a few minutes.

A little farther along and we saw the dark shape of the shed. "That's where me da' keeps the feed," I said. "There's a little burner in there, too, so he can make tea."

"That's your hiding place?"

"No. I reckon if anyone was lookin' for 'im, they'd look in there."

"*I* would."

We passed the shed, staggering a few more yards, and came

to the place where the undergrowth was thick and matted. "In here," I said. "He can hide in here."

"Where?"

Behind the shed, hidden in the deepest part of the wood, a cluster of shrubs grew so large and close and thick it was as if there was a solid mass of green, spotted with large flowers the color of blood. Hawthorn and rhododendron were tangled there among other plants that had names Dad had told me but I'd forgotten. In the winter it looked like an impassable huddle of dark sticks and knotted wood, but now, when summer was in full swing, it was a beautiful growth of leaves. And only I knew that to one side, close to the foot of a sycamore tree, there was a single place where the sticks and the twigs that supported those leaves didn't meet. It was a spot where I'd cut the branches with my own penknife to allow me to crawl inside, where there was a hollow large enough for me to stretch out and lie down. In there — in *my* place — I could almost stand up straight, and I could probably have cut away enough height for that if I'd wanted to, but I liked the area just as it was.

I led Kim around the shrubs and showed her the entrance to my hiding place. "Right here."

We bundled the German through the hole in the tangle of twigs and leaves and creepers and pulled him into the cavernous interior. Toward the back grew the thick trunk of another sycamore, so we leaned him against it and sat back to stare at him.

Our souvenir.

"You think he's dyin'?" I asked. "I don't want him dyin' in here."

"He's not dying," Kim said. "At least, I don't think so. He's just hurt, that's all. Hurt and tired."

"Prob'ly scared, too."

"Yeah."

Somewhere not too far away, a scream pierced the night.

"What on earth was that?" Kim said.

I looked at her just as the sound came again. Loud and shrill, a high-pitched noise that was a cross between a scream and a dog's bark.

"Really," said Kim, "what *is* that noise? It's horrible. Sounded like someone being murdered!"

"It's not horrible," I said. "I hear it all the time. When I hear it at night, it makes me feel cozy."

"That noise makes you feel cozy? You're madder than I thought."

Again, the scream split the night.

"It's a fox," I said. "Maybe a vixen looking for her cubs."

"Well, I don't like it," she said.

"It's just a country sound. You're not scared, are you?"

"No. Not scared. Just a little . . . concerned, that's all. It's creepy."

Lying back against the tree, the German airman said nothing. I shone the flashlight at his face but he didn't react. His eyes were closed, his arms hanging limp at his sides, his legs stretched out and relaxed so his feet had splayed out sideways to make a V shape.

"Is he dead?" I whispered, cocooned in our mixture of darkness and orange light.

"I don't think so. No. He can't be. Maybe we should check."

"Check?"

"Listen to his chest," she said. "Then we'll know."

"*I'm* not doing it," I said when I saw how she was looking at me. "You wanted to bring 'im here."

Kim scratched her head. She took a deep breath through her nose and blew it out of her mouth, puffing her cheeks. "All right."

I pulled out the pistol. "I'll make sure he doesn't try anythin'." I pointed it at him, right at the bright orange circle cast by the flashlight.

Kim crawled over on all fours, moving slowly. Closer and closer.

When she was right beside him, she stopped.

"Go on," I said.

Kim looked back at me and made a face to show she wasn't scared, but it quickly passed and I saw her real feelings right there, as if they'd been painted on her. She was just as scared as I was.

Out in the field, the fox screamed again.

Kim leaned close, turning her head to put an ear against the man's chest. She paused, then moved closer until she was touching him.

When the airman reached up and grabbed her hand, Kim almost jumped through the tangled web of twigs above us. He gripped her tight, not letting go, as if he had summoned the last of his strength.

I jumped, too, dropping the pistol onto the damp soil at my knees, but in the orange light I saw the man open his eyes. He looked at Kim, so close to his face, her wrist held tightly in his fist, and he opened his mouth.

"*Danke*," he said, then let go, his hand dropping beside him as if all his strength was gone.

Kim shuffled back as quickly as she could until she was beside me again, and I reached down to grab the pistol. I could hear Kim breathing hard.

"We should go," I said.

"Yeah." Kim held her water bottle in her hand and considered it. "I'll leave it for him."

"You sure?" I asked. "Looks like a canny water bottle. If it was mine, I'd wanna keep it."

Kim looked at it, then shook her head and threw it gently so it landed on the German's lap. "He needs it," she said.

We backed out of the den, both of us pretending not to be scared, and walked quickly back to the creek, crossing through the woods without caring about brambles and nettles and thistles. The next morning my legs itched and there were scratches all over me, but right then I didn't notice them at all. We hurried on, jumping the babbling burn this time, heading back to the barbed-wire fence, and escaping out into the field. Only then did we slow down a little, but I still felt as if there was something watching us; as if something might be following us.

"I nearly jumped out of my skin," Kim said. "He gave me such a scare."

"Me too."

"Not as much as me," she said. "The way he grabbed me. I thought I was going to die."

"And I dropped the gun," I said. "It slipped right out of me hand."

"It was fun, though, eh?"

"Fun? I thought I was going to wet meself."

"Wet yourself?" Kim started to laugh. "You wet yourself?"

"No. I said I *thought* I was going to."

Kim burst out laughing, bending double and putting her hands on her knees to support herself.

"Shh!" I said. "The soldiers'll hear." But I couldn't help feeling the laughter coming to me, too, riding up inside me, uncontrollable, until I couldn't stop myself. And then we were both laughing, releasing all the tension and fear that had built up that night. We laughed and laughed until our sides hurt, and we were still giggling when we started walking again, heading back across the field.

We quieted down going up the hill and avoiding the wreck, and when it was time for us to part, Kim punched me on the arm. "Wet yourself," she said. "That's a good one."

"Do you think he'll still be there tomorrow?"

"Where else would he go?"

"Nowhere, I s'pose."

"Then we'll go back first thing. Take him something to eat. Do you think you can get anything?"

"We haven't got much." I thought about the tripe we'd had for tea and, for some reason, that made me think of the body in the plane.

"You must be able to get *some*thing."

I tried to think what I could take without Mam noticing. She sometimes baked biscuits, but she'd know exactly how many she'd made, and if there was any bread left, she'd know exactly how many pieces. If there was meat — which there wasn't — she'd know exactly how much. The only thing I could think of was my sweets ration.

"A couple of barley sugars?" I shrugged.

"We'll have to do better than that," Kim said. "We can't have him starving to death."

"Maybe we should just tell someone where he is. Let them —"

"Shoot him?"

"You *really* think they would?"

"What else? You heard the sergeant."

I didn't want that to happen. The German had looked so scared when I'd pointed the gun at him, I could hardly imagine how he must have felt. And I didn't want him to die because of me. I thought about what Kim had said earlier, about wanting someone to look after my dad if something happened to him, and I tried not to imagine him, tired and scared, having to face an angry sergeant and a line of soldiers with guns.

"I might be able to get some food," Kim said, pushing my thoughts away. "Aunt Hillary's a bit batty, so she probably wouldn't notice if something went missing. We'll have to get some supplies from somewhere, though, so have a good think about it."

"All right."

"And how about a blanket? You think you can get one of those?"

"I s'pose I could try. Do you think . . ." I thought about what I was going to say and took a breath. "Are you *sure* we shouldn't tell someone?"

"Not yet," she said.

Then she stopped and looked at me for a moment before turning and running toward the village. "See you tomorrow!" she called back. And then she was gone.

A KNOCK AT THE DOOR

I hardly slept the rest of that night and, when I did, my dreams were so clear I would have thought I was awake if it weren't for the strange things I saw. Crashed airplanes, the sky filled with falling parachutes like a million jellyfish floating in clear water. Falling bullet casings and balls of fire. There were moments of darkness, too: the thickest, oiliest blackness, filled with the stink of cooked meat. For a time I felt as if I were falling into a deep pit filled with the burnt bodies of dead soldiers, their eyeless faces staring up at me from the dark. Their bony hands reached out for me, clothed in the tattered remains of their ruined uniforms. Then I was yanked away, to watch soldiers moving across green meadows in the height of summer. And I saw Kim's face in my muddled dreams, too. I saw her turned-up nose and her black hair, cut like a boy's.

And when first light pushed around the cracks in the black-out curtains, I woke up with a mixed feeling of excitement and dread when I remembered what we had done.

I tugged back the curtains and reached under my bed to pull out the shoebox where I kept all the cigarette cards Dad had given me to collect. Then I climbed back into bed, sat up against my pillow, and opened the box, moving the cards aside to take out the pistol.

There were bits of mud clogged in it, and I was careful not to drop any of the dirt on my bed covers. I held it out and pointed it at the foot of the bed, just as I'd pointed it at the airman last night.

It still didn't seem real. Even with the gun right there in my hand, heavy and hard and metal. Even then, it didn't feel as if it had happened to me — more like someone had told me about it, or I'd imagined it.

But it *was* real. Last night, Kim and I really *had* captured a German. We had sneaked out in the night and we had taken him to my secret place. My throat went dry at the thought of how many rules we'd broken, and for a moment I was smothered by a feeling of such guilt that I had to stop myself from rushing to Mam's bedroom to tell her what had happened. A small voice in my head was telling me it was the right thing to do. The grown-ups could take over then. They'd deal with everything. They'd find the German and I'd have nothing more to worry about. Except for getting into trouble, of course.

And Kim would get into trouble, too, and she'd call me a sneak and hate me. And maybe the German would be killed and it would all be my fault. And there was also the other thing — what Kim had said about how we should look after the German so that if something happened to my dad or her brother, then they would be looked after, too. As if, somehow, our actions would affect the actions of someone else a thousand miles away. I was so desperate for Dad to be safe, so desperate for him to come home, that maybe it was worth a try. Maybe it *would* be bad luck to tell the grown-ups about the German. Bad luck for Dad.

I put the gun back in the box and hardened my nerve. I wouldn't do anything without talking to Kim. We were in this together. I wasn't going to tell on her.

As I slipped the box back under my bed, I remembered what we'd talked about before we parted last night, about needing supplies for our prisoner. So I climbed out of bed and put on my bathrobe before creeping from my room and heading downstairs. It was early, but Mam would be up soon, so I went as quietly as possible, going through the kitchen and into the scullery.

Over on my right, there was a heavy white sink that we filled from the pump outside, using a bucket. Some of the houses in the village had taps in the kitchen, but ours was too far out and they hadn't run in the pipes yet. We didn't have gas either, so Mam did all the cooking on the range that took up most of the right wall.

In the far corner, a side door went out into the garden, but we hardly used it, so it was usually blocked by the mangle. Beside it, along the back wall, there were some uneven shelves and, because it was coldest there, there was a stone slab where Mam put the meat and butter under a sieve to keep it fresh.

I stood for a moment, the stone floor cold on my feet, looking at the shelves, wondering what on earth I might be able to take. We really had so very little. There was a nearly empty tin of Lingfords baking powder that had been there forever, a can of National Dried Milk, and a packet of dried egg. There were one or two other tins and boxes, but nothing that wouldn't be missed or that would be of any use to our German. I checked the bread bin but there were only four thin slices left. There were a few vegetables in a basket on the floor. On the cold slab, under the sieve that kept the flies away, there was a small knob of butter on a metal plate, a chunk of cheese that wasn't much bigger, two paper packets, and a tray of five eggs. I stared at them, deciding if I had time to risk looking in the packets. If I was going to do it, I'd have to do it right now, before Mam came down. The longer I waited, the less time I'd actually have to take anything.

I made up my mind and opened the first packet, careful not to crumple the paper. Inside, two thin rashers of bacon. They were fatty, with very little meat on them, but I knew I couldn't take them. Mam would know. Two rashers of bacon was a luxury, and she'd be saving them for something special.

I wrapped them back up and opened the second packet, seeing what was left of the piece of tripe. White and rubbery and foul. It was only a small piece, about the size of my hand, but I thought I might be able to take a tiny slice, so I hurried to the drawer and took out a sharp knife. I cut a piece of tripe no thicker or longer than my little finger, and then I wrapped the main piece back up again before cleaning the knife, drying it, and putting it back in the drawer.

When I went to the cold slab to collect my thin strip of tripe, I realized I didn't have anything to wrap it in. I glanced around for something but, as I did, I heard creaking upstairs. Mam was coming.

I looked down at my tiny piece of tripe, like a white worm in the palm of my hand, and felt a pang of guilt. I was stealing.

That's what I was doing. I was stealing from my own mam so I could feed the enemy. Except, I told myself, he wasn't just the enemy: He was a scared, wounded, hungry enemy. Anyway, I wasn't doing this just for him, I was doing it for my friend, too. For Kim. And I was doing it for Dad — so someone would do the same for him.

I put the tripe into the pocket of my robe and turned to leave the scullery. And that's when I did something very silly. I reached out and grabbed an egg. One of the five eggs sitting in the tray. I slipped that into my pocket, too, then I turned and hurried out, closing the door behind me.

When I came out into the hallway, Mam was at the bottom of the stairs, dressed and ready for the day.

I stopped.

"Mornin', pet." Mam smiled. "What are you doing up?"

"Nowt."

Mam's expression changed. The smile faltered as if she'd seen something in my eyes. Maybe she'd seen right through me. She had looked into my head and seen exactly what I'd been up to.

"Is somethin' the matter?" she asked.

"No." My heart was beating fast now, and there was something inside me that wanted to blurt it all out and tell her what I'd done. I was sure she was looking at the egg-shaped bulge in my bathrobe pocket.

"Well, off you go, then, and get dressed. I'll get breakfast."

"All right," I said, moving past her, taking the stairs two at a time. I could almost feel her eyes on my back, watching me with suspicion as I went into my bedroom and closed the door behind me.

My hands were shaking when I took my bounty from my pocket. I held them out in the palm of my hand and stared at them: the first things I had ever pinched from Mam. A sad-looking piece of tripe covered in fluff from my pocket and a single brown egg. I had stolen, but I'd done it to help someone. I felt good and bad at the same time.

I put the egg in my satchel and picked the fluff off the tripe, looking around, wondering what to wrap it in. The only thing I had that would do the job was the comic on the floor beside my bed. I'd read it a few times already, but I didn't like the idea of ripping it, because if I took an old comic book back to the shop, Mr. McPherson let me have a new one for a cheaper price. Perhaps if I took a tiny piece from one of the pages, he might not notice. But as soon as I thought it, I began to feel like a criminal. I'd already stolen food from Mam, and now I was thinking about cheating Mr. McPherson. I decided that I'd rip part of one page, and then I'd tell him I ripped it by accident. Maybe I'd even be able to bring the ripped piece back and put it inside the comic. That way I wasn't trying to cheat him, I was just telling him a little white lie.

So I tore a small piece from one of the inside pages of my Dandy comic, and I wrapped the worm of tripe inside it before putting it next to the egg in my satchel.

Then I dressed and went downstairs.

Mam was in the kitchen by then and she smiled when I came in, giving me a hug and kissing the top of my head.

"Hungry?" she asked.

"Starvin'."

Mam had cooked one of the rashers of bacon I'd seen on the

slab. I'd smelled it as soon as I'd come out of my bedroom, and the first thing I'd thought of was the dead airman in the plane last night, but I pushed the thought away. My stomach was grumbling, and I wasn't going to let anything put me off my food.

My plate was already on the table — there was one rasher of bacon, with a single fried egg and a piece of bread. The bacon looked smaller now that it had been cooked. It was tiny, curled up next to the egg, and I ate it very slowly, savoring the taste.

Mam was sitting opposite me, sorting through her sewing box. There was a pile of clothes on the seat beside her: everything that needed mending. There was a steaming mug on the table, too, but I knew we'd almost run out of tea, so Mam was drinking hot water. She'd be saving the tea for another time.

"You not havin' anythin'?" I asked.

"I've had some toast," she said. "Now it's time to make do and mend."

That's what the posters told us all to do. "Make Do and Mend." That meant instead of wanting new things, like clothes, it was better to mend the ones we already had. Like my shoes with the cardboard to cover the holes, or my worn-out shirts and trousers, and there wasn't a man in the village who didn't have a patch on the elbow of his jacket. Even Mr. Bennett's jackets had patches. I think it might have been Mam who'd sewn them for him.

I watched her pick up a sock and put her finger through a hole in the toe, then I went back to eating my breakfast.

"I could have sworn we had five eggs last night," Mam said, taking me by surprise.

My hand stopped in midair, my fork a few inches from my mouth. I looked up at Mam. She was putting a wooden mushroom-shaped object into the sock, just behind the hole.

"But there were only four this mornin'."

I put the fork into my mouth, taking the small piece of bacon, the metal prongs grating against my teeth.

"You don't know anythin' about that, do you?"

I shook my head, chewing slowly. The bacon suddenly tasted like cardboard. "Uh-uh."

Mam nodded as she threaded wool into a thick darning needle. "There isn't somethin' you want to tell me?"

Once again, it was all on the tip of my tongue. But I couldn't tell Mam. I couldn't tell her I'd stolen the food. "No," I said.

Mam continued to look at me. "Are you sure?"

"Aye."

"So what *were* you doing downstairs this mornin'?" she asked.

"Nowt."

"I see. So I wonder why the dishcloth was wet, the tea towel's been used, and there's an egg missing." She looked up at me from her darning. "As if, maybe, someone dropped an egg and thought they could clean it up without me noticing."

I stared at her.

"Don't lie to us, Peter. What were you doin' in the scullery? Looking for somethin' to eat?"

I nodded.

"Did you take anythin'?"

"No."

"Good. We have to save what we've got," she said. "You can't just take things."

"I was hungry," I said, adding lying to my list of crimes. "I thought . . ." I shrugged.

Mam leaned forward. "I know it's hard — you're a growin' lad — but we haven't got much. We can't just help ourselves. There's two of us."

"I really didn't take anythin'," I said. "I promise."

"That's not the point, Peter. You thought about it, but breakin' the egg made you think again, didn't it?"

I hung my head. "Sorry." And I really *did* feel sorry. For everything. But not sorry enough to come clean and tell the truth, I suppose.

"Hm. Well, lucky for us, the hens are canny layers, so we'll probably have another four eggs this morning." Mam looked at me for a long moment, then shook her head. "All right. Just don't do it again."

I nodded.

"Eat up, then. It'll be gettin' cold."

I ate slowly, trying to enjoy my breakfast, but somehow it didn't taste quite right anymore. I looked up from time to time, watching Mam darning my sock, and I felt bad that I'd lied to her. But I'd done it for a good reason, hadn't I? I'd done it for Dad and Kim and Josh and to help the airman who was sitting out there in the woods, probably starving. Maybe even dying.

"What do you think Germans eat?" I asked.

"What's that?" Mam stopped and glanced up at me.

"What do Germans eat?"

She went back to what she was doing. "Whatever made you ask that?"

"Nowt. Just wondered, like."

"Well . . ." She thought about it. "I don't know. I s'pose they probably eat the same things as we do."

"Bacon and egg?"

"Maybe."

"And bread and cheese?" I asked.

"Aye, why not?"

"And what do they do?"

Mam rested the darning on her knee and looked at me. "What on earth are you talking about, pet?"

"I mean . . . well, I don't know. Are they like us? I know they don't talk like us, but do they do the same *things* as us? You know, like go to the shops and sleep in a bed and sit at a table for breakfast and . . . you know — the same things as us."

"I s'pose they do." Mam raised her eyebrows as if something had occurred to her. "I haven't ever met any Germans, but I s'pose they're probably not so different from us at all."

"Not so different," I repeated. "So why do they want to bomb us?"

"I'm not sure they all do," Mam said.

"So, they're not all bad, then?"

"Course not. Just like not all the lads in the village are like Trevor Ridley."

"Not even them what fly the planes?"

Mam looked at me with a puzzled expression. "What's all this interest in Germans?"

"Just wonderin'," I said, standing up and taking my plate from the table.

"Is this 'cause of that plane yesterday?"

I shrugged.

"Well, you don't need to worry about it, because you're never going to see any Germans in this country. Brave men like your da' —"

"And Kim's brother," I said.

"Aye, and Kim's brother . . . Brave men like them are keeping us safe. So that's enough of that talk for now."

"All right." I was putting the plate in the sink when there was a knock at the door.

"Someone's early," Mam said, looking at the clock, then at me. She furrowed her brow as if thinking, then her face fell and her mouth hung open, her lips making a shape like an *O*, her eyes widening.

I knew what was wrong. As soon as I saw her reaction, I understood what she was afraid of. She was afraid of the telegram boy, the one who came early to give wives and children the message that their husbands and fathers were dead.

"Go into the scullery," she said.

I didn't argue. I just nodded and felt something cold squeeze my insides as I left the room, moving like I was floating, a million terrible thoughts in my head. But one of those thoughts was louder than all the rest. Something had happened to Dad. He was hurt or lost or . . . or worse. Except that couldn't be. I'd helped the German. I'd hidden him and helped him, and that meant Dad would be all right, didn't it? That was what Kim had said; that was what we'd decided.

I stood in the middle of the room and listened as Mam went to the door. There was a moment of quiet, then she laughed and came into the scullery with a relieved smile on her face, and I knew I was right. Nothing had happened to Dad. He was fine. And maybe, just maybe, we'd had something to do with that.

"It's for you," she said. "Your new friend."

Kim stepped out from behind her, raising a hand. "Morning." She was dressed in the same shorts and shirt as yesterday, and had her satchel slung across her.

"What's wrong?" she asked me as Mam went back to the kitchen. "You look like you've seen a ghost."

"No one ever comes this early," I said. "We thought you were the telegram boy."

Kim drew in a sharp breath and put a fist to her mouth. "I'm so sorry."

I nodded and we went back into the kitchen, where Mam poured us both a small glass of milk.

When I sat down, Mam put her hand on mine and squeezed it. "Dad's fine," she said quietly. "I know it."

I smiled at her.

"So you're from Newcastle?" Mam said, looking up at Kim. "Here to keep safe?"

Kim nodded and wiped her mouth on her forearm.

"Well, let's hope we don't get too many more planes comin' down on our heads, then, eh?" Mam said.

"At least there's no bombs," Kim replied.

"Oh, we get our fair share of those," Mam said. "Still, I s'pose it's worse in the town . . ." She stopped herself and looked at us, putting her hands on her hips. "Listen to me gabbing on when I've got things to do," she said. "Go on, you two, get yourselves out. But don't go too far. I don't want you back in those woods again."

"But Mam —"

"No buts, Peter. I don't even want to think about what almost happened yesterday."

"But it's morning, Mam, the Germans won't come now."

"They came yesterday when it was light. And anyway, there was a parachute, wasn't there? There might be one of them Germans outside our house right now." Mam turned to look at the door as if, for a moment, she really thought there *was* a German outside. And when I saw that look on her face, seeing her suddenly realize that there might be an enemy on the loose near our village, I had to think quick or she wouldn't let me go out.

"He'll be long gone," I said. "I know *I* would be if it was me. An' if he isn't, then he's prob'ly dead."

Mam shuddered, and I wondered if I'd made things worse, but Kim stepped forward and put her hand on my shoulder. "It's all right, Mrs. Dixon, I'll make sure we don't go too far. And if there's any sign of trouble we'll come right back. I promise."

Mam stopped with her mouth half open, and she looked at Kim. When she closed her mouth, there was a faint smile on her lips. "Well, that's very refreshin'." Then she narrowed her eyes. "All right. Just stay out of trouble, the pair of you. An' I want you straight back if there's any sign of it."

Mam collected our glasses, taking them to the sink, and while she had her back to us, Kim took the chance to lean over and whisper in my ear. "Did you get a blanket?"

I shook my head. In all the confusion of stealing food, I'd completely forgotten about trying to get hold of a blanket.

Kim made a face to show her annoyance.

"Back in a mo'," I said, thinking I'd run upstairs and get a blanket. I needed to get my satchel, too, with its cargo of tripe and egg.

"What is it now?" Mam asked.

I looked at her and then at Kim, an awkward moment. "Err . . . my penknife."

"Do you really need it?" Mam asked.

"Course I do," I said.

"Lads." She looked at Kim for understanding but received none. "Go on, then, go and get it."

I rushed upstairs, wondering how I was going to smuggle a blanket out of the house. We had a few spare in the cupboard and I hoped Mam wouldn't miss one, but I didn't know how I was going to get it past her.

I could hear them talking downstairs as I opened the cupboard and grabbed a heavy pink blanket from the pile. I stuffed it up my shirt, but that was no good. It looked like I'd eaten a whole cow, and the corners were sticking out, so I went to my bedroom and thought about putting on a coat, but Mam would think it strange — I *never* wanted to wear a coat.

Then I had an idea.

I opened my bedroom window, which was at the back of the cottage, and threw it down into the garden. If I ran straight out, I could collect it before we headed over to the woods. I grabbed my satchel and left my room.

On the way downstairs, I remembered the pistol under my bed. I stopped and stood for a moment, deciding we'd need protection if we were going to see the airman, so I went back to my bedroom, took the pistol out of the box, and stuck it in my satchel.

"Ready?" Mam asked when I came into the kitchen. "Got the all-important penknife?"

I patted my pocket.

"And your satchel, I see. What d'you need that for?"

"Just 'cause." I put one arm across it as if to stop her from taking it.

"You got something in there?"

"No. Nowt."

"A lot of nowt goin' on this mornin'," Mam said. "Are you two up to somethin'?"

"No," I protested. "It's just for . . . stuff. Souvenirs." As soon as the word escaped my lips, I knew I shouldn't have said it.

"Souvenirs?" Mam said. "You'll not be going near that crashed plane. If I find out you've been anywhere near there, I'll tan your backside so hard that —"

"We won't go anywhere near it, Mrs. Dixon," Kim stepped in again. "I promise."

"And you?" Mam looked at me. "You promise, too?"

"I promise," I said, glad she hadn't made me promise not to go to the woods. She said I wasn't allowed, but that wasn't the same as making me promise.

"And try not to get all clarty," she said, coming closer, taking the sleeve of my shirt between her finger and her thumb. "Marks like this aren't easy to get out."

I glanced down at the dirty brown stain on my sleeve, knowing straightaway that it wasn't mud from the field. It was blood. German blood.

"Off you go, then," she sighed.

But before I could open the door, there was another knock.

I glanced over at Mam again and, once more, she had that look of worry in her expression, as if she was expecting bad news. Only this time she didn't tell me to go into the scullery. Instead, she brushed down the front of her dress and put a stern look on her face, then she strode to the door and pulled it open.

When I saw Mr. Bennett standing on the step, I let out my breath. I hadn't even realized I'd been holding it.

Beside Mr. Bennett was the man who'd been giving the orders at the crash site yesterday. The lieutenant had his feet together as if he was standing to attention. His hands were behind his back and his chin was jutting out, pointing straight at the door. Behind him were Sergeant Wilkes and another two soldiers, with their rifles over their shoulders.

Mam reached out to put her hand on the doorframe and I thought I saw her legs give way slightly at the knees. She steadied herself, swallowed hard, and forced a smile. "Gentlemen."

Mr. Bennett cleared his throat. "I'm sorry to disturb you so early, Mrs. Dixon . . ." And then he saw it, too. He noticed the way Mam was standing, supporting herself on the doorframe, and he suddenly looked concerned. "Oh, no, Mrs. Dixon, really, it's nothing to worry about. Everything's all right. Lieutenant Rogers just wanted to ask you a few questions."

My mother took a sharp breath. "Oh. Oh." She looked back at me. "I thought . . . Oh." She came back into the kitchen and sat down on the chair where Kim had been sitting. "Oh, thank goodness for that."

"May we come in?" Mr. Bennett asked.

"Aye. Aye, of course," Mam said. "Please."

Mr. Bennett stepped in and the officer came with him, removing his cap. Sergeant Wilkes and the other two soldiers remained outside when the officer closed the door behind him.

"I'm so sorry to have worried you," Mr. Bennett said, coming over to Mam, reaching out for her shoulder but stopping short of actually touching her. "I should have said something straightaway. I'll remember next time." He glanced back at the officer. "I should've thought that when you saw the soldiers you'd think . . ." He shook his head and looked at me. "Hello, Peter. How are you?"

"Fine."

Mam waved a hand at me. "It's all right, you two go and play."

The lieutenant stepped forward, putting his cap under his arm. "Actually, it might be better if they stay."

LIEUTENANT WHATSHISNAME

The lieutenant wouldn't sit down. Mam asked him to, but he just stood there with his shiny boots on our clean floor, his heels together. Mr. Bennett looked uncomfortable, as if he wanted to sit down but wasn't sure what to do because the soldier was still on his feet. Mam stayed on the chair anyway, and Kim and I went to the other side of the table and sat down.

Mr. Bennett was wearing a checked shirt and a tie. He put his hand on the back of his head and rubbed it, smiling at Mam, telling her again that he was sorry.

The lieutenant had taken off his cap when he came into the cottage, and now it was tucked under his arm. "As I'm sure you know, a German plane crashed close to your home yesterday afternoon."

"A Heinkel," Kim said.

"Yes, quite." The lieutenant eyed her closely. "As you say, a Heinkel."

"Are you sure you won't sit down?" Mam said. "I could make you a cup of tea. It'll be weak, but we have a little milk." She was still shaky; I could hear the tremble in her voice.

"No. Thank you, madam. I shan't be long." He stood up even straighter, if that was possible. He was so stiff and straight it was a wonder he didn't crush the cap under his armpit.

"As I was saying" — he cleared his throat — "there were no survivors at the crash site and my men are guarding it now. However, a parachute was seen in the vicinity of the village."

"Yes, Peter told me about that," Mam said.

"Peter?" the lieutenant asked.

"Me *son*."

"Ah. I see. Well. Some of my soldiers discovered the parachute late yesterday evening; at least, they found what was left of it. Some children found it a couple of miles away, tangled on a fence, and by the time we got to it, most of it had been cut up and taken away."

"There'll be a few of the ladies wearin' silk underwear very soon, then," Mam said.

"I beg your pardon?"

"The silk from the parachute," she explained. "The ladies use the silk to make underwear."

"Hm. Quite. Well, putting that aside, it was unfortunate there was no sign of the person who may have used the parachute."

"He got away, you mean?"

"Yes, that's exactly what I mean. But not to worry, madam," said the lieutenant. "He looks to have come down in some trees, so he may well be wounded or dead, but my sergeant has a nose like a bloodhound and we'll have the Jerry" — he cleared his throat again — "we will have the *German* before the day is out. You can bet on that."

"I'm not a bettin' person, lieutenant." Mam seemed to have overcome the shock of seeing the soldiers at the door, and her mood had darkened. She was annoyed at them for frightening her.

"Of course not, madam."

"The lieutenant would like his men to have a look around, Irene, that's why we're here," said Mr. Bennett. "He wants to check all the buildings on the estate. It's nothing to worry about, just a precaution, really. I'm sure the German is long gone by now. Probably broke free of his parachute and is strung up dead in a tree somewhere."

"Oh, that's horrible," Mam said.

"Sorry. What I mean to say is that Lieutenant Rogers's men will find him if he's here."

"Precisely," said the lieutenant.

"So would it be all right to have a look around the garden, check the cellar, that sort of thing?"

"I s'pose so," Mam said. "If it'll help."

"And I see you have a shelter in the back garden, madam. I'd like to —"

"Help yourself." Mam stood up.

The lieutenant removed his cap from under his arm and started to head back to the door.

"What will you do if you find 'im?" I asked. "If he's alive, I mean."

He stopped and turned to look at me. "Well, that's to be seen, young man. But don't you worry yourself about it; it's all in hand."

"Will he be shot?"

"Don't you worry, Peter," said Mr. Bennett. "The soldiers will hunt him down."

"And shoot 'im?"

"Nothing for you to be concerned about," said the lieutenant. "I imagine it's all a bit of a game to you."

"I'll have you know my lad understands exactly how serious this is," Mam told him. "My husband is away fightin' and my son knows exactly what his father is fightin' *for*. I've made sure of that and we're both very proud. We might not be soldiers, but that doesn't make us simpletons, you know."

"I apologize." The lieutenant flushed and I couldn't help exchanging a look with Kim.

"Well, I think you'd better go and carry out your search, then," Mam said, going to the door and pulling it open. A lovely smell of fresh fields came in on the warm breeze, and I could see the sergeant and the other two soldiers standing there, slouching against the fence. They snapped to attention as soon as the door opened.

"And if there's anywhere else you can think of, madam. Anywhere a fugitive might be hiding."

Mam took a deep breath and looked up at the ceiling. I imagined her trying to think of all the places a man could hide and I hoped she wouldn't remember Dad's shed in the woods.

"No," she said. "I can't think of anywhere."

"And you two should keep close to home," the lieutenant said to Kim and me. "We don't know where this man might be . . ."

"Prob'ly dead," I said, looking over at Kim and then back at the lieutenant. "You're prob'ly wastin' your time gettin' all them soldiers to look for 'im."

The lieutenant eyed me closely. "Hmm. Well, if you see anything — anything at all — I want you to tell your mother and she'll come straight to me."

We both nodded without saying a word.

Mr. Bennett followed Lieutenant Rogers outside and gave Mam a smile before she closed the door on them.

"Stuffy old so-and-so," she said under her breath.

"Mr. Bennett?" I asked.

"No. That Lieutenant Whatshisname. Telling me you think this is all some sort o' game. Cheeky beggar." She shook her head. "Still, I s'pose he's just doin' his job, tryin' to keep us all safe."

"Come on, then." Kim grabbed my hand. "Let's go out." She pulled open the door and we hurried out.

"Don't go too far, remember," Mam called, but we had already closed the door and were heading round the back of the house.

Mr. Bennett was gone — I could see him walking along the path toward the village — but the soldiers' vehicle was still parked on the lane and one of the men was standing by our Anderson shelter, while the other had gone down to poke about inside. I wasn't sure why they were bothering — I could see from where I was standing that no one was hiding in there.

The sergeant was close to the wall beneath my bedroom window, looking up, holding a blanket.

Kim ran over to him and snatched it from his hands. "I've been looking for that," she said, running back to me.

The sergeant whipped his head around to watch us. "What are you up to?" He narrowed his eyes in suspicion.

"Nothing." Kim pulled my shirt to make me follow her.

"And where are your masks?" he called after us as we ran through the gate and over the path. "You're supposed to be carrying your gas masks."

"Can't hear you!" Kim shouted, and looked at me with a mischievous smile.

"Don't," I said.

"I'm not scared of him."

"Well, I am. And we'll have to go round," I said. "Can't have him watching where we go."

"Did you see that Lieutenant Whatshisname's face when your mum told him off?" Kim asked as we climbed the hill. "He was standing as straight as a board with his shiny boots and his gun on his belt, and your mum made him blush."

"I don't think she liked him."

"I'm not surprised," Kim said. "That other man liked her, though, I could tell."

"Mr. Bennett?"

"Yeah. He seemed nice."

"He's all right, I s'pose."

Kim looked at me. "You don't like him much?"

"Not really."

"Why not? Who is he?"

"He's the one owns all this land," I said. "And Bennett Hall."

"So your mum and dad work for him?"

"Not Mam."

"So why's he not fighting? He's not too old."

"He was at Dunkirk," I told her. "Said he got injured or somethin' and now he gets to stay at home."

"Oh." Kim took a deep breath and nodded as if she suddenly understood something. "I see."

"No. That's not why I don't like him," I said.

"Why, then?"

"'Cause he always comes to our house."

"You mean because he likes your mum."

"Don't say that." I turned on her. "Not ever."

Kim put up her hands. "Sorry. I didn't mean anything by it."

I sighed. "I know. It's just, that's what Trevor Ridley always says to us, and he *does* mean somethin' by it. He says Mr. Bennett is Mam's fancy man."

"Is he not married?"

"He was. She died, though, before the war."

"Oh."

We were nearing the top of the hill and I stopped as something occurred to me. "D'you think he's lookin' for a new wife?" I asked. "Maybe he thinks Mam —"

"No," Kim said. "And don't worry about what that boy Trevor Ridley says. Next time we see him, I'll give him a bloody nose, how about that?"

"I'd like to see you try."

"You're on."

I smiled at that, but then something else came to mind, making the smile drop away. "Do you think he knew?" I said. "That sergeant?"

"Knew what?"

"That we found the German?"

"How could he?"

"He found the blanket, didn't he? And you heard what the lieutenant said about him having a nose like a bloodhound. Them dogs can sniff out anything." I thought about the way he had looked at Kim when she'd snatched the blanket from him. Was it suspicion or surprise? I couldn't be sure, but whenever I thought about him, I remembered the wolfish grin I'd seen yesterday on the hillside.

"He doesn't know anything," she said. "How could he?"

"Maybe you're right."

"Of course I am. Didn't you know? Girls are always right."

RECONNAISSANCE

At the top of the hill, we got down on our tummies like commandos watching an enemy base. We stayed low behind the bushes and kept out of sight. The sheep that were grazing there took no notice of us, hardly even looking up.

By the wreck, three soldiers had their backs to us. They weren't Home Guard, like they'd been when we went into the plane last night. These were real soldiers. Young and fit and well armed. They were sitting facing the broken plane and, as we watched, one of them stood up and went to the fuselage, looking in. I could hear him saying something, but couldn't make out the words.

"What they doin'?" I said. "You think they found somethin'?"

"Just guarding, that's all. Stopping people from taking souvenirs."

"People like us?"

Kim smiled. "Yeah. And maybe they're waiting to see if the German'll come back."

I could smell her again, just like yesterday. Cheap soap. But it smelled so much better on her than it did on me and Mam.

"He's not going to, though, is he?" I said.

Kim shook her head, and I thought about what we'd seen inside the plane last night. "Maybe they're guardin' it so nobody goes inside and sees what we saw," I suggested. "Imagine if one of the bairns climbed in there and saw the dead man. And it's prob'ly dangerous, too." A thought struck me. "Hey, I wonder if there's any unexploded bombs in there, like. Maybe *that's* why they're guardin' it."

"It's probably all of those things," Kim said, standing up. "I'm going to find out."

"What?" I looked up at her with alarm. "No."

She was taking off her satchel, pulling the strap over her head.

"What if *he* comes?" I said. "That sergeant?" I felt sure he'd know what we had done if he looked into our eyes.

"He won't," she said. "He's out searching. But even if he does, I can handle him. You stay here and look after this." She dropped her satchel on the ground next to me. "I'll be back in a minute."

I tried calling to her, not sure whether to go after her or do as she'd said, but she was already trotting down the hill toward the soldiers, so I laid low and watched.

The three soldiers didn't notice Kim until she was close to the bottom of the hill. It was the one who'd been looking into the fuselage who spotted her. He came forward, his voice loud, but I couldn't make out the words. He whipped his rifle from his shoulder and pointed it at her while the other two jumped to their feet, dropping cigarettes and pointing guns.

Kim put her hands up and stopped as they approached her.

115

She looked small, all the way down there at the bottom of the hill, beside those soldiers. When I was with her, it always felt like she was tall, but from where I was now, she looked like a little boy in her shorts and shirt. She wasn't scared of the soldiers, though, and I could hear her talking to them. I felt myself puff up my chest in pride that she was my friend.

I saw Kim pull something out of her pocket, her identity card, and hold it out to the soldier who'd first spotted her. He took it, slinging his rifle over his shoulder, and looked it over for a moment before passing it back. After that, the other two lowered their rifles and lit cigarettes. I could see them offer one to Kim, and I was sure I saw her reach out and take it. They talked for a while, the soldiers smoking, and then Kim came back up the hill. The soldiers watched her until she was at the top before they sat down again, this time facing in different directions.

Kim passed over the crest of the hill, then crouched down and crawled back to where I was lying by the bushes.

"What did you do that for?" I asked

"Recon."

"Reckon?"

"Reconnaissance," she said. "Find out what's what. See what's happening."

"And *did* you find out?"

"We were right. They've already had a few little 'uns down there this morning, some big 'uns, too, so they're guarding it to stop people from taking souvenirs. The bodies aren't there anymore, though. They took 'em away first thing this morning. Also, they're waiting in case the German comes back."

"He's really got them runnin' around, hasn't he?"

"*We've* got them running around," she said with a smile.

Once again, I felt a pang of guilt and fear. "He needs help, though. There must be someone we can tell. How about Mam?"

"He's got *us*," Kim said. "He doesn't need anyone else. We agreed on that. Anyway, she'd just tell Lieutenant Whatshisname, and then they'd shoot him."

I wasn't entirely sure that was exactly what the lieutenant had said, but even so, I thought Kim was right. If I told Mam about the German, she would definitely tell the army and, if the sergeant was anything to go by, there were a few of them just itching to kill someone.

"Maybe he'll die anyway," I said.

"Maybe he will." Kim looked at me. Then I noticed she had a cigarette behind her ear.

"What's that for?" I asked.

"It's for him," she said. "All soldiers smoke, don't they? My brother does and I bet your dad does, too."

I shrugged and, for a moment, it wasn't a German out there in the woods anymore; it was my dad lying there, waiting for us to bring him a blanket and a cigarette and something to eat.

"Right, then." She took her satchel from my hands and shuffled back, away from the crest of the hill. "Come on. Let's go and have a look at our souvenir."

We couldn't go into the woods through the hole in the fence because the soldiers might have seen us, so we went in farther along. The wire was tight enough for us to climb, and I draped the blanket over the top rung to cover the barbs before we clambered over. There were one or two fluffs of wool snagged where the sheep had wandered too close.

"D'you think he'll still be there?" Kim said as we made our way among the trees.

"Don't know."

"You all right?" she asked.

"Aye."

"Scared?"

I looked at her. "A bit."

Kim tightened her lips and nodded. "Me too."

I stopped and took a deep breath. "It's not too late to go back," I said. "We could get someone . . ."

Kim stood beside me and glanced back the way we'd come, then stared forward into the woods as if she were having second thoughts. She bit at the inside of her cheek, then shook her head. "No. That could be Josh. Or your dad. We should help him."

"I dunno. Maybe we —"

"Come on," she said. "He's our souvenir. We found him. And it's up to us to look after him."

"All right." But I wasn't really doing it for him — I was doing it for all those reasons that had been spinning in my head this morning. Most of all, though, I was doing it for my new friend, Kim.

We walked side by side where we could, but there were times when I had to take the lead. My legs were still scratched and stinging from our rush through the woods last night, so I was careful to avoid those things now that it was daylight. I felt important leading Kim. She was older than me by nearly a month; she was taller than me and she was braver than I was, so it felt good to be in the lead, showing her where to go. She probably never would have found her way back to my hiding place if I hadn't been there.

Farther in, we jumped across the burn using the stones that jutted from the surface. I looked down at the clear water creek and thought about how I used to build dams when Dad was tending to the pheasants on the other side. It always used to start out with me following him around, watching what he did to look after the birds. There were small cages with boxed-in sections for hens that were laying, and there were open pens for the older chicks, and I'd help put out feed but then I'd get bored and come down here to the burn.

"Maybe we should build a dam sometime," I said to Kim. "You ever built a dam?"

"No."

"You need to get loads of stones and twigs and make a wall. Then clog it all up with mud to stop the water from getting through."

"Sounds fun."

"I used to do it when me da' was working. Sometimes it would get really big, and once I even made the water into a deep pool that lasted for days and days, until there was a hard rain and it overflowed and washed away."

"So where *is* your dad?" Kim asked. "Do you know?"

We were on the other side of the creek now and I picked up a long stick, swinging it at the tall nettles. "Africa."

"Hey, that's where my brother is, too. At least, when we last heard from him. He came home for a few days after Dunkirk, but then he went away again."

I suddenly felt a pang of jealousy because my dad hadn't come home. "*My* da' was in Dunkirk, too," I said. "He wasn't in no plane, though. He was right there on the ground."

"So?"

"Well, I mean, it was more dangerous for the soldiers, wasn't it? Bein' on the ground and everythin'."

"Planes can get shot down, you know."

"Aye, but —"

"Like yesterday, remember. It's just as bad."

I sighed. "I know. I didn't mean . . ." I shrugged.

"It's all right."

"We heard about it on the wireless, like, about Dunkirk. All them men coming back from France. Mam said maybe me da' would come home after that. He didn't, though. Went straight to Africa. We had a letter from him sayin' he was there for . . ." I tried to remember the words he'd used. I could picture them, in my dad's handwriting. "'For the *duration of the emergency.*' That means until the war's over."

"He didn't even come back for a few days?" Kim said. "That's not fair."

I swung at the nettles again, swiping the tops off a whole clump of them, sending pieces of leaves fluttering through the air, then I stopped and looked at the green sap left on the end of my stick.

"They'll be all right." Kim punched my arm. "Giving Hitler a run for his money, eh?"

"Aye. Winnin' the war." But I knew we were both thinking the same thing. My dad and Kim's brother were out fighting the

Germans, and we had one right here in the woods. And we were looking after him.

"It's different," Kim said, as if she'd read my mind.

"Aye." And although I couldn't explain it, this *was* different. All those Germans we heard about on the wireless were different. They were not men, they were faceless, helmeted and armed, marching across places I knew the names of but had never seen. France, Norway, Africa. They were airplanes dog-fighting over the English channel; they were bombers casting a shadow over our cities. They were the *enemy*.

Our German was different. He was a real person. He was here, he had a face, and he was in trouble.

NOT MUCH OF A
GERMAN

Coming closer to my secret place, I slipped a hand into my satchel to take out the gun.

"Oh no." I stopped.

"What's wrong?" Kim asked.

I held up the pistol for her to see. "It broke." There was slimy egg yolk all over the pistol, adding to the dirt that was stuck in the gaps in the metal.

"You brought an egg?"

I nodded, feeling awful. I'd stolen food from Mam and now it was ruined. It was no use at all.

"And you put it in your satchel with the gun? What did you expect?"

I shrugged and shook my head. All the effort I'd gone to this morning was wasted.

"Well . . ." She looked at me and stopped. She could see I was upset and annoyed with myself. "Oh, never mind. You got a blanket and that's brilliant. Just wipe the gun on the grass over there."

I went to the trunk of a hazel tree, where the grass grew in tufts as high as my wellies, and I squatted down to wipe the pistol clean. Kim crouched beside me.

"It's all right," she said. "It doesn't matter."

"Of course it matters," I said. "I took it from *Mam*. I thought it was all right because I was going to use it to help someone, but now I've broken it and . . ." I sighed and picked up a twig to flick some dirt from a crevice on the gun. "We've got nowt to spare as it is."

"You think it's bad *here*?" Kim said. "It's even harder in the city. There's gardens here and loads of vegetables, but in Newcastle most of the gardens are blown up and —"

"We've still got hardly anythin' and we can't afford to go breaking stuff, or giving it away. Maybe we shouldn't be helping 'im."

"He's our souvenir."

"Aye, but he's not, though, is he? He's a person and, well . . . maybe we *should* tell someone. Let someone else look after 'im."

"Look after him?" she said. "They'd just shoot him. You said so yourself."

"Did I?"

"Yes, you did."

"Aye. I s'pose so." It all felt like such a mess.

"Come on." She stood up and put out a hand to pull me up.

I reached out and took it. It was warm and soft. And when I was standing, she let me hold it for a moment longer before I let go and we continued on through the woods, going straight to my secret place: the place where we had hidden our souvenir.

At the end of the main street in the village, there was a notice board that used to show drab flyers about dances, or church services, or about the village fair. Now, though, there were colorful posters telling people to DIG FOR VICTORY or MAKE DO AND MEND. There were even posters telling people not to talk about the war because German spies lurked round every corner and hid behind every bush.

When the posters first went up, there were too many people crowding round the notice board to see them, but then they were everywhere. They were in the village hall, in the grocer's, and even on the wall inside the butcher's instead of pictures of lamb chops and mince.

One of the posters was put up so we'd know how to spot the enemy if they invaded — as if we wouldn't be able to tell by the fact they'd be shooting at us. There was a picture of a German sailor standing next to an airman wearing a blue-gray jacket with gold on the collar and matching trousers tucked into long black boots. He also had a hat with an eagle on it, pulled tight over his golden hair. I'd felt ashamed when I first saw the picture because I thought the uniform was really sharp, and because my hair was a similar color.

But the man we'd captured didn't look anything at all like the drawing pinned up behind Mr. Shaw's counter. Our German was completely different.

It was dim inside the tangle of shrubs, but some light cut through the gaps, and it was clearer than it had been in the flashlight. I could see that he was sitting in the same position, with his back against the sycamore, his arms loose by his sides, and his legs outstretched.

He was wearing an all-in-one suit, more like overalls, gray except for the torn left sleeve, which had a good deal of dark brown dried blood caked on it. There were pockets on his thighs, and he wasn't wearing a hat of any sort. I was also surprised to see he didn't have golden hair. His hair wasn't even as blond as mine; his was a sort of brown color. What Mam would have called "mousey." His skin was pale, but much of his face was dirty, and there were streaks of mud and scratches, too. One long cut ran from the top of his head right along the side of his face and curved around to his chin. It didn't look deep, but it had bled a lot. Both of his eyes were closed, and his chin was resting on his chest.

The other thing I noticed was the smell.

"Stinks in here," I whispered, noticing a dark stain around the front of the airman's overalls. When I realized what it was, I felt a great surge of embarrassment for him and glanced away. "You think he's wet 'imself?"

"Maybe. Probably. He's been here all night."

I'd never heard of a grown-up doing that before and it made me feel even more sorry for him. I thought about how terrible Dad would feel if it had happened to him and, somehow, it seemed even worse than being shot down. "He must really be in a bad way."

"Looks like he hasn't even moved."

"He looks *dead*," I said, putting the gun on the ground beside me. "D'you think —"

"No, I can see him breathing."

I looked closely, watching his chest, and saw that Kim was right.

She knelt facing the airman and opened her satchel, removing a paper napkin, which she laid out. Onto it she placed a handful of broken biscuits and a raw carrot. She also took out a cloth, a clean rag, and a bottle of Dettol antiseptic.

"It's all I could get," she said.

I opened my satchel and looked inside. The egg had soaked into the leather and begun to stiffen. I'd have to wash it later, otherwise it would start to smell. I took out the small package of paper and unwrapped it to show my piece of tripe. "That's it," I said. "Apart from the egg."

"Tripe? Can you eat it raw?"

I stared at the pitiful thing and shrugged. "Don't know."

"Can't risk having a fire to cook it."

I crumpled it back into the paper and sighed. "It's no good then, is it? Wasted." A stab of guilt poked at my insides. Wasting food was the worst crime.

"No, it's good," Kim said. "He'll just have to eat it raw."

"You reckon?" I wondered if she was just trying to make me feel better.

"Of course. Put it with the rest."

So I put it beside her offerings and we stared at the bits and pieces. It didn't look like much.

"We'll have to get more than this," Kim said with a sigh. "It's not enough."

"How?"

She thought for a moment. "I might be able to get a few more things. A slice of bread, a small piece of meat. I'll try to get something that's cooked. Maybe sneak out a bit of my lunch or tea."

"I can try that."

"You ever get the rations from the shops?"

"Sometimes."

"Well, next time see if you can keep a bit; bring it here."

I nodded, feeling a tinge of shame that I was sitting here, in front of a German airman, discussing how I was going to steal food to feed him. But underneath it all, I felt as if I was saving his life.

"And we'll need something for him to wee in," Kim said.

"What?"

"Well, you're right about it stinking in here, and what if he needs to go for a you-know-what? He needs a chamber pot."

"A gazunder? Can he not just go outside, like?"

"Not sure he's in any state to. He can hardly walk. Haven't you got a spare one?"

I shook my head. "Just the one under me bed."

I tried to think what we could bring for him. If I ever needed a pee when I was in the woods, I just found a good tree. Anything more serious and I ran home to the netty — a small wooden outhouse at the bottom of the garden that was painted a faded and cracked green. There was a gap under the door that the winter wind blew right through and I sometimes begged to use the commode in Mam's bedroom if I needed a sit-down, but she always said no. That was only for use at night.

"We used to have an old coal scuttle," I said, "but that went to the scrap collection. Don't think we've got anything else. Nothing Mam wouldn't miss, anyway."

"Well, see if there's anything you can find. I'll have a look, too."

We waited a while longer, saying nothing, but still he didn't wake up, so Kim edged forward and put her hand out. She touched his shoulder, a quick poke, and drew her hand away.

Still he didn't move.

This time she put her hand on his shoulder and shook him, making his whole body wobble. For a moment, I thought he was going to slide sideways and fall over, but instead he moaned and opened his eyes. Just a crack.

Kim jumped back to sit next to me and I put my hand down to touch the pistol.

The German looked at us as if he was trying to remember where he was. He blinked hard and shook his head, a tiny movement as he looked about. And then he remembered.

He opened his eyes wide, panicking as he tried to push himself up. Immediately he gasped in pain, lifting his right hand to his left arm, putting his legs up to shuffle away from us. He turned his head from side to side like a cornered animal searching for an escape route, but there was nowhere for him to go, so he just cowered there. The sound of his heavy breathing filled the cocoon of foliage.

"Don't think we're going to be pushovers," Kim said to him. "We might be children, but we're English and we're tough." She knelt up very straight and puffed out her chest. "Show him the gun, Peter."

"Hm?"

"Show him the gun."

"Oh. Aye," I said, gripping the pistol and holding it up.

The German cringed and put up his good hand, holding it out in front of his face. He said something in German, but all I heard was a lot of sounds, and the only one I could pick out was the one he had said last night. *"Bitte."*

"Don't *point* it at him," Kim told me.

"But you said to —"

"I said *show* it to him, not point it at him."

"All right." I lowered it and put it down.

"Are you thirsty?" Kim asked him. She picked up the bottle she'd left last night and shook it. "There's not much in it."

"We can always get more," I told her. "From the burn."

"Thirsty?" she asked him again, shaking the bottle. "You want a drink?"

"Wasser," he answered. "Wa-ter."

She unscrewed the cap and gave it to him. He put it to his lips and I watched to see if he did anything strange, but I couldn't see anything that made him different. On some of the posters, the Germans looked like they had no faces, just half-closed eyes looking at us from the shadow beneath their helmets. Or they were dark monsters, sighting along the barrels of their rifles. On one of them, the enemy was a mustached cross between Hitler and the devil — his red face topped with horns that stuck out from his side-parted black hair. But as I watched him drink, I realized the man we'd brought into my secret place wouldn't have stood out if he'd been waiting in the queue at the grocer's. A change of clothes and he would have looked just like everyone else. He wasn't very frightening at all.

When he'd drained the water bottle, I took it back and replaced the cap. Kim handed him the broken biscuits and the carrot, putting the paper napkin on his lap.

The German eyed them with suspicion.

"We'll get some more water," Kim said, holding up the bottle and nudging me. "Come on."

We left him to his food and crawled out.

When we were at the creek, Kim squatted beside the clear water and submerged the bottle. I jumped up onto the tire swing that hung by a thick rope from the bough of an old tree, and watched the bubbles rising in the burn.

"I like your swing," Kim said.

"Me da' put it up for us," I said, swaying gently, legs dangling, the tire twisting slowly so that one moment I was looking at Kim and the next I wasn't.

"That should do it," she said, taking the bottle from the water and screwing the top back on.

"He's not much of a German, is he?"

"What do you mean?"

"You've seen the posters. They always look different. Like they're monsters or somethin'."

Kim looked confused at first, then she smiled and laughed through her nose. "You don't really think they all look like devils, do you?" She came over and put a hand on the tire to stop it from revolving.

"Well, no, but . . . I dunno . . . That's what they're like on posters. Or they're blond or they're angry or . . . *something*. But he's not scary at all. He's sort of . . . well, sort of sad, and you can't help feelin' sorry for him."

Kim tightened her mouth and nodded.

"He just looks like us," I said.

"You're right," she agreed. "No different at all."

For a little while we stayed like that, not saying anything. Me sitting in the tire and Kim standing beside me, holding it still.

"Every time I look at him, it makes me think of Josh," she said eventually.

"Me too. About me da', I mean."

"Have you heard anything?" she asked. "Any letters?"

I shook my head. "You?"

"Not for ages," she said. "I hope he's all right."

"Me too."

"And I can't stop thinking about how I wish someone would look after him if anything like this happened to him and . . . well . . ." She shrugged.

"He looks really scared, doesn't he?" I remembered how I'd pointed the gun at him, and that's when I realized I'd made a terrible mistake. All the time I'd been thinking about how sorry I felt for the German, I had forgotten about something important.

"Oh no," I said, slipping out from the tire. "I left it inside. The gun. I left it in there with 'im."

"What?" She stared at me. "Why did you do that?"

"I forgot about it."

Kim took a deep breath and let it out in a big rush. "Well, there's not much we can do about it now."

"Are we going back?"

"Do you want to?" she asked.

I looked at the tangle of sticks and leaves that hid the German from view. "What if he shoots us?"

"Do you think he will?"

I imagined the airman inside, pointing the gun, ready to kill us. A moment ago I'd been feeling sorry for him, but now . . . "No." I shook the thought away. "Of course he won't. It probably doesn't even work, anyway; it's so full of muck."

"So do you want to go back?"

I swallowed hard, thinking for a moment before I nodded. "Aye."

"You sure?"

"Not really."

I went first; it was only fair that way, because it was me who had forgotten to bring the gun with us. I held my breath and crawled in, cringing, waiting for whatever it would feel like to be shot and killed, but the German was still sitting against the tree trunk eating his carrot. The pistol was exactly where I had left it, as if he hadn't bothered with it at all. He was sitting forward now, though, as if he'd noticed his wet patch and was trying to hide it from us.

I let out my breath and shuffled farther in to sit with my legs crossed, so the pistol was just on one side and Kim was on the other.

The German looked up at me and took another bite of carrot. The vegetable snapped off in his front teeth and we could hear him crunching it. Kim and I sat as far away as possible from him, staring almost as we might stare at a curiosity at a traveling fair — or an animal in a zoo.

The German continued to chew.

"What's your name?" I asked.

He stopped chewing.

"Peter," I said, touching my finger to my chest. "Peter." Then I pointed at Kim and said, "Kim."

The German swallowed. He ran his tongue around his mouth and said, "Peter." He pointed at me with the half-eaten carrot, then swung it to my right and pointed it at Kim. "Kim."

We nodded and he nodded.

He looked at us, his eyes sliding from me to Kim and back again. Then he sniffed hard and touched his own chest with the bitten end of the carrot. "Erik."

"Erik." I glanced at Kim. "Doesn't sound foreign at all."

"Erik," he said again, forcing a smile to his lips, but I could see he was in pain, even if he wasn't as afraid of us anymore.

When he'd finished eating, he folded up the paper napkin and handed it back. Kim replaced it in her satchel and offered him the cigarette the soldier at the wreck had given her. Erik took it, putting it into his mouth. He looked very grateful to have it, and waggled his hand in front of it until we realized we had no way to light it.

"Sorry," Kim said, holding out her hands and shrugging.

The German patted the pocket on his left knee, and unzipped it, putting his hand in and taking out a silver gas lighter that he used to light the cigarette. He took a deep suck on it and tipped back his head before letting the smoke drift out. Immediately, the small space was filled with the smell of tobacco, making us both cough.

As the German smoked, Kim unscrewed the cap of the water bottle once more and wet the cloth she'd brought. She edged closer to the German and held it toward his face.

"I should clean your cut," she said.

At first he flinched away, but then he nodded and allowed Kim to gently wash the dry blood from around the long gash on his face. It was crusted thick in places, and when she rubbed a little too hard, Erik winced and his gaze met mine before he looked down at the bare, compacted soil, almost as if he was ashamed.

Kim wafted the smoke away as she cleaned the dirt and blood from his face, and when she sat back, we could see what Erik really looked like. Kim had been right when she said he was only a young man, perhaps even still a teenager.

She dabbed some of the Dettol onto the scratch using the

cloth, then she put her fingers to the place where his sleeve was ripped and parted the material to look inside. She wrinkled her upturned nose and took a deep breath. "That's quite a scratch."

"Maybe he did it on a tree when he was comin' down."

"Maybe. Give me your knife," she said.

"Why? What you gonna do?"

"I need to cut the rest of his sleeve."

"What?"

"His arm needs to be cleaned," she said. "It looks really bad."

"Shouldn't we get a doctor or somethin'?"

Erik was watching us closely now, trying to follow our conversation, and he stiffened at the word *doctor*.

"It's all right," Kim said. "I've seen people clean wounds before. Bigger wounds than this."

Erik was looking from me to Kim and then back again, desperation coming to his eyes as he started to shake his head.

"Where?" I put my hand in my pocket and started to take out my knife, but hesitated.

"Where d'you think? Dad's a doctor and Mum's a nurse," she said. "I've been to the hospital loads of times. I did tell you."

"Did you?"

"I think so."

"Nein," Erik finally said, taking us both by surprise. "No. No doc-tor. No."

"It's all right." Kim sat back and held her hands out to him. "No doctor." She looked at me. "We don't need a doctor. I can do this. I promise."

"But —"

"We can't tell anyone, Peter. You know what they'll do to

him. We have to look after him ourselves. Just give me your knife; it'll be fine."

I sighed and took out my penknife, opening the blade and passing it to her.

Erik pulled back when Kim put the steel close to his arm, but she smiled at him. "Don't worry," she said. "It's fine."

It was strange watching Kim cut away the sleeve and clean Erik's wounded arm. For that short time, she didn't look like a child. She looked more like a little adult because she seemed to know exactly what she was doing. She didn't hesitate or panic or worry about anything she was doing. And when she had cleaned the wound, I watched as she disinfected it with the Dettol and cut the rag she had brought, making it into a good, tight bandage.

"That's *amazin'*," I said when she was finished. And I thought how proud her mam would have been to have seen her bandage him like that. "Really brilliant. You'll be a brilliant nurse, like." I even imagined, just for a moment, that one day I might be wounded, and Kim could be *my* nurse.

Erik put his right hand to the dressing on his left arm and nodded. "*Danke*," he said.

"You're welcome." Then she looked at me. "It'll do for now, but it'll need to be changed. We'll have to get proper bandages from somewhere. It could get infected otherwise."

"Doctor Jacobs has some," I said, remembering how he'd taken care of me just after the plane crash. "I saw them in his medical bag." And I knew, as soon as I'd said it, what was coming next. I could already see Kim's mind at work.

"Hmm," she said. "Then we'll have to find a way to get hold of that bag."

BROKEN BONE

When I got home for lunch, there was something cooking on the range in the scullery.

"What's that?" I asked, lifting the lid to see what was bubbling inside.

"Stew," Mam said. "Mr. Bennett came round."

"Again?"

"Don't make that face; he brought this meat for us." She came over and took the pan off the heat.

"What kind?"

"Meat." She wasn't any more specific than that, and I didn't ask. Sometimes it was better to not know exactly what meat you were eating.

I washed my hands and took two bowls from the sideboard so Mam could ladle out a small amount of the stew for each of us. It didn't look like there was much meat in it, just a few pieces. Mostly it was potatoes.

At the kitchen table, I scooped some up onto my spoon and blew on it before tasting.

"Better than tripe?" Mam asked.

"A bit."

"We're lucky Mr. Bennett looks after us."

I bit into a soft chunk of potato and felt it burn the tip of my tongue.

"He's really very nice, pet. I wish you didn't always look so sulky when he comes here. He likes you, you know."

I didn't say anything.

"And it's good to have someone to help out."

"*I* can help," I said.

"You *do* help, pet. But there are some things you can't do."

"Like what?"

Mam sighed and shook her head: "Well, I s'pose he can get things for us. He has connections. He gets food and . . . and remember that bag he got you for your gas mask? A proper army one."

It *was* a good bag, I couldn't deny that. A real soldier's gas mask bag that I thought about not using because it had been Mr. Bennett's, but it was too smart to leave unused. I'd almost forgotten he'd given it to me.

"I can get things, too." I tried not to sound and look sulky like she'd said. "I can get us a rabbit."

Mam nodded. "That's true. When you bring one home it's always a good one."

I made a mental note to check my snares when I went out that afternoon. I should have checked them this morning — Dad told me I should never leave them too long — but I'd had a lot on my mind.

"Any letters?" I asked. "Anything from Da'?"

Mam shook her head and reached over to pat my hand. We

ate in silence for a while, then she said, "So what have you been doing this morning?"

"Playin'."

"Not going too far, I hope."

"No."

"And what exactly do you play?"

"Nowt really. Just . . ."

Mam gave me one of her looks. Eyebrows raised, chin down.

"We're making a dam in the burn," I said. It probably popped into my head because I'd thought about it earlier, when we'd been in the woods, and I told myself it was only a half lie. I wasn't lying about where we were, just about what we were doing. And Mam knew I liked to dam the burn in the woods.

"I thought I told you not to go into them woods." Mam looked cross.

"No. You said not to go in the afternoon."

"Did I?"

"Aye."

Mam looked unsure. "I don't like you going there. Not after what happened yesterday." Then her brow creased. "And with that German prob'ly wanderin' about . . ." She looked as if she was trying to fix on something right at the back of her mind, something that didn't want to be remembered.

Then it came to her. "What about your da's shed?" she said. "Doesn't your da' have a place where he keeps all his pheasant things?"

"Aye." I tried to keep my face calm. "What about it?" I knew what was coming next.

"Maybe he's hidin' there. The German."

Dad used to say swans were clever birds. He said they looked all calm and peaceful gliding on water, but if you looked underneath, you'd see feet paddling away like mad. That's how I felt right then, trying to pretend I wasn't worried.

"Can't be," I said. I didn't want Mam to see that underneath I was beginning to panic. Our German wasn't in the shed — but he wasn't far away. "No one can get in there. It's all locked up and only I know where the key is."

"You haven't been inside?"

"Never," I said. "It's me da's stuff."

"What if he's broken in, like?"

"He couldn't have. Anyway, I've been near there; the hut's fine."

"Still . . . I don't know about you goin' all the way out there. I don't like you bein' in the woods if —"

"I showed Kim the tire swing me da' made for us," I said, changing the subject.

Mam stopped and stared. Then the corners of her mouth turned up into a gentle smile. "I remember when he made that," she said. "Luggin' that tire out there so you could swing on it while he was carryin' on with them birds of his." Mam was in the middle of lifting her spoon to her mouth, her hand hanging in the air, and she turned to look out the window as if she were going to see Dad out there gathering his bits and pieces. It made me look, too, but there was nothing there. Just the garden.

"Are you all right, Mam?"

She blinked and shook her head ever so slightly, then smiled. It wasn't a proper smile, though, and I thought she looked very sad. "Just thinkin'."

"He's comin' back," I said. "You'll see. It'll all be over soon and he'll come straight back. I know he will."

Mam put her hand on mine and squeezed. "You're a canny lad, Peter. Such a good lad." She took her hand away and turned her head so I couldn't see her. When she spoke again, it sounded as if something had caught in her throat. "Simon Jenkins came round earlier. He wanted to know if you were comin' out. You used to be good pals with him."

"Mm."

"You should call on him this afternoon."

"I told Kim I'd play with her."

"You're very friendly with that lass, aren't you?"

"She's nice."

"It's good for you to have new friends, but you mustn't forget about everyone else."

The last time I'd played out with Simon Jenkins he'd said something about how we always had more than everyone else, and we'd had an argument. It probably didn't mean much to him, but it did to me. It was bad enough that Trevor Ridley was always talking about my mam and Mr. Bennett; I didn't need to hear it from my friends, too.

"She's a right little tomboy, I should imagine," said Mam.

"You mean Kim?"

"Who else would I be talkin' about?"

"Aye, I s'pose she is."

"She even looks like a lad with her short hair. She'd be bonny if she let it grow."

"She *is* bonny," I said. "Anyway, that's what I like about her; she's not all girly dresses and frilly socks."

"Well, just you make sure you stay out of trouble. Come straight home if you see anythin'. And be careful when you're near the burn. It only takes a —"

"— few inches of water to drown. I know, Mam. I'll be careful."

"Course you will, pet."

After lunch Mam made me wash the dishes, and then she gave me the ration book and sent me down to the village.

"Got your identity card?" she said.

I patted my pocket to let her know I had it on me. I was supposed to carry it all the time, just like we were supposed to carry our gas masks everywhere, but sometimes I forgot. I'd been stopped before, over on the links, just like they'd stopped Kim that morning when she ran down the hill. One of the soldiers had stepped forward with his bayonet pointed at me and told me to show him my identity card. I don't know if he thought I was a German spy or that maybe I was leading an invasion, and at first I thought he was just joking, but he was very serious.

"Go on, then," Mam said. "And then you can go out and play."

I ran all the way to the village, because Kim had said she'd meet me on the hill at two o'clock and it was already after one.

When I came out of the grocer's, I could see a group of boys at the end of the road, close to the green. They were watching the Home Guard practicing, and I knew who it was straightaway. Trevor Ridley and his friends.

I turned and walked away, quickly heading home, but Trevor had seen me, and called out as he ran up behind me with his two friends.

"What you got there, then?" He poked at the bag in my hands. "Rations?"

"Aye."

"What d'you need rations for? I thought you got everythin' you need from his lordship. That's right, isn't it?" Trevor said. "Mr. Bennett gives your mam whatever she needs."

Beside him, Adam Thornhill snickered like an animal, raising his upper lip to show those oversized teeth that made me think of horses.

I ignored them and tried to walk away, but Trevor stepped round to block my path.

"So what you got in there you can't get from Mr. Bennett, eh?" Trevor grabbed at the bag and, when I tried to pull it away, it ripped, the contents spilling onto the pavement. A small piece of meat wrapped in paper; a bottle of milk, which smashed; a few sugar cubes that burst from their wrapping and skittered onto the road.

I stood and stared at those small white cubes just lying there. I didn't care too much about the milk, but the sugar cubes meant something. They were the one luxury Mam and I shared, but now they were lying in the road. I wished, just for a second, that I had my satchel with me. I wished I could put my hand into it and pull out that German gun and point it at Trevor Ridley. It might not work, but it would give him the fright of his life, and he'd wish he hadn't made me mad. But even the thought of it felt so wrong, and I was relieved when I heard Mr. Shaw shouting from across the street.

The older boys stood their ground as Mr. Shaw came closer and stopped on the other side of the road.

"What're you lads up to?" he asked.

"Just sayin' hello to our friend," Ridley replied.

"Well, go and say hello to someone your own size," Mr. Shaw told him.

"What if we don't want to?"

"You want to watch yoursel', son, or you'll be feelin' the back of my hand." Mr. Shaw started to come across the road. "Now clear off."

The boys stayed a second longer, then they made a move, walking back along the pavement as the butcher came to my side.

"You all right, son?"

I nodded.

"You want to hit 'im next time," Mr. Shaw said. "Get the first clout in. It's the only way with lads like them. Hit 'em once, canny hard, and they leave you alone. I did the same thing when I was a lad."

It was easy for him to say — Dad told me Mr. Shaw was strong enough to lift a whole pig onto a hook without any help, so I don't suppose Trevor Ridley scared him much.

"You sure you're all right?" Mr. Shaw stooped to look into my face. He lifted a hand to scratch his nose, and I saw he had a small piece of pink mince stuck on one fingernail.

I nodded again. "Fine."

"Come on, then, let's get this lot picked up." Mr. Shaw crouched to gather up the wrapped meat, and I squatted beside him, collecting the spilt sugar cubes. One or two were broken, but most were intact. I picked up the broken ones anyway, dusted the dirt off them, and put them in the bag.

Walking along the path on my way home, I saw Kim coming

toward me from the hill. The strap of her satchel was across her chest and she was carrying something in her right hand.

"Saw you coming. Where've you been?" she asked. "I've been waiting."

As she came closer, I saw she was holding a long-handled pan. It was white; black in the places where the color had cracked and come away.

"I was in the village."

"What's the matter?" she asked, seeing my mood straightaway.

"Trevor Ridley. He split the bag and spilt all me rations."

"You should've hit him." Kim hefted the pan as if she was going to swing it at someone.

"That's what Mr. Shaw said."

She put her arm around my shoulder. "So, what rations did you get?"

"Not much. Some meat and sugar, that's all."

"Can you take something?" she said. "For Erik? I've got a few things — a piece of bread and some vegetables. And this." She lifted the pan. "You know, for a toilet."

"Won't your aunt miss it?"

"Probably not. It was right at the back of the cupboard. Looks like it's for big stews or something, and we've never got enough of anything to need such a big pan. Wasn't easy to sneak it out, mind."

"Wonder why it didn't go for scrap."

"Maybe she's saving it for after the war."

"Don't think I'd want to eat anything out of it after our German's used it," I said.

Kim made a face and stuck out her tongue. She put her hands

to her throat as if she were choking. When I'd stopped laughing, she pointed at the bag. "You gonna take something, then?"

I thought about it, my feelings all muddled. I didn't want to take anything from Mam, but I couldn't say no to Kim. She'd already managed to get a few things and it wasn't fair if I didn't get anything.

"I s'pose so," I said. "Maybe some of the sugar, like." I took out some of the broken pieces and put them into Kim's satchel along with the other provisions. "I can tell Mam I dropped them." And Kim looked so pleased to be getting more things for Erik that I added, "Maybe I can get something else tomorrow. I'll try not to break it this time."

Kim waited outside while I took the rations home and explained to Mam what had happened. There was no point in lying about it, because Mr. Shaw had seen everything, so I told her what Trevor Ridley and his friends had done.

"I'll speak to their fathers," she said. "Nasty little —"

"No."

"Then I'll take a belt to 'em meself."

"Mam, leave it alone."

"Well, we have to do something, pet. I'll not have them lads treatin' you like that. And making a mess of our rations . . . your da' would give 'em a right hidin' if he was here."

"It's all right," I told her. "I'll sort it out."

"Then make sure you do. We can't lose our rations. You know what your da' would say? He'd say give the lad a bloody neb and he'll leave you alone."

"That's what everyone says."

"Because it's true."

"I don't want to talk about it. I'll sort it out meself."

Mam looked at me for a long while, squeezing the small parcel of meat in her calloused fingers. They didn't used to be like that, but now all she ever did was scrub and dig. "Tell you what," she said. "Next time it happens, I'll go to his father and get this sorted out once and for all. Better yet, I'll grab him when he comes for the pig slops. In the meantime, it's up to you. How about that?"

I shrugged.

"Good. Well. That's that, then."

Erik actually looked pleased to see us when we arrived. He was awake and sitting up, not so confused and afraid anymore. The smell in there was even worse this time, and I noticed there was a dark, damp patch on the soil, close to the base of the tree. It looked like he'd tried to put soil over it, but the ground was hard and dry.

Kim opened her satchel and took out the food, laying it on a napkin. She put the pan next to Erik and said, "Toilet." She pointed at the stain on the soil, then at the pan. "Toilet." Then she put a cloth over the top of it.

For a second, Erik looked away as if embarrassed, then he held up the water bottle Kim had left for him and tipped it upside down to show us it was empty. "Wa-ter."

"I'll go." Kim took it from him.

"No, don't leave me . . ." I started to say, but Kim was already outside, going back to the burn, leaving me alone with Erik.

For a moment we just looked at each other. I couldn't help feeling a little afraid. I was alone. In the woods. With a German.

I was thinking about scuttling out behind Kim when Erik pointed at me.

"Peter," he said.

I stared.

"Peter," he said again.

"Aye." I nodded and put a hand on my chest. "Peter."

"Peter. *Freund*," he said.

"Froind? What's that?"

Erik put his hands together and wove his fingers as if he were about to pray. *"Freund."* He unclasped his fingers, pointed at me, at himself, and said it again. *"Freund."*

"Oh," I said as it dawned on me. "You mean *friend*? We're friends? I don't know about that . . ." I let the idea roll around my head, thinking about how we'd helped him, fed him. "Maybe, though. Aye. I s'pose so. In a way. Friends."

"Friends," Erik tested the word. "Peter, Erik, *friends*," he said. "Friends. *Danke.*"

"You're welcome."

Then he leaned forward and pulled up the left leg of his overalls and, for the first time, I noticed that he had taken off his boot. He rolled down the sock and I saw that the skin was black-and-blue and swollen.

Erik pointed at it and made a motion with his hands that I didn't understand, so I shook my head at him. He prodded a finger at his ankle and winced, tightening his eyes. "Ah." He looked at me and made the motion with his hands once more.

He could see I still didn't understand, so he looked around him, feeling the ground behind until he lifted it up and showed me a dry twig. He pointed at his ankle, then took the stick in both hands and snapped it.

"It's broken?" I said. "You broke your ankle?" It would explain why he hadn't left the den. He wasn't just afraid; he couldn't walk.

"*Ja.* Bro-ken."

Just then, Kim came back in with the water bottle.

"You can bandage a cut," I said to her. "But can you fix broken bones?"

The way it turned out, Kim did know something about broken bones. She knew more than I did, anyway.

"We'll have to make a splint," she said.

"How do we do that, like?"

"All we need is some good straight wood to put against his ankle and something to tie it with. It might even be just a sprain."

"I don't know," I said. "Cleanin' a cut and putting on a bandage is one thing, but this is . . . Do you not think he needs a doctor?"

"No." Erik said. "Doctor, no." He was shaking his head and waving his hand, one finger pointing up. "No. Doctor, no. *Bitte.*"

"There he goes again," I said.

"He's frightened," Kim argued, "and so would I be. You think they're going to let a doctor treat him? You think Lieutenant Whatshisname is going to let him just walk into the hospital? Or that sergeant?"

"Maybe they would," I said. "Maybe they'll make him better and take him somewhere safe. A prison for soldiers. I mean, if it was me da' what found him, I'm sure he wouldn't just shoot 'im."

"Is that what you think?"

"Aye."

"Your dad's in the army, though, isn't he?"

"Mm."

"Then he's probably out shooting Germans right now. It's what they do. But look at him," she gestured. "He's so frightened."

"Me da' would never shoot someone like that," I said. "I just know it. He never would."

"So he would help him, then? I know my brother would."

"Aye, but . . ."

"Or d'you think he'd turn him over to someone like that sergeant — so he could shoot him?"

"I don't think Doctor Jacobs would —"

"Doctor, no," Erik said. He was shaking his head at us, his eyes wide. "Doctor, no. *Bitte.*"

"See," she said. "He's terrified. And I keep thinking about Josh; if it was him sitting in here all scared and dirty and . . . I just feel like we have to help him. Like we have to do whatever we can."

And then Erik started saying something in German, putting his hands on either side of his ankle and pretending to wrap something around.

"He wants us to make a splint," Kim said. "Isn't that what your dad would do?"

"I dunno. Maybe."

"And what you'd want someone to do if it was *him* who was hurt? Your dad, that is."

"I s'pose."

"Come on, then," she said. "All we need is a good piece of wood."

DAD'S SHED

It was a long time since anyone had been into Dad's shed, and now I stood at the door, staring at the padlock. It was thick and heavy. A dirty silver color, with a single bead of something brown that had once been a sticky liquid but was now as hard as a stone.

"Me da' was the last person to come in here," I said. "Prob'ly the last person to touch this lock."

I had been with him that day, the last time he came into the woods, so he could give the shed a fresh coat of creosote to protect it from the weather while he was away.

"Where's the key?" Kim asked.

"Right here."

The shed stood on a base of slats that kept it a few inches off the ground to stop the damp from getting in, and when I slipped my fingers into the space just below the door — as I had seen Dad do many times — I cringed at the thought of what creepy-crawlies might be lurking under there. Spiders and wood lice and earwigs. But I didn't feel any of those things. What I felt was cold and hard and metal.

I stood up and held out the key.

"Go on, then," Kim said. "Open it."

There were a few spots of rust, and I had to force the key into the lock. Once it was in, though, it turned easily and the clasp popped up. I slipped it from the latch and put it into my pocket. Then I took a deep breath and opened the door.

The right side of the hut was shelved from ceiling to floor. The other side had a short bench built from unplaned wood, and there was a chair and a stool. Dad used to sit on that chair, with the door open, smoking a cigarette and drinking a cup of tea. I would sit on the stool and eat a biscuit. We didn't always say much, but I liked being with him.

There was a strong odor of damp wood and dust and creosote and paraffin. It was a smell that made my chest tighten with memories of Dad. I swallowed hard and tried not to think of him sitting on that chair, opening a pack of cigarettes and holding out the card for me to add to my collection.

"You all right?" Kim asked.

I took a deep breath and stepped inside.

"What's that?" Kim said, pointing to the heater on the bench.

I went to it and put a hand on it. "To keep the shed warm," I said. "Burns paraffin. One of me da's jobs was to stop people stealin' the birds, so he used to come out at night if there was poachers about."

"Did he stay out all night?"

"Sometimes, like. I used to try to get 'im to take me with 'im, but he always said it wasn't much of an adventure sittin' in the woods all night."

"I bet it would be *great* fun."

"He said he'd let me when I was older. I'm prob'ly old enough now, but he's not here, is he?"

There were a few shotgun cartridges on the bench, too. Waxed paper tubes with brass bases — some used, some not. Kim came into the shed and picked one up, lifting it to her nose to sniff it.

"Shotgun cartridges," I told her. "Whenever I found 'em in the woods, I picked 'em up, 'cause if they were different from me da's, they might help tell 'im who'd been shootin' where they weren't s'posed to."

"Then what?"

I shrugged. "Call the police, I s'pose."

Under the bench, there were rolls of wire mesh and roofing felt for building pheasant pens, and there was a short-handled ax leaning against the wall. Cobwebs that had once stretched from the ax to the corner of the shed now hung limp and abandoned, a dry spider husk dangling from a single thread, spinning in the breeze.

The shelves were a treasure trove of the bits and pieces Dad needed for his job. There was a folding knife next to a tall metal flashlight, and beside that an old satchel that Dad had put away because the strap had come off and needed to be fixed. There were boxes of nails and tacks, bundles of string and thick cord, a rope, a pile of rags, a container filled with paraffin, a tin of oil, bags of feed, and a rattle that he used to scare away the crows. There was a toolbox, too. A large blue metal box.

"There should be a saw in there," I said, slipping my satchel over my neck and leaning it against the wall.

The toolbox was heavy, so I slid it to the edge of the shelf and half lifted, half dropped it to the floor. I opened it up and, as if it knew we wanted to use it, Dad's tenon saw was right there on the top. I took it out and ran a finger along the flat edge of the blade. It was still shining, as if Dad had used and cleaned it just yesterday, and I could see my smudged reflection in the shining metal.

"You miss him a lot," Kim said. It wasn't a question.

"Aye."

"I miss my dad, too. And my mum."

"At least you know where they are."

"Not my brother, though. Not Josh. I don't know where *he* is."

"No. I s'pose not."

Kim sat on the stool and leaned forward, putting her forearms on her thighs. She clasped her hands together so she looked like she was praying. "How come you don't play with anyone else?" she asked.

I touched a finger to the teeth on the saw. They were still sharp, still bright. There was a trace of oil on the blade because Dad had oiled everything, saying he wanted to make sure it was all still in working order when he came back from winning the war.

"I do," I said.

"Not since I met you."

"You're different," I said. "You don't say things like other people do. Anyway, I can't tell anyone else about Erik, can I?"

"No." She looked up at me. "All that stuff Trevor Ridley says, it's just because he's jealous, you know."

"I know."

"You shouldn't take any notice of it. You shouldn't worry what people say about —"

"I don't." I traced the saw's jagged blade with one fingertip.

"That man who was at your house: Mr. . . . what was it?"

"Bennett."

"Yeah. Well, he's just looking after you and your mum. For your dad. He's not trying to take his place."

"He never could," I snapped.

"I'm just saying, that's all. It's good to have someone watching out for you."

"Aye, well, I don't want to talk about it."

"Not even to me?"

I shrugged. "I just wish me da' would come back. Or at least that we could get a letter from 'im."

"Me too," Kim said.

I looked up at her and saw the sad expression on her face. I didn't like it. I didn't want Kim to be sad. I wanted her to be bright and smiling and full of adventure and mischief like she normally was. It was as if Erik was there to keep us busy, and as soon as we stopped thinking about him, we thought about all the other things happening around us.

"Come on," I said, standing up. "Let's get this wood."

I left the shed and went over to one of the bird pens. Kim stayed where she was for a while, and I could feel her watching me, but I didn't turn around.

There were four pens in a line, like small houses among the trees and the overgrown nettles.

"What are they for?" Kim asked, coming to stand beside me.

"For when they lay eggs," I said. "They lay them in there, and when the chicks are a bit older, they go into those." I pointed to a row of larger pens where Dad used to keep the young birds. They looked a lot like cages, about waist height and twelve feet long. They were made from posts and crosspieces of square-cut wood, covered with wire mesh that was supposed to keep the birds in and the foxes out. Dad had covered part of each pen with roofing felt that was bent right over one side, giving the birds some shelter from the wind and rain. Dad had built them all, carrying the wood out here and putting them together. I'd helped, standing by, holding nails, passing him tools until I'd grown bored and gone down to play at the burn or sit in the tire swing. I remembered how he'd sweated when he built them, and I didn't like the idea of damaging one of them now. I promised myself that when it was all over, I'd find some wood and I'd repair it, make it just like it was, so that when Dad came back from winning the war, everything would be just as it should be.

"Maybe we can get some wood somewhere else," Kim said, probably seeing the look on my face.

"It's all right. This is more important."

I took a deep breath and stamped hard on the corner of one of the pens, snapping the place where the wood had been nailed together. Then I slipped it out from the wire mesh that kept the birds inside the run, so I had a long pole of square-cut wood, about six feet long. I took it to a pile of rotting logs and put one end against them so the pole was far enough from the ground for me to cut it with the saw. The teeth of the saw bit into it easily, and within a few minutes I had my first short length of wood for a splint.

"You think this'll do?" I turned around, holding it up to show Kim.

"That looks good," she said. And then she did something that took me by surprise. Instead of punching me on the arm like she normally did, she leaned over and kissed me on the cheek.

"What was that for?" I asked, wiping it away.

She shrugged. "I don't know. For being my friend, I suppose."

I cut a second length of wood, about a foot long, and we took a piece of cord from the shed before putting everything away just as we'd found it. I even used an old rag to clean the saw and wipe over a thin layer of oil to protect it.

I took a last look around, trying not to see Dad sitting at the bench, and then I picked up my satchel and was about to pull the door shut when I stopped.

"What?" Kim asked. "What's the matter?"

I put my hand into my satchel and took out the gun I'd found at the wreck. "I don't like this," I said.

Kim didn't say anything, so I turned to look at her.

"When I saw Trevor Ridley earlier on, I thought if I'd had it with us I coulda pointed it at him. He woulda left me alone."

Kim listened.

"Erik looked scared when I pointed it at *him*," I said.

She nodded.

"It didn't feel right. I didn't like it. And anyway, we don't need it, do we? I mean, Erik doesn't want to hurt us. He's our friend, right?"

"Our friend?"

"That's what he said. And we *are* lookin' after him, so I s'pose he is, sort of."

"Mm." She nodded slowly. "I suppose. Why don't you lock it in the shed?"

"That's what I thought. Me da' will know what to do with it when he gets back home."

I went back into the shed and put the gun on the shelf beside the toolbox, then I came back outside and closed the door.

I snapped the padlock into place and slipped the key under the shed again before we went back to Erik. It felt good not to have the gun anymore. It felt less like he was the enemy. Less like he was our prisoner and more like he was our friend.

In the den, Kim used the pieces of wood, putting them on either side of Erik's ankle and wrapping the cord around them.

"This should keep everything from moving about," she said, tying it off.

Erik touched the makeshift splint and nodded his approval. *"Gut."* He gave her a thumbs-up. *"Gut."* He even slapped the splint as if to show us how strong she had made it.

"So will that make it better?" I asked.

"I think so. At least it'll stop it from getting worse."

"Someone at school broke their wrist one time," I said. "Fell down the stairs or something and had to go to the hospital. He had a plaster mitten round his wrist after that. Does he not need one of those?"

"A cast? No. The splint does the same thing."

"You sure?"

"I think so. Anyway, it might not even be broken." Kim looked at me, and for the very first time since we'd hidden Erik away, I saw something new in her eyes. I wasn't sure what it was, but I think it was doubt. Kim had been sure about cleaning and disinfecting Erik's wound, and she had been sure about hiding him from the soldiers to save him from being shot, but she wasn't sure about the splint. She wasn't *positive* that it was the right thing to do, but Erik looked pleased with it, so it was enough.

We gave Erik some water and tried to talk to him, but we couldn't do much more than smile at each other, make signs, and say a few words. Some of the words he said sounded a bit like English ones, but not many. And every time we ran out of signs and words, Erik would touch the splint on his ankle and give us a thumbs-up. He'd point at Kim and say, "*Gut* doctor." If I'd ever been worried about what we were doing, Erik's smiling, relieved expression made me feel as if it was the right thing.

"I reckon we need to get him some clothes," Kim said after a while. "His *stink*."

"And they're all ripped up."

"Yeah. I don't think I can get any, though, what about you?"

"I might be able to." I wanted to be as useful as Kim had been. But the idea that had come to me, the way I could get some clothes, I didn't like it one bit.

When it started to get dark, we refilled the water bottle and left Erik to spend another night alone. I told Kim to go straight home, I needed to check my snares, but she wanted to come with me, so we went deeper into the woods, past the pheasant pens.

"I should've checked 'em already," I said. "But I haven't had time. I was puttin' them out when I heard the sirens. Just before the plane crashed. And after that . . ." I shrugged.

Kim nodded.

"S'posed to check 'em mornin', afternoon, and evenin' in the summer."

"Why?"

"Leave a rabbit too long in a snare and a fox'll get 'im. Or maybe crows or magpies. And it's cruel to leave 'em strugglin'."

Kim looked at me, raising her eyebrows. "Isn't it cruel anyway?"

"Nah," I said. "Least, it doesn't have to be. It's no worse than shootin' 'em, and we can't do that."

"Wouldn't it be easier?"

"We might need the cartridges, like. If the Germans come. Anyway, there's more skill in this. You have to set the snare just right."

We came to the far edge of the woods, where the land rose by about a foot and the fence ran along the top.

"See all the burrows?" I said. "And fresh droppings?"

Kim nodded.

"They used to be all out in that field when it was grass," I said. "This time of day there'd be loads of 'em. Rabbits all over. Not so many now that there's no grass, though."

Coming to my first snare, I crouched down and put my fingers in it, showing Kim how it worked. "Trick is to put it in just the right place, right over the middle of the beat."

"The beat?"

I looked at Kim. "That's the place where the rabbit puts his feet, see. It's called the beat." I touched the ground, showing her the patches worn thin like footprints. "That's where he hops."

Kim nodded with fascination and looked as if she was waiting for me to go on. It felt good to be telling her this, and it reminded me how I felt when Dad taught me.

"The loop's got to be just the right height, too," I said. "And wide enough. See, a rabbit runs with his ears up, so there's no point in makin' the loop small; and you need to get him when he's runnin', not walkin'."

"What's that?" Kim pointed to a place a few feet away where I'd set another snare. There was a tuft of gray fur caught in the wire and the noose was pulled tight.

We went over and I pulled the fur away, feeling how soft it was between my fingers. I gave it to Kim and let her feel. "Looks like we got one," I said. "Think a fox took 'im, though."

I'd set five snares, and all were empty, so we reset them, then made our way back through the woods and headed home.

"D'you think Erik ever goes out?" I said to Kim as we crossed the burn. "Comes out of the den, I mean."

"Not from the smell of him. Anyway, he probably couldn't walk on that ankle."

"What about now that he's got a splint? He might try and go out now. Or d'you think he's too scared?"

"I should imagine he's scared most of the time," Kim said.

"How about you? Are you scared?"

She stopped and looked at me. "Of what?"

"What d'you think they'll do if they find out what we've done?"

"They won't find out."

"And what are we going to do when he's better? Erik can't stay in there forever."

"Don't worry," Kim said. "The war will be over soon and then he can go home. It'll all be forgotten."

That night the prime minister's voice was on the wireless. He was talking to the people of London, I think, but it felt like he was talking to all of us. I sat on the floor with my legs crossed, looking up at the sideboard and listening. He had a strange voice, not like anybody I knew. He said the words differently from people in my village, different even than people like Kim and Mr. Bennett, but I liked listening to him. He always made me feel proud that Dad was out there fighting to make us all safe.

Mr. Churchill was talking about how terrible the Nazis were and he said that our hearts went out to the Russians in their struggle because they'd just been invaded now. He said that if the people of London were asked, they would say to Hitler, *"You do your worst, and we will do our best."*

When he said those last words, there was a lot of clapping and I almost put my own hands together, even though I wasn't exactly sure what he meant.

When the clapping died down again, Mr. Churchill told us that it was our turn soon, that it was time the enemy should be made to suffer in their own homelands the way they had made us suffer. But it wasn't going to be easy.

"We do not expect to hit without being hit back," he said, *"and we intend with every week that passes to hit harder. Prepare yourselves,*

then, my friends and comrades, in the battle of London, for this renewal of your exertions. We shall never turn from our purpose, however somber the road, however grievous the cost, because we know that out of this time of trial and tribulation will be born a new freedom and glory for all mankind."

There was more clapping and cheering — a *lot* of it — but when I looked at Mam, sitting on the settee, and saw her expression, she didn't look proud or excited. She didn't look as if she wanted to clap or agree. She looked afraid.

I stood up and went to sit beside her. I leaned close so she'd put her arm around me. "What does it mean?" I asked.

"It means we're goin' to attack them and they're goin' to attack us back. It means it's goin' to get worse before it gets better," she said. "Much worse."

"But it'll all be over soon, won't it?"

Mam squeezed me right against her, but she didn't smile. "Sometimes, Peter, I think it's going to last forever."

AIR RAID

I'd been in bed awhile when I heard the wail of the air-raid siren starting up.

Mr. Charlton, who owned the pub, was one of three people in the main village who had a telephone. He was also the ARP warden, so if there was a chance of a raid, he would get a call and it was his job to go out and crank the Carter siren that stood on a tripod outside the pub. And when it started to whine, someone would rush out and crank the other sirens — one outside Mr. Shaw's butcher shop and one outside the baker's at the other end of the street. People used to laugh about Mr. Charlton patrolling the streets at night, wearing his tin hat and his overalls and shouting, "PUT THAT LIGHT OUT!" or "CLOSE THOSE CURTAINS!" but, really, he had an important job — and one of the most important things he did was sounding the siren to let us know that German planes had been spotted and a raid might be coming.

And right now they were coming.

Mam hurried into my room and was by my bed as I heard the unmistakable drone and buzz of planes approaching.

"Get up," she said. "Quick."

I threw back the covers and jumped out of bed. I was wide awake; no time for sleepiness.

"Get your robe and your mask. Quick."

I put on my robe as quickly as I could and grabbed my gas mask — still in its original box, but now kept in the army bag Mr. Bennett had given me.

Somewhere out in the night came the first thump of a bomb hitting the earth.

"Quick!" Mam said again as she took my hand.

We went downstairs together as more bombs dropped, sounding closer and closer. I could hear the whistle as they fell from the sky.

"They're close," I said, feeling panic rise in me.

"Not *that* close," Mam said, but I was sure I felt the house shudder as we reached the bottom of the stairs and hurried across the kitchen.

Mam yanked the door open and the air-raid siren suddenly became louder. The high-pitched whine pulsed outward from the village center, filling the quiet spaces between the whistles and distant explosions.

Mam didn't say a word as we rushed out. She just held my hand as if she would never let it go, and dragged me across the garden toward the Anderson shelter.

It was a beautiful night. The air was clear and cool. But the sky was filled with terror as we ran across the lawn, my bathrobe catching in the breeze, my bare feet soft on the soil and the grass.

In the distance, farther up the coast, I could see the powerful beams of searchlights pointing at the sky, and I could hear the quick thud of the anti-aircraft guns firing at the planes. I could see fires, too, a strange orange glow that shimmered just on the edge of the horizon. But the planes sounded closer now, their angry buzz getting louder and louder as they approached. And the whistle and thump of their bombs followed them.

Ahead of us, at the bottom of the garden, the Anderson shelter sat low, half buried in the ground. We ducked down inside, squeezing past the sandbags that protected the entrance. Mam made me go first, climbing backward down the little ladder, then she followed and pulled the door shut behind us, sealing us into the cramped metal tube.

We were half underground. The bottom of the door was about level with my head. There was a bunk bed on one side of the shelter, pushed right up against the corrugated metal, and a rickety table against the far wall. There were garden tools there, too, propped against the table and lying on the floor. We didn't use the shelter often, but Mam made sure there were always a couple of blankets and a few damp board games. There were one or two books, as well, and a candle that she now lit, scraping matches in the dark until it was alight. On the concrete floor, insects scuttled to find the dark corners.

It was a warm night, which made it more comfortable in the shelter. In the winter Mam would light the paraffin heater, and the steel walls would drip with condensation.

Mam sat on the bottom bunk beside me and put her arms around me and we stayed like that, in near-darkness, staring at the opposite wall.

Outside the explosions continued to thump and boom, coming closer, like the footsteps of a giant stomping toward us, determined to kill us. I could hear the high-pitched whistle as the bombs dropped from the planes, falling to the ground with deadly effect. My whole body tensed in preparation, waiting for a direct hit as the whistle shrieked toward the earth. I squeezed my eyes shut, and every time one landed, I flinched, and prayed that it was the last.

I wanted to put my hands over my ears to block out those sounds. The sounds of real nightmares, not imaginary monsters in the dark. But I kept my hands in the pockets of my robe and I stared ahead at the damp metal wall of the shelter, where the reflection from the candle glimmered a dull orange.

"Prob'ly on their way home," Mam said. "That's what it is." She squeezed me and looked down. "They're not after *us*, you know."

I nodded and tried to be strong, but I was scared. The bombs had never been so close before.

"They're droppin' whatever they've got left," Mam said. "That's all. It means the planes aren't so heavy when they go back."

Or maybe, I thought, they were bombing away the barbed wire and the pillboxes and the mines on the beach, getting ready for an invasion. I swallowed hard and squeezed my eyes shut as another explosion shook the ground, raining dirt and dust from the ceiling.

I thought about my new friend, Erik, curled up inside my hiding place, with the heavy pink blanket I'd taken from the cupboard. I wondered if he was afraid when he heard the planes, if it made him think about the men who'd died when he'd crashed. And I thought about Kim, wondering if she was safe down there in the village. I was reminded of the story she told me about the house on her road in Newcastle — the one that was hit by a bomb.

Mam held me tight and looked down at me. "It's not so close as it sounds."

But even as she said it, there was a loud whistling that seemed to be right above us, and Mam wrapped her arms around me. After just a few seconds there was a tremendous boom and the whole shelter rattled and shook. Muck fell from the ceiling again, and the candle snuffed out, leaving us in darkness.

"Did they hit us?" I said into the silence that followed. "Did they —"

"No," Mam said, and she took her arms away. "No. We're all right."

For a moment I was left alone in the damp darkness, then I heard her moving about, the rattle of matches in a box, then the flare of a flame. When the candle was relit, Mam came back and held me as the planes passed over, and their noise faded to a calm drone, and then nothing, as the planes turned out to sea and headed back to wherever they had come from.

And even then, we didn't move.

Outside, the air-raid sirens had stopped wailing and the only sound was that of the shelter's iron casing settling into place.

"I think that's it," Mam said.

I didn't reply. We sat in silence for a long time, waiting for the all clear, and when that continuous note screamed from the sirens to tell us it was safe, it made me jump. I shook myself.

"Can we go back inside?" I asked.

"I think so."

When we yanked the door open and stepped back out into the night, it was as if nothing had happened. The sky was clear, the air was cool, and the darkness was as quiet as it was supposed to be.

Back inside the house, there was a large crack running the length of the kitchen ceiling, and a big section of plaster had fallen away. It had landed right on top of the table and broken into pieces. There was pale dust everywhere.

Mam didn't say much. We were both too numb to say much of anything at all. She just tutted and went to get the broom and the dustpan. Together we cleaned up the mess, throwing the pieces out into the garden, and when it was done, Mam warmed some milk and we sat at the kitchen table to drink it.

"Well," she said. "That was an adventure."

"I hope Kim's all right."

Mam forced a smile. "She'll be fine. The bombs were close, but not that close. No one really wants to bomb *us*."

I hoped she was right.

The following morning, Mr. Bennett came round just after nine o'clock. Mam opened the door with the usual worried expression she wore when someone came so early.

"Just wanted to check everyone was all right," he said, looking at Mam and then smiling at me. "Quite a raid, wasn't it?"

"We survived," Mam said, inviting him in and looking up. "A bit of damage to the ceiling, but that's all."

"I saw the plaster outside," he replied, stopping just inside the door and following Mam's gaze. He sucked his teeth as he looked at the place where the plaster had come away, and at the long, deep crack that ran almost the whole length of the kitchen. "Anything I can do to help?"

"Not really. Thank you."

"That crack looks bad. Maybe I could get someone to look at it."

"I'm sure everyone's got better things to do," Mam said.

"I'll see if someone can help. There's a little bit of cleaning up to do in the village, but after that, maybe someone can have a good look at it."

"Is everyone all right?" Mam asked.

"Well, a few bombs came close," he said. "One or two on the beach, but no one was hurt. A few windows broken, that's all."

"Thank goodness."

"Is there anything you need? Anything at all?"

"No. Thank you," Mam said. "That's very kind of you to come and check on us."

Mr. Bennett hesitated on the step, pursing his lips and nodding. "Well, you will let me know if there's anything, won't you?"

"Yes. Of course. Thank you."

When he was gone I asked Mam, "D'you think Mr. Bennett's lookin' for a new wife?"

"What made you say that?" Mam knelt in front of me and put her hands on my shoulders.

"I was wonderin' if that's why he comes here all the time."

Mam smiled and brushed her finger across my cheek. "You know I love your da', don't you?"

I nodded.

"And that I'll wait for 'im?"

"Forever?" I asked.

"Aye," she said. "Forever and ever."

SLEDGEHAMMER

Kim didn't come that morning like I'd hoped she would. I'd been thinking about her all night, and when she didn't come round, I started to worry. I couldn't get that house on her street in Newcastle out of my mind.

"She'll be fine," Mam said. "Mr. Bennett already told us no one was hurt."

"Can I go and check?"

"Of course you can. But stay out of trouble. And don't get in anyone's way . . ."

I was out the door before she finished what she was saying, running past the gate and heading down the track. I'd never been to her aunt's house before, but I knew where it was. The way it turned out, though, I didn't need to know, because when I came to the high street, I saw Kim standing near the corner, watching the adults cleaning up the mess.

"What about all that last night?" she asked as soon as I was beside her. "Fancy those bombs coming so close. The village is in a right state."

"You should see our kitchen; the roof nearly fell in," I

exaggerated. The fear from last night was all gone. Now, in daylight and under a clear sky, everything was exciting again.

"I'll bet it's nothing like this."

"Mr. Bennett said it was just a few broken windows," I said, feeling both annoyed and relieved about missing what had happened here.

"Well, it's a bit more than that. All the shop windows are smashed and the street's covered in glass. There's a few houses that have lost all the slates from the roofs, like they just slipped off. And there's places all along the beach where bombs have exploded. You should see it."

"You think Erik's all right?" I asked.

Kim's expression became serious. "The bombs didn't go over there," she said.

"I bet he's scared, though. Can you imagine? We should go and check on him."

"We will," Kim agreed. "Come and have a look here first, though. We're right here, and you don't want to miss out."

So we went onto the high street and witnessed the destruction caused by bombs falling so close to the village. Kim had been right about the windows. The front of Mr. Shaw's shop was a jagged mess, and there was a large pile of glass lying on the pavement right in front of it where someone had started to tidy up. The greengrocer's, the baker's, the post office, all the shopfronts were smashed, even though brown paper strips had been gummed across them to stop them from shattering. A lot of the chunks were still stuck together in strings, almost like Christmas decorations, broken pieces hanging loose, but that was all the strips had done. In fact, there was hardly a window on the high street that wasn't at least cracked. And there were pieces of roof tiles everywhere.

"Did anything actually get hit?" I asked, looking around at all the people who were helping to tidy up. "Houses, I mean?"

There were at least half a dozen men from the Home Guard, in uniform, sweeping the road and collecting debris in coal shovels. Mr. Charlton, the pub landlord, was there, decked out in his blue overalls and black tin hat with a white *W* on the front of it. Mrs. Charlton was standing beside him, wearing similar overalls, but her helmet had *ARP* painted on it. It looked like they were arguing about something, which wasn't a big surprise because they were always arguing, and most people said she should be the warden, she was so bossy.

There were proper soldiers there, too, come from their billet at Bennett Hall to help clear away the mess while Sergeant Wilkes strutted around making sure they were following orders. A large brown horse stood in the middle of the street, harnessed to an open cart, and the men were throwing the rubbish into that. The horse didn't seem at all bothered by what was happening.

"I don't think there were any direct hits." Kim surveyed the activity as if she hadn't already seen it. "But there's a right old mess. Pretty scary, though, eh? Last night."

"Aye."

"We were all squashed into the shelter like sardines," she said. "The Higginses next door haven't got one, so they all came in, too."

We walked along the high street, heading toward the beach, and when we came past the green and over the path, I could see the mess of tangled barbed wire and the giant holes in the sand where the bombs had struck.

"They really *were* close," I said.

"As if they were trying to hit us," Kim agreed.

And for a while we stood in silence looking at the damage. The gray sea continued to break on the beach as if nothing had happened. Just offshore, a gull moved in the wind, its wings held out.

Kim sat on the grass and I looked down at her. "We should go and see Erik now," I said.

"This might be a good time to get supplies."

I sat down beside her. "What kind of supplies?"

"I saw your Doctor Jacobs helping to clean up. He had his bag with him." Kim turned to me, the breeze rustling her hair. "Maybe we could get some bandages or something."

"How?"

"We could pretend we got hurt. He'd have to look at us and, while his back's turned, we could take something from his bag."

"You mean *steal* it?"

"Erik needs it," Kim argued. "He's our friend and we have to look after him."

"Aye, but —"

"If we don't change the bandage, it could get infected."

"Hmm . . ."

"Listen." Kim turned to face me. Her legs were crossed and her knees just touched my thigh. "We could go and help for a little bit — with the cleanup — and then I could pretend I hurt myself. When the doctor's looking at me, you can take something from his bag. It'll be easy."

"Really?"

"Of course."

"I don't know," I said. "What if we get caught, like? Me mam would kill us if she found out. And Doctor Jacobs is so nice, and —"

"Please, Peter." Kim put her hand on mine. "We have to do it for Erik. He needs us."

I looked down at her hand and sighed. "Hurt how, though? It would have to be good."

Kim wrinkled her nose, thinking about it. "A cut, maybe."

"There'd have to be blood for that."

Her shoulders sagged. "Maybe just a sprain or something, then."

"A sprain?" I shook my head. "That wouldn't work." And then I had an idea. I took my penknife from my pocket and opened the blade. "I could cut meself with this. It's sharp, so it wouldn't hurt."

Kim looked a little unsure.

"I'll do it now." I put the blade against my palm. "I'll say I cut it on a spelk of glass."

"I'm not sure, Peter."

And I wasn't sure either. I didn't know how much it would hurt or how much blood there would be. But something made me do it. Perhaps it was the look on Kim's face. There was something like fear in her eyes, but there was a twinkle there, too. A kind of awe that I would do it, and I knew she'd be impressed if I did.

I gritted my teeth and drew the blade across my skin. There was a sharp stinging sensation, but I cut further, separating the surface flesh, and when I took the knife away, the blood welled in dots along the cut, bulging, growing, and joining.

"Did it hurt?" Kim asked, staring.

"Not much." I put the knife away, feeling very brave, and squeezed the cut so more blood pushed out — enough for it to begin to run down to my wrist when I held my hand up. "Hey, maybe we won't have to steal anything," I said. "Maybe the bandage for this will be big enough for Erik."

"I shouldn't think so." Kim shook her head. "Anyway, *you'll* need it."

"Aye, true." I watched the dark red trails winding down my arm. "So you really think this'll work?" I asked.

"Of course it will."

We went back into the village, where Doctor Jacobs was helping with the cleanup. He was standing next to the green, leaning on a broom handle, talking to one of the other men from the Home Guard. He had his medical bag slung over one shoulder.

As soon as he saw us coming over, he stopped what he was doing and said, "Hello, Peter. What's happened this time?"

I had kept my hand up all the way from the beach, so the blood had made a good pattern running past my wrist and onto my forearm. It looked very impressive. As I came closer, Doctor Jacobs saw the blood and began to take his bag from his shoulder.

"How did this happen?"

"A spelk of glass," I said.

"Well, we'd better have a look at it. Sit down on the grass."

For a moment, I felt like a real wounded soldier. The Home Guardsmen were all around and there was broken glass and roof tiles all over the street. And here I was, sitting on the battlefield being looked after by the medic.

Doctor Jacobs rummaged in his bag, pulling out a few bits and pieces, asking me to hold my hand out.

"Any news from your dad?" he asked as he went to work.

"Not for a while. Mam says it takes time for letters to come from Africa, though."

Kim sat beside him, close to the bag, and while the doctor was focused on me I saw her slip her hand in.

"What's goin' on here?"

Kim snatched her hand away and looked up as Sergeant Wilkes approached.

"You been in the wars?" he asked.

"Cut his hand on some glass." Doctor Jacobs hardly even glanced at him. After the way Sergeant Wilkes had spoken to him the other night at the crash site, I wasn't surprised.

"Glass?" he asked, coming to stand right behind me so I could feel him looming over. "How'd you manage that, like? I thought the lads had swept it all up. And I didn't see you cleanin' up, son."

The sergeant was looking down at me, with his hands on his hips, and while his attention was on me, Kim's hand was back in the medical bag.

"And what about you, bonny lass?" He turned to look at her and, once more, Kim snatched her hand away.

"Eh?"

"I didn't see you cleanin' up either," he said, tilting his head to one side and narrowing his eyes. "How'd he manage to cut himself on glass?"

"We were sitting by the links," she said. "There was a bit in the grass. Must've got blown over there by a bomb or something."

With a frown on his face, Sergeant Wilkes glanced out at the sea, then looked at us each in turn, really staring. "You two should be carrying your masks," he said. "What if this place was teeming with gas, eh? What then? And do you want to get into trouble with the warden?"

"No, sir," I said. "Sorry."

"Hm, well." He sniffed hard. "Don't let me catch you without 'em again." He turned toward the sea once more and nodded. "I s'pose I should go and have a look, then. See how bad it is." He paused and took a deep breath. "And keep away from there. You know it's dangerous."

"Any luck finding the German?" I asked. I thought it was a good time to see if they were any closer to finding Erik, but I had to blurt it out before I lost my nerve.

Sergeant Wilkes studied me, doing that thing where it seemed like he was looking right into my head. "Don't you worry about no Jerries," he said, leaning forward. "We'll have 'im soon enough, you mark my words. I'll find 'im before the week is out."

"Then what?" Kim asked.

"What d'you mean?"

"Well, what will happen to him?" she said.

"If I get my hands on him?" He grinned. "Not your concern. If I told you, it would make your toes curl up in your boots." He winked and lifted one hand in a mock salute. "As you were, little soldiers." And with that, he turned and marched away, boots crunching on the road.

"He gives me the creeps," I said.

"Me too," said Doctor Jacobs with a smile. "But he's just doing his job. I should keep away from him, though, if I were you."

We both nodded, and as soon as the doctor went back to dressing my wound, Kim stuffed her hand back into the medical bag.

"So. No German yet, eh?" I said, trying to keep his attention on me.

"Not so far as I know."

"And they've no idea at all where he might be?" I glanced sideways at Kim.

"Not yet," the doctor said.

"Prob'ly long gone by now," I suggested as Kim grabbed a handful of whatever she could and whipped it into her satchel.

"Oh, I don't know about that. They're beginning to think he might be hiding somewhere close." Doctor Jacobs looked up at me. "So you be careful where you play and who you talk to."

"If it was me, I'd get away."

"Where would you go?" he asked.

I shrugged. "Up the coast. Look for a boat, maybe."

"Hm. Well, they'll find him, one way or another."

By now, Doctor Jacobs had finished cleaning the cut, and when he reached into his bag for something else, he stopped. He turned and opened the bag with both hands, peering inside, then looked up at Kim's innocent expression.

"I could have sworn . . ." He looked into the bag, then at Kim, again. "Hmm," he said. "I thought I had more than this. Very odd." Then he shook his head and took out a small bandage for my hand.

When he'd finished, he sent us on our way, telling us to be careful and stay out of trouble, but we hardly took any notice of him. We just wanted to be away from him as quickly as possible, escaping with our stolen medical supplies and going to Erik.

"Good idea trying to get some information out of him," Kim said. "You'd make a good spy. And trying to throw them off the scent was clever, too — up the coast to look for a boat? I like that."

"Don't s'pose it'll do much good," I said.

"You never know. It's worth a try."

About halfway along the street, I changed my pace, walking more slowly.

"What's wrong?" asked Kim. "Why have you slowed down?"

I stopped and spoke to her, still watching the boys standing in front of the notice board. "Maybe we should go back and help clean up."

"What are you talking about? We need to go to Erik."

"I just think . . . maybe we should help. You know."

"Wait a minute," Kim said. "Is this because of that boy Ridley over there?"

I shrugged.

"Don't be so silly," she said. "After everything we've done. You and me just captured a German soldier!"

"Not really captured," I said.

"Well, maybe not, but we got him, didn't we? There's soldiers looking all over for him, but *we've* got him. I reckon you're braver than any of those monkeys, so what's the matter with you?"

When she said it that way, it did sound silly, but I couldn't explain it right then. I didn't understand my own feelings. Trevor Ridley frightened me because even when I tried to make him leave me alone, he always overpowered me. He and his friends always got the better of me. And then there were the things he said about Mam — about Mr. Bennett taking a fancy to her — and those things made me so mad. And what made it worse was that sometimes his comments got right under my skin and I wondered if they were true. Maybe Mam *was* going to forget about Dad. Maybe she *was* going to go and live with Mr. Bennett. He came round to our house so much, it could have been true and, even though deep down I was sure it wasn't, Trevor Ridley was always there to add a grain of doubt.

"You're not going to run away," Kim said.

I looked along the street at the boys.

"And anyway," she went on, "I promised you that the next time he said anything, I'd give him a bloody nose. Come on." She put her arm around my shoulder and I reluctantly walked with her.

Trevor Ridley had spotted us coming and was ready with something to say as soon as we came close. "Oh look, it's that baby Peter Dixon and his evacuee lass. Or is it a lad? I can never tell."

I started to walk past them, but heard Kim say beside me, "Looks like one of the pigs escaped from your dad's farm."

"Don't try to be clever," Ridley said, coming to stand in front of us, with his friends behind him.

"A *fat* pig," Kim said.

I just wanted to walk away, but I couldn't leave Kim on her own. Anyway, being with her made me feel stronger, so I stood straight beside her, trying to make myself look taller. "A fat, clarty one," I said, and my whole body tingled with fear and excitement.

Trevor Ridley raised his eyebrows. "Feelin' brave, are you? Finally got a friend, so you're feelin' brave." He looked Kim up and down. "Even if she is a lass."

"At least I'm not a fat pig," she returned.

Ridley stared at her, tightening his jaw, then looked at me. "I saw what you two just did."

My heart stopped.

"Saw you with your hand in the doctor's bag." He looked at Kim and narrowed his eyes. "What're you two up to, liftin' stuff off the doctor?"

My mouth was dry. I could hardly speak. "Nowt," I said, my tongue clicking. "We're not doing nowt."

Ridley sniffed hard and came closer. "Maybe I should go tell 'im what I saw."

"We didn't do nowt," I said again.

Ridley lifted a hand and jabbed his index finger right against my chest. "You're a liar, Peter Dixon, and you're in a lot of bother."

Kim shrugged. "No one would believe you. Everyone knows what you're like."

"What's that s'posed to mean?" Ridley snapped his head round to look at her.

"Just that you're a liar and everyone knows you're trouble. *Especially* the doctor," she said. "*Especially* after he caught you at the wreck the other night."

Ridley dropped his hand and narrowed his eyes. "What d'you know about that?"

Kim shrugged again.

"Who told ya?"

"No one. I just know."

Trevor looked flustered for a moment, knowing he wasn't going to get anything else out of her, but he wasn't one for just giving up, so he turned to me and sneered. "Your mam gone to live with his lordship yet? Or is she waitin' for your da' to get shot first?"

Even Cummings and Thornhill were shocked by that, and one of them took a sudden breath in surprise.

"Take that back," Kim said. "Take it back now."

"Why don't you try making me?" he said. "Or are you —"

But before he could finish, I stepped forward and swung at him harder than I imagined I was able. I tightened my fingers into a fist and hit Trevor Ridley square on the nose as hard as I could. I felt the cartilage squash under my knuckles, and he sat down on the pavement as if he'd been hit with a sledgehammer.

Behind him, the other boys took a step back.

I shook the pain from my hand and looked at my knuckles, and then down at Trevor Ridley, who was staring up at me, one hand on his nose.

Kim stepped forward, looking at the other boys, raising her fists like a boxer. "Anyone else want to have a try?" she asked.

None of them answered. It was as if they were all too stunned to react. Bob Cummings and Adam Thornhill just stared, mouths open. Even *I* felt as if I'd been frozen to the pavement, and it was only when Trevor began to get to his feet that Kim tugged my shirt.

"Let's go," she whispered.

I stepped back, not quite believing what I'd just done. Kim pulled me.

"Now," she said.

Bob and Adam had come to life again and were reaching down to help Trevor stand.

Kim yanked me hard this time.

"Run!" she said.

And with those words, the spell was broken and we both turned and ran. We raced along the pavement, and we kept on going until we reached the end of the street. Turning the corner, we ducked between some houses and came out onto the road at the bottom of the fields. We stopped by one of the concrete roadblocks and looked at each other.

"That was brilliant," she said between breaths.

"My hand hurts. It was my bad hand, too. The one I cut."

"Yeah, but it's worth it, isn't it? I mean, you should have seen their faces. Ha! You should have seen *your* face. I think you surprised yourself more than anyone else."

I still couldn't quite believe I'd hit Trevor Ridley, knocked him right down on his backside, but I'd looked back at him as we ran away, and I'd seen him get to his feet and point after us.

"This isn't going to be the end of it, though, is it?" I said.

"Course it is," Kim said. "He won't bother you again, not now. Everyone knows that if you stand up to bullies, they leave you alone."

"I'm not so sure." I had seen the look on Trevor's face and it scared me. "I don't think he's gonna forget about this. And he knows we took stuff outta Doctor Jacobs's bag."

"Doesn't matter."

"D'you not think we're in trouble?" I asked as we crossed the road and headed over the field toward the hill.

"Because of the supplies? No. I don't think so."

"What if he tells someone?"

"Who would he tell? Anyway, no one would believe him."

"I just can't stop thinking about it. This isn't the end of it. What if —"

"*I* can't stop thinking about that punch," Kim said. "Does it still hurt?"

"A bit."

She stopped and took my hand in hers. "Doesn't look bruised," she said.

I watched her as she turned my hand over, studying it closely.

"Can you waggle your fingers?"

I moved them about.

"I reckon you'll live," she said, rubbing the fingers between both hands for a moment. "What about your cut?"

I shrugged. "It's fine."

"Let me see."

I let her pick away the edge of the bandage with her fingernail, then pull it back to reveal the cut. "It's still bleeding."

"Only a bit."

"I've got an idea," she said. "Give me your knife."

"Why?"

"You'll see."

I fished the penknife out of my pocket and gave it to Kim. I watched her open the blade and put the cutting edge against her palm. Without taking her eyes off me, she gritted her teeth and pulled the blade along her skin. It wasn't a big cut, but when she squeezed it, the blood oozed out. Then she folded the knife and gave it back to me before taking my hand and pressing the two cuts together.

"Blood brothers," she said. "Or blood brother and sister."

"Aye."

We held our hands together like that for a while, both of us squeezing hard and looking right at each other. When we let go, I put my hand to my mouth and sucked away the blood.

"You gave him a right good wallop," Kim said, sealing the end of the ritual. "Just what he deserved." She put her arm around my shoulder, and we walked toward the hill, best friends.

RABBIT

Kim re-dressed Erik's wounded arm with our stolen bandages while I emptied the pan. I was glad he'd put the cloth over the top of it because the smell in the den was awful, and there was a lot of weight in the pan. I took it into the woods and turned my head as I flung it into the undergrowth. Afterward, I swooshed it about in the deepest part of the burn and went back to Kim and Erik. It was only as I returned that I realized I hadn't been worried about leaving Kim alone with him.

When everything was cleaned up, we gave Erik the food we'd managed to get, and we all sat looking at each other. Talking was difficult because Erik hardly knew any English and we hardly knew any German, but we managed to communicate in simple ways. Sometimes it made us laugh when we were all making shapes in the air with our hands, pointing, looking up in the hope of inspiration. Kim had a nice laugh, quiet and sweet, but sometimes she snorted and slapped her leg if something was really funny. Erik didn't so much laugh as smile, showing a slightly crooked row of front teeth.

That day, he dusted his hands across the ground in front of

him to make it flat, and took a stick. He drew a shape in the dirt and pointed at it, saying, "Deutschland."

I knew the shape and we knew the name. There was a map of the world on the wall in the classroom at school, and the teacher had shown us where Germany was.

Erik put the stick close to one edge of his drawing and said, "Hamburg." Then he wrote the word into the dirt. He tapped his chest and said, "Erik, Hamburg."

"You're from Hamburg?"

"Hamburg," he said, nodding.

Then he said something else in German that we didn't understand and left us shaking our heads, so he rubbed away his drawing and started again. This time he drew a long blob and pointed at it, saying, "England." Then he drew another blob and said, *"Norwegen."*

"Norwegen?" I repeated, and looked at Kim. "Is that Norway?"

"You were in Norway?" Kim asked him. We knew where that was, too, because they'd showed us that at school. The Germans had invaded and taken it over last year.

"Ja. Norway. *Norwegen."* Erik patted his chest, then he thought for a second before pointing at me and saying, "Peter *farter?"*

As soon as he said it, Kim and I looked at each other and smiled. The smile turned into a laugh, and Kim did that thing where she snorted and slapped her thigh. We laughed so much there were tears in Kim's eyes, but when I looked at Erik, he was confused, so I stopped myself laughing and said, *"Farter?"* Then I put my lips on my forearm and blew, making a loud, wet sound.

Erik looked even more confused now. *"Furzen?"* He shook his head. *"Nein.* No. *Vater. Papa."*

"He means *father*," Kim said, wiping away the tears. "I think he wants to know where your dad is."

Suddenly it wasn't funny anymore, and I was thinking about Dad. It didn't seem right that we were laughing and he was out there somewhere, far away, and we hadn't heard from him for such a long time.

"Africa," I said. "He's in Africa."

"*Afrika.*" Erik nodded. "Bad," he said. "War bad."

"*Germans* are bad," I replied.

Erik stared at me, shaking his head.

"So why do you keep bombing us?" I said, but he couldn't understand, so I pointed at him and put my hands out as if I were an airplane. Then I made bomb noises and pointed at myself. "You bomb us. Germans are bad."

Erik stared for a while longer. "*Nein,*" he said. "No. No. *Nazi* bad. German *gut.*" He put his hand on his chest. "Erik. Nazi. No."

When we left, Kim and I went farther into the woods to check the snares.

"Mam says maybe all Germans don't want to bomb us," I said.

"She's probably right. I suppose they're not all Nazis. Like Erik; he's not, is he?"

"So why was he in the plane, then?"

"He probably had to be," Kim said. "You think everyone *here* really wants to go and fight? I bet your dad would rather be at home with you and your mum. I know Josh would rather be here."

"Aye." It was Dad's duty to go, I knew that, and Mam said he'd gone away to protect us, but I couldn't help thinking Kim was right.

"So maybe Erik didn't want to go either," she said.

"I never thought about it like that. People being made to go to war. Sounds unfair."

"Lots of things are unfair," Kim said.

"I s'pose." I thought about Dad not being allowed back after Dunkirk like Kim's brother was, and I thought about how he had gone to fight while others had stayed at home. People like Trevor Ridley's dad. The more I thought about it, the more unfair it felt, and that made me feel even more sorry for Erik. Maybe he'd never even wanted to go up in a plane. Maybe he never wanted to fight anybody. And, for the first time, it occurred to me that he must have a mam and dad, too. Sisters and brothers, even, or a girlfriend or wife or something. They were probably all at home right now, wondering where he was. Maybe they were worried, too — worried because they hadn't had a letter from him, just like we hadn't had one from Dad.

The first two snares we came to were empty, but when we came to the third, I saw straightaway that the slack had been pulled tight against the peg.

"I think we got one," I said, hurrying over.

Kim ran alongside me, asking, "Where is it?"

I got down on my knees and beckoned her close. "Under there." Close to the snare, there was a tuft of undergrowth that the rabbit was using for cover. The animal was crouched low to the ground, its ears pinned right back.

Kim leaned close, putting her hand on my arm. "That's amazing," she said. "You got one."

"*We* got one. You helped put these out."

She nodded, her mouth slightly open.

"It looks so soft," she said. "And look at its eyes."

I took the tethering cord in my fingers and held it firm as I reached out to clasp the rabbit around the back of the neck. Gripping it that way, I grabbed its back legs with my other hand and pulled it from the undergrowth, holding it out for Kim to see. The rabbit hardly struggled at all. Its legs kicked once or twice, but that was it.

"What now?" Kim asked.

"Break its neck."

Kim grimaced.

"Turn around if you don't want to see," I said.

"It's all right." Kim nodded. "Go on."

I held the rabbit's head close to the ground and twisted as I pulled the hind legs back, giving a good tug, and felt the rabbit go limp.

"That's it?" Kim asked.

"That's it."

For a while, Kim sat with her legs crossed, looking at the rabbit laid out on the ground in front of us.

"I've eaten rabbit," she said after a while. "Quite nice, really. Never seen one killed, though." She looked up. "I suppose you've done that lots of times, have you?"

"A few. I don't really like doin' it. I don't *want* to do it, but we have to."

Kim thought about it for a moment. "What does it feel like?"

"Doesn't feel like anything . . . I . . . No, it *does* feel like something. It feels like Mam's gonna be happy. It feels like there's something better than tripe to eat, and it feels like we won't be hungry tomorrow." I thought about letting Kim take it home — she *had* helped to set the snares, after all — but I knew how pleased Mam would be. She loved rabbit. And one time, when I brought one home, she saw me from the kitchen window and she said it reminded her of watching Dad come home with a rabbit for the pot.

"Maybe I'll try next time," Kim said. "Be a proper country person. Like you."

"You sure?"

"Of course."

"It's just . . . you look a bit shocked."

"Not shocked," she said. "I think it's brilliant. You just caught an animal and now you're going to take it home to eat. What could be better than that?"

And the way she looked at me — that was the first time I realized Kim felt about me the same way I felt about her.

Kim didn't say much on the way back, but she kept looking down at the rabbit I was carrying. I had its hind feet in my right hand, its head hanging toward the ground, and I felt so good. All around the world, the war raged. Bombs were being dropped and bullets were being fired, but right here, in these woods, I felt happy. I was with my best friend, and I was about to make Mam happy.

For a few moments, everything was just as it should be.

THE SOLDIERS COME

Two days later, the soldiers came. They weren't German, but we were just as afraid of them when we heard them coming through the woods.

Kim and I had come over the top of the hill as usual, sneaking past the men guarding the wreck. There were only two of them there that day, and neither of them seemed very alert, leaning on the now-cold pieces of twisted metal, chatting and smoking. They were wearing waterproof coverings to protect them from the drizzle that filled the gray morning air, and looked as if they were draped in sheets, like green ghosts guarding the wreckage. We were so used to seeing them, we'd almost forgotten there might be soldiers still looking for Erik.

"I saw that boy Trevor following me before," Kim said.

"Really?"

"Mm. He was with those other two, waiting on the street near my house. Don't worry, though, I gave them the slip."

"What did they want?"

"Not sure."

"I don't like the idea of them tryin' to follow you."

"I'll be all right," Kim said.

"What if he gets you on your own, though? Or what if he follows you to the woods?" I stopped and looked round, half expecting to see Ridley and his friends right behind us.

"I'll be extra careful from now on," Kim said. "I promise." She knew as well as I did how bad it would be for Erik, and for us, if anyone found out we were hiding him. We'd come too far to tell anyone now. Mam always said that if you tell a lie, it can get bigger and bigger, and I was beginning to understand what she meant.

Inside the woods it was damp, and the smell lifted out of the soil and filled our nostrils. A good, earthy smell. Everything seemed alive despite the drizzle and the clouds. The past few days had been hot and sunny, and everything was grateful for the cool air and the wet. It made everything look greener.

Erik always looked afraid when we first came into the den, and he'd taken to holding a stick at the ready, as if there was anything much he could do with it. He'd hold it in front of him, pointing the sharpest end, but as soon as he saw us, he'd put it down and smile. I think if it had been me stuck inside that den all the time, I'd be pleased to see just about anybody. It was a good place to go for some peace and quiet, or maybe to play for a while, but I wouldn't have wanted to live there.

The smell was better that day, and the pan was empty. And when I picked up his water bottle, expecting it to need refilling, it felt heavy.

I held it out to Kim. "He hasn't drunk any. You think he's all right?"

"Maybe he's not thirsty."

Erik gestured at us, making us watch him. He put the first two fingers of his right hand on the ground as if they were the legs of a little man. He made them walk away from him, then pointed at his chest and tapped his stick before walking his fingers through the air toward the entrance to the den.

"You've been out?" Kim said. "Using a stick?" She looked at me. "He's been out."

"Is that safe?"

"It means he can walk," she said. "See. We've made his ankle better." She pointed at his ankle. "Good?"

"*Ja. Gut,*" Erik said. "*Gut.*" He gave us a thumbs-up.

"Mustn't have been broken." Kim looked relieved. "So it *was* a sprain after all."

"And you can take your aunt's pan back," I said.

"I'm not sure she'd want it. I know I don't want to —"

And that's when we heard them.

Somewhere outside, a little way off, we heard voices coming closer.

Erik froze. His thumb was still out, but his eyes widened and he looked at us. From one to the other he looked at each of us, then he dropped his hand and reached for the stick.

I felt my heart quicken. My legs turned to stone.

". . . got us bloody tramping around looking for him," said a voice. "Why the hell would he be so close? He's prob'ly long gone by now."

"God help him if he's not," said another. "He wouldn't stand a chance."

"All them bombs . . . I find one of them Jerries here, he's not going to know what hit him."

194

"Be quiet." A third voice. One I recognized. "With you lot thumping around like a herd of elephants, any German would hear you a mile away." It was Sergeant Wilkes.

"He's probably dead anyway, Sarge," said one of the voices that had spoken before. "At least he ought to be."

"Shh."

For a while there was just the sound of men moving through the woods. The occasional swish of a low branch catching on a uniform, the snap of a twig beneath a shiny boot. And then a splash and Sergeant Wilkes said, "Oh, bloody hell. Now I'm gonna be sloshing around all morning."

"They're at the burn," Kim whispered.

I shook my head at her and put my finger to my lips, still staring at Erik, who was now looking at us in a strange way.

Outside, the boots moved through the woods, coming closer and closer.

"I'm telling you, if I find this devil I'm gonna make him pay for this." The sergeant's voice was unmistakable.

And in seconds, the soldiers were almost right on top of us, just a few feet away. Erik was terrified, pressed back against the trunk of the sycamore, gripping his stick in trembling hands.

"There's a shed," I heard one of them say, and I imagined them all pointing their rifles at Dad's shed, expecting a deadly German soldier to leap out at them.

"All right, stand back," said the sergeant. "Be ready. We'll have to check it."

Everything was quiet for a moment. Then a rattle.

"There's a padlock," said one of the soldiers. "He's not going to be in there."

"We have to be sure," Sergeant Wilkes replied. "These Jerries are sneaky, you know. Break it open."

Straightaway, I thought about the gun on the shelf and I turned to stare at Kim. I tried to remember if the gun was in plain sight; tried to remember if I'd left it in front of or behind the toolbox. If the soldiers saw it, they'd know something was up.

I felt my heart hammering. My body seemed heavy, my skin cold and clammy. I was as afraid now as I'd been when the planes had come and Mam and me had run to the shelter. Perhaps more. All three of us sitting motionless in my den, protected from the soldiers by nothing more than some sticks and leaves. If all the foliage had suddenly fallen from the thick tangle of undergrowth, we'd have been left sitting in the open just a few feet from the soldiers. I was almost too frightened to breathe, in case they heard me. Terrified they'd find us, or the gun, or both.

I felt Kim take my hand in hers, and she squeezed it tight when we heard the sound of something hard being smashed down on the padlock.

Again, everything went quiet.

I imagined the soldiers stepping into the shed and seeing the gun on the shelf. I imagined them calling for more soldiers so that they were everywhere, searching every inch of the forest, looking under every bush and behind every tree.

"Nowt in here," said one of the soldiers. "Looks like no one's been in here for a while."

"Anything been moved about?" the sergeant asked.

"Not that I can tell."

I felt a tiny sense of relief that they had not found the gun.

"Right, then, let's move on."

"What *is* all this stuff?" one of the soldiers said. "Looks like some kind of cages."

"Doesn't matter. Let's move on."

"There's one here that's broken, Sarge. And it looks recent."

"Aye, it *does*." And there was something in Sergeant Wilkes's voice that made me imagine him narrowing his eyes like I'd seen him do before. And I remembered how the lieutenant had said he was like a bloodhound.

The voices were quiet again for a while, and then came the words that struck fear right into us. We knew we were going to be discovered as soon as we heard Wilkes speak again.

"All right, you lot," said the sergeant, "spread out. I want this whole area searched. Don't leave any stone unturned."

We cowered in our hiding place like snared rabbits, not daring to breathe or move or think as the soldiers moved around us. We could hear their boots on the soil. I even thought at one point that I heard one of them inhaling heavily not more than a couple of feet away from me as he investigated the area around the hut.

And then, without any warning, a bayoneted rifle pierced through the foliage to my left. It broke through with little more than a swish and a rustle, and the pointed blade thumped into the soil just a few inches from my thigh. We all whipped our heads around to stare at the length of black steel spike slung beneath the barrel of the Lee Enfield rifle. We watched as it twisted, drew back, and disappeared almost as quickly as it had come in.

"Could be in here," said the sergeant. "Hidin' like a little rat."

Then it struck through again, this time hitting the soil between Kim and me.

"You in there, Jerry?"

The third time it intruded into our den, the bayonet missed Erik by inches.

"I'll stick you like a pig."

On the fourth time, it drew blood.

The bayonet drove through the leaves and tangled branches, nicking Kim's right calf, raking across her skin, tearing a ragged scratch. She immediately put her hand to her mouth to stop herself from shouting out in pain, her other hand squeezing mine.

We waited for the bayonet to come through a fifth time, each of us drawing our legs up, making ourselves as small as possible. My muscles were tensed so hard they felt like they were on fire. But the bayonet didn't appear again. Instead, there was a shaking and rustling as if Sergeant Wilkes was kicking in frustration at the tangle of branches and leaves.

"Ah, there's nowt in here," he said, sounding out of breath.

"Clear over here, too."

"Nothin'."

The voices all agreed there were no Germans hiding in the area, and we heard them regroup by the shed. I looked at Kim, seeing the pain in her eyes, but she still held one hand clamped firmly over her mouth, and the other was still squeezing mine.

"Right, let's move on," said the sergeant. "And keep the noise down. You're soldiers, not schoolgirls."

We listened to them moving off into the woods until there was no more sound. But even then we all sat in silence, not daring to speak.

For a long time we said nothing, and the blood trickled along Kim's calf, soaking into the top of her sock, running down and dripping into the soil. The dark earth drank it up like water, drawing it down as we sat there, too afraid to say anything because the soldiers might come back.

It was Erik who moved first. He shuffled over to where Kim was sitting and took hold of her satchel. He removed a clean cloth and pressed it to the wound on her leg. He held it there, letting the blood soak in, then took it away and inspected the wound.

He sucked in his breath and shook his head. The emotion that he most commonly showed in his expression was fear, but now I saw something else in Erik's eyes. It looked a lot like anger.

He dabbed at the wound, cleaning the blood away. It wasn't deep. The bayonet hadn't left a bad cut on Kim's calf, and the blood made it look much worse than it was. Really, it wasn't much more than a scratch, the kind of thing that might have happened climbing over the barbed-wire fence — which was what she would tell her aunt when questioned — but that wasn't what was on my mind. Something else was bothering me much more. Something else weighed down on me like a heavy, dark blanket that had fallen from above and covered me, making me afraid and angry and surprised, but I couldn't quite put my finger on what it was.

"He just stabbed right in here," Kim said. "He just stabbed away without knowing who was in here. It could have been anyone."

And that's what was bothering me. Her words described exactly what I was feeling. The sergeant had thrust his bayonet into the undergrowth without knowing what might have been in here. He gave no thought to the fact that children might be playing in the woods, hiding because they were afraid. But, most important, Sergeant Wilkes had thrust his bayonet in here because he thought there might be a German soldier hiding inside. And it confirmed for me what I had doubted all along. The soldiers meant to kill Erik. They meant to catch him and kill him.

The whole world had turned upside down — it was the British soldiers who terrified us now, not the Germans.

I looked at Erik, his injured ankle with the homemade splint, his bandaged arm, and his torn flight overalls. I watched the way he carefully wiped the blood from Kim's calf and took the Dettol from her satchel to disinfect her wound. I watched him do those things and I wondered how someone could kill him in cold blood. He wasn't bad.

Kim was braver than I would have been. I could see that she was scared and hurt, but she didn't cry. Not a single tear escaped her eyes. She gritted her teeth and squeezed her eyes shut, but she didn't cry.

"I don't think they saw the gun," I said.

"They were looking for a man," Kim replied, wincing as Erik poured some of the Dettol onto the cloth and dabbed at her wound. "But you'll have to move it. Hide it better."

"I will," I said. "Right now."

I crawled out quietly, afraid that the soldiers would come back, but there was no sign of them anywhere. They were long gone.

I went to the shed and collected the broken padlock before going inside. It didn't seem as if the soldiers had moved anything. As Kim said, they were looking for a man, not for something as small as a gun. I made myself calm down and went into the shed, taking the gun in one hand and opening the toolbox with the other. I lifted out some of the tools and put the gun inside before replacing them. I couldn't imagine any reason why the soldiers would look for a German inside a toolbox. The gun would be safe there.

With that done, I hung the padlock back on the clasp and positioned it so it looked as if the shed were still locked. It didn't occur to me that if the same soldiers came back, they'd think it strange that the lock had found its way back onto the door.

When I returned to the den, the cut on Kim's leg had more or less stopped bleeding, so Erik tied the cloth around her calf and sat back.

"Thank you," she said to him.

Erik smiled and nodded once, but the smile fell away quickly, and he looked at the ground between his feet as if he were ashamed of something. And I knew exactly what was wrong. If it weren't for him, we wouldn't be here. We wouldn't have had to lie and steal. And Kim wouldn't have been hurt.

Erik thought it was all his fault.

SNAP

After lunch, I went out and sat on the top of the hill to watch for Kim. The wreck was still down there, its tail section sticking up in the air, displaying the crooked cross they called a swastika. Two soldiers were still guarding it. Maybe both of them had been with Sergeant Wilkes when he stuck his bayonet into our hiding place. I picked up my stick and held it like a rifle, aiming down at the soldiers and sniping them where they stood, making shooting noises to myself.

When I was certain they were well and truly sniped, I turned round so I was looking back toward the village, and I strained my eyes for any sign of Kim, but there was none.

I stayed prone, lying on my stomach with my arms folded in front of me, and I rested my chin on my forearm. The day had warmed up since the drizzle this morning. The sky had cleared and the sun was out. It was warm, with a cool breeze coming over the sea, wafting up toward me. It carried the smell of salt and seaweed.

The village looked small from here. Just a few houses with a high street that had a couple of shops and a pub. Beyond that, the links were a hotchpotch of green where the grass grew long and tough, and brown where the sand lay. There were two pillboxes on the links now, one at each end of the bay, like punctuation marks. They were gray concrete hexagons with slits on each side so the soldiers could point their heavy machine guns in any direction. I tried to remember what the bay had looked like without them, but I couldn't. It was beginning to feel as if they'd always been there, and as if they always *would* be there, and that made me think about what Mam had said the other night. About the war lasting forever. I hoped it would be over soon so that Dad could come home and Erik could go back to wherever he had come from and everything would be normal again. Mr. Bennett would go back to being Dad's boss, and . . . and Kim would go home. I didn't want that. I'd only known her a few days, but already I felt as if she was the best friend I'd ever had.

I waited almost an hour before I decided Kim's aunt must have kept her in. She was probably angry about the state she'd been in when she got home. I thought about going to call on her, but when I saw figures cross the road and come to the edge of the field in the distance, I decided not to. I knew straightaway it was Ridley and his friends, so I pulled back and slipped down the hill, out of sight. I ran to the trees, where I found a good spot and climbed into the crook of an oak, to a place where I could see both the top of the hill and the wreck.

I sat quietly, wondering if there was another reason why Kim hadn't come out. Maybe she'd seen the boys waiting to follow her and had decided to stay in. I probably would have done the same thing.

It was a while before the boys reached the crest of the hill. They made no attempt to hide themselves from the soldiers. Instead, they marched straight down the other side to talk to them. The soldiers didn't even hold out their rifles or ask for their identity cards, and I thought they must have been there before. The soldiers must have known who they were.

I didn't stay to watch anymore — it made me too angry — so I dropped down from the tree and went to see Erik.

When I crawled into the den, the first thing he said was "Kim?"

"She's not comin'." I shook my head. "Prob'ly in trouble."

"Doctor?" he asked.

"I s'pose."

I opened my satchel and took out the food I'd brought for him. "I brought this, too," I said, showing him some small pieces of scrap paper and the stub of a pencil I'd found in a drawer in the sideboard. I'd been looking for a pack of cards when I had spotted the paper Mam and Dad used for keeping score. "So we can write things down or draw pictures. And I thought you might be bored, so I brought some playing cards." I knew he couldn't understand me, but it seemed right to talk to him. I couldn't very well have said nothing.

He replied by speaking in German.

Erik took the pack of cards and opened it. He split them in half and flicked the ends together, shuffling the cards so they made a mechanical ripping noise when he flicked them. He dealt out a number of cards to each of us and picked up his own, but I shook my head.

"I don't know any card games," I said. "Except for Snap. Mam and Da' tried to teach me some others, like, but I could never remember how."

Erik shrugged, gathered the cards back together, shuffled them once more, then fanned them out so they were facing the ground and offered them to me.

"You want me to take one?" I reached out toward the cards and made a pinching motion.

"Ja." He nodded at the cards.

I took one out and turned it around to show him, but he shook his head, saying, *"Nein."* He twisted my hand around so the card was facing me again.

"Don't show it to you?" I asked. I pretended to turn the card, then shook my head as he had done, and held it to my chest so he couldn't see it.

Erik nodded and took the card back. He shuffled the deck again and held them out in the same way.

I picked one and looked at it — the seven of clubs — but this time I didn't let him see. Erik then shuffled the rest of the cards, split them, and held one half out to me, tapping the top card.

"Put it back?" I asked, offering the card toward the pile.

"Ja." He continued to tap until I returned the card to the deck, then he put them all together, shuffled them, and fanned through them until he said, "Ha!" and took one out. With a flourish, he slapped it on the ground in front of him.

It was the two of hearts.

"No." I shook my head.

"No?"

"No."

"Hm," he said with a confused look. He fanned through the cards again, shaking his head. Then he shrugged and showed me the cards, gesturing for me to look through them. I looked at each one, but none of them was the seven of clubs.

"Ah!" Erik said, holding up his hands. He snapped his fingers and leaned forward, reaching behind me. When he brought his hand back, he was holding the seven of clubs.

"How did you do that, like?"

Erik laughed and reshuffled the cards, showing me the trick all over again, but after a while it wasn't clever anymore, so I taught him how to play Snap. He seemed to have played something like it before, and it didn't take him long to learn. We had a few games, then I watched him eat the bits and pieces I'd brought for him.

"It must be dead scary," I said, making him look up at me. "Bein' stuck in 'ere after that plane crash and the bombings an' everythin'."

Erik nodded, but I knew he didn't have a clue what I was saying.

"I know *I'd* be scared. Me da' would, too, I s'pose. Prob'ly not as much, though."

Erik tore off a piece of bread with his teeth and washed it down with a swig of water.

"Kim thinks that if we look after you, then maybe someone will look after me da' or her brother. Sort of like doin' a good deed. If something happened to 'em, I mean."

Erik stopped chewing. *"Bruder?"*

"Hm?"

"Bruder," he said again, then thought hard for a second. "Bro-ther."

"Brother?"

"Ja. Peter, Kim, bro-ther?"

And then I understood. "No, I'm not Kim's brother. No. Friends."

"Ah. Friend." He nodded once, as if that had cleared everything up for him. "Erik bro-ther," he said, touching his chest.

"You have a brother?"

"Ja," he said. *"Bruder."* He put the water bottle down and stretched out his leg so he could get his hand into the pocket of his flight suit. When it came back out, there was a piece of paper in his fingers. He looked at it with a sad smile and then passed it over to me.

Except it wasn't a piece of paper, it was a photograph. There wasn't much background to see apart from the very left edge of a stone house that seemed to have been built in the middle of a field with woods in the distance. It reminded me a lot of Hawthorn Lodge. In the foreground, Erik and a younger boy were standing with a man in a suit and woman wearing a flower-patterned dress. Erik was wearing some kind of uniform, but the younger boy was dressed in shorts and a shirt, with a sleeveless pullover, knee-length socks, and shoes. If it hadn't been for Erik's uniform, I would have thought the photograph might have been taken right here in my village.

"Konrad," Erik said, tapping the younger boy. "Bro-ther."

"That's your brother?" I asked. "And your mam and da'?"

"Konrad." He tapped the boy once more, then moved his finger first to the man, then the woman, saying, "Papa. Mama."

"Are they fightin'?" I asked. "Your brother and your da'? Are they fightin' in the war?" I pointed at his brother and then held my arms out like I was a plane.

"*Nein.* No." Then he said something in German but I didn't understand a word of it. He paused for thought, then patted his chest. "Erik," he said, putting his hand to the top of his head as if he were measuring himself. "Konrad." He dropped his hand to chest height, then pointed at me. "Konrad. Peter."

"Haven't got a clue what you're sayin'." I shook my head.

Once again Erik thought hard, then his face lit up and he took the scrap paper I'd brought and wrote something on it in pencil. When he turned it round for me to look at, I could see the numbers *14* and *19*.

Erik pointed at the number *19*, then at himself.

"You're nineteen?" I said. "And your brother is fourteen?"

"*Ja. Bruder.* Konrad." He tapped the *14* again.

"He's like me: too young. I'm twelve." I took the pencil and drew the number *12* on the paper and patted my own chest.

Erik smiled. "*Ja?*"

"Yes," I said. "Ya. Kim, too."

He gave me a thumbs-up.

"And your da'?" I asked. "Your papa?"

"Papa . . . Papa . . ." Erik tried to think of a way to tell me. "Papa school."

"School? Your da's in school? But that doesn't . . . Oh, you mean he's a teacher?"

"*Ja.* Teacher."

It was so normal. I hadn't really given much thought to what Erik's family might be like — in fact, I hadn't given much thought to whether he even had one — but now that I knew, they just sounded so *normal*. Not like the posters. Nothing like that at all.

"I wish me da' was here," I said, passing the photograph back to him. "It's not fair. I miss him so much." I put a hand to my mouth and swallowed hard, determined not to let Erik see me upset.

"War bad," Erik said, leaning across to pat my shoulder. "War bad."

"Aye."

He sat back and said something in German, making me wish I could talk to him, but all I could do was shrug and shake my head.

Erik took another bite of the bread and held it up. *"Danke,"* he said. "Peter *gut*. Erik *gut*. Friends."

"Aye," I said. "Friends."

When he'd eaten, he showed me that the water bottle was empty by shaking it from side to side. I reached out to take it from him, but he pulled it away and shook his head. *"Aussen."*

"What?"

"Aussen," he said again, and pointed at himself, then at me, then at the entrance to his prison.

"Out?" I said. "You wanna go out?"

"Ja. Out."

I thought it might be dangerous, especially after the soldiers had been here just that morning, but I supposed they probably wouldn't come back so soon. Also, I felt sorry for Erik being stuck in the den all the time.

"All right," I said. "Why not?"

Erik looked taller and bigger when he was outside. He walked much straighter now, although he had a definite limp because of his ankle. He supported himself with his stick, using it like a shepherd's crook, and he managed very well. Kim had done a good job of patching him up.

Erik was like a soldier returning from the battlefield. He was still wearing the gray flight overalls, which must have looked quite smart when they were clean and new, but now they were torn and caked with soil and blood. One leg was rolled up to make room for the splint, and because he didn't have his boot on, his sock looked very grubby. I'd told Kim that I'd try to get some clothes for him, but I'd avoided it until now. I knew what I'd have to do to get them and I couldn't quite bring myself to do it. Looking at him now, though, I decided I would have to.

We went to the burn and I offered to take the bottle, but Erik wouldn't let me. He struggled to his knees and filled it himself. And when it was done, he stayed where he was, sitting by the burn, looking up at the trees and the blue sky beyond.

"Beau-ti-ful," he said, taking me by surprise. "Beau-ti-ful," he said again, closing his eyes and letting the sunlight fall through the treetops to touch his skin. He let out a deep sigh, then put out his left foot and plunged it into the burn.

"Ahhh," he said. *"Gut."*

I sat beside him and put my fingers in the water. Despite the warm day, the burn ran almost as cold as ice.

Erik leaned over to dip his own fingers into it, flicking the water at my face.

"What did you do that for?" I said, wiping it away. "That's freezin', that is."

Erik looked at me, his face serious, then a smile cracked across his lips and he started to laugh.

"Oh, you think that's funny? Well, how about this?" I said, flicking water at him from my own fingers.

Erik flicked back, so I cupped my hand in the water and threw it up into his face. It hit him with a splash, showering clear water over his shoulders, into his short-cropped hair, and he shut his eyes, the cold shocking him. When he opened his eyes again, he was laughing. A good, happy sound that made everything go away.

There was no war in that moment. There were no enemies. There was no hiding. There was only two people, like brothers, playing in the woods.

We splashed each other in a flurry of water, each of us laughing, until we heard voices. Erik stopped and cocked his head to one side, putting a finger to his lips. "Shh."

I took my hands out·of the burn and listened.

Footsteps. Voices.

Someone else was in the woods.

I stared at Erik as if mesmerized, and remembered the soldiers who had broken into Dad's shed — how Sergeant Wilkes had stabbed his bayonet into the undergrowth, cutting into Kim's leg.

A twig broke somewhere out in the trees and it was like an alarm breaking the spell. We had to get away. We had to hide.

I shook my head and stood up, offering a hand to Erik. Quickly, I helped him to his feet and supported him as he limped back to our hiding place.

"Who's there?" Sergeant Wilkes's voice came from among the trees beyond the burn. "Come on out."

It was always him. Whatever happened, the sergeant was always there, as if there were ten of him spread all over the village. Mam would have said he was like a bad penny.

"We heard you. We know you're there."

The sound of his voice coming closer sent shivers along my spine and all I wanted to do was hide, but as I was about to crawl into the den, something occurred to me: Sergeant Wilkes knew someone was here. If I hid with Erik, he would have his men search this place again and again. They would scour it until they found Erik, and they would kill him. The bayonet that had cut Kim was proof of that. And even if they didn't find him, they would post men in here, or they would keep coming back, and this place wouldn't be safe anymore.

Sergeant Wilkes had heard us, so he would have to find someone or he would not stop looking. The only thing I could do was to let him find *me*. It was the only way to protect Erik.

I grabbed my satchel and my stick and put out my hand, telling Erik to stay where he was, then I turned and ran back to the burn. I jumped over it and went toward the sound of people moving in the woods. I got as far away from Erik as I could, and waited for the soldiers to come to me.

"We're going to find you. There's no hiding," they were saying.

I stopped and put my hands in the air.

"I'm here," I said. "It's just me."

"Who's '*me*'?"

"Peter Dixon," I said.

"Well, stay where you are."

In a few moments, I saw two soldiers coming through the trees, rifles pointed out in front of them. Sergeant Wilkes was there, just like I thought. I didn't know the other one, but I'd seen him in the village before. He looked about the same age as Erik except he was quite short — not much taller than some of the older boys at school — and he had a hard look in his eyes, as if he wanted to hurt someone.

They came right over to me, still aiming their weapons.

"It's always you, isn't it?" the sergeant said. "Poppin' up wherever I go. What is it this time, eh? What you doin' in here?"

"Nowt. Just playin'," I said. "I was dammin' the burn."

"This place is out of bounds."

"I didn't know."

"You live in that cottage yonder, don't you?"

"Hawthorn Lodge," I said. "Just over the hill."

Sergeant Wilkes watched me with suspicious eyes, then relaxed a little and lowered his rifle. He waved a hand, telling the other soldier to do the same.

"All right, then," said the short one. "Let's see your identity card."

"Don't be a clot, Banks," said the sergeant. "I know who he is. He's always hangin' about with that lass — the one what looks like a lad."

"She doesn't look like a lad," I said.

"So where is she?" the sergeant asked.

"What?"

"We heard voices," said Banks, still with that hard look in his eyes. "You're not hidin' something, are you?"

"Hidin'? No. Course not."

"So who were you talkin' to? I'd bet that lass is round here somewhere. The pair of you are always hangin' about like you're up to somethin'."

"She *was* 'ere," I said, thinking fast. "That lass, Kim. She got scared and ran off when she heard you. Said she was going home."

"Got scared?" the sergeant asked.

"Well, she *is* a lass," I said.

The soldiers both laughed, and that seemed to make them relax even more.

"Right, then — you, come with us." Sergeant Wilkes stepped aside and waited for me to go past him, then both soldiers followed me out of the woods, and when we came to the barbed-wire fence, I saw that Trevor Ridley and his friends were waiting.

"Told you there was someone in there," said Trevor. "Might've known it would be *him*. I'll bet that lass is in there somewhere, too."

"Haven't you lot got homes to go to?" said the sergeant as he climbed over the fence, snagging his trousers. "Haven't you got better things to do than drag me out here for this?"

"We thought it might be somethin' good," Adam Thornhill said. "That escaped German, maybe."

"Aye," Bob Cummings managed. "That escaped German."

"But all they found was you." Trevor looked at me, then turned to the soldiers. "Couldn't you have just shot 'im?"

As the second soldier, Banks, went over the fence, he snagged his trousers, too, except his didn't come off so well. They had caught fast and he couldn't swing his leg over, so he sort of hopped on the spot for a while, trying to release them from the barbs. Trevor Ridley couldn't stop himself from laughing, and the soldier was none too pleased.

"Get lost," Banks said once he'd freed himself. "Or maybe I'll think about shootin' *you*." He came so close to Trevor that their toes were almost touching, and he looked at him with a menacing stare. Their eyes were almost level, but Banks looked even meaner than Trevor did.

"You wouldn't dare."

"Just try me." He stepped even closer to Trevor.

Trevor looked at me and sneered, actually lifting the corner of his lip. "I'm still going to get you, squirt."

"Not now, you're not," Banks told him. "Go on, push off."

Trevor Ridley and his friends backed away a few steps and then stopped. Trevor pointed at me, saying, "I mean it," then he turned and the three of them walked away.

"I reckon you want to stay away from him," Banks said to me when Trevor was gone. "Nasty piece of work."

"Couple of years and the army'll have him," Sergeant Wilkes muttered. "*And* you." He pointed at me. "Stay out of them woods. There's a German soldier on the loose and he's likely to skin you alive if he finds you."

"Why would he do that?" I asked.

"What?"

"Why would he skin me alive?"

"What are you talking about?"

"Well, if you were in Germany and you found a German lad, would you want to skin 'im alive?"

Sergeant Wilkes thought about that, looking at me as if I'd spoken a foreign language.

"Well," he said eventually, "of course not. I'm not German, am I?"

SPY

Mam stood up in surprise when I came in through the kitchen door.

"There you are," she said, smoothing down her dress and smiling. "I was just tellin' Mr. Bennett how you're out all hours of the day and goodness knows what you get up to." She cast a glance at him and then lowered her eyes.

"No good, I should think," said Mr. Bennett. He was at the kitchen table, the chair half pulled out so he was sitting sideways on it. He would have been close to Mam when she was sitting down.

"You all right, pet?" Mam asked. "You look a bit pale."

"I'm fine," I said, but I was still getting over the shock of almost being caught with Erik in the woods. All of that disappeared, though, when I came right into the kitchen, because there was a smell coming from the open door of the scullery that made my belly groan in pleasure.

"What's that?" I asked.

"Mr. Bennett brought us a chicken."

"A whole one?"

Mam nodded and grinned. "A whole one."

"Well," he said, smiling and looking at Mam and then at me. "She was hardly laying at all anymore, so she wasn't much use just scratching about. She's probably not got much meat on her, but I thought it would be a good treat for the two of you."

"I was going to save it for tomorrow, but then I thought, let's have it today," Mam said. "For a treat."

"Well, it *is* Sunday, so what more perfect time for roast chicken?"

I wasn't sure what to say. I didn't like it that Mr. Bennett came to the house so much, mostly because of what Trevor Ridley said, but the thought of a whole roast chicken was almost too much to bear. I couldn't possibly be sulky under those conditions.

"I've asked Mr. Bennett to eat with us," Mam said. "It's the least we could do, isn't it, pet?"

I nodded reluctantly.

"Well, don't just stand there gawpin'," she said. "Go and wash your hands."

The smell in the scullery made my mouth start to water as soon as I went in there. It was such a thick and rich aroma that it seemed to swell around me. My belly groaned again and I put a hand on it and looked across at the range, imagining the chicken roasting inside. No stinking tripe being boiled today.

I washed my hands in the sink, scooping water from the enameled bowl beside it and rubbing them briefly with the lump of soap that was there. It was misshapen and knobbly because it was the leftover pieces of all the old bars, squeezed together to make one big enough to use.

Mam came in behind me when I was drying my hands and kissed me on the back of the head. "Aren't we lucky?" she said, "Rabbit one day, chicken the next."

And when I looked at her, I could see how happy she was. I hadn't seen her that happy in a long time. I was both pleased and disappointed. Pleased to see her that way, but disappointed it wasn't because of me. It was because of Mr. Bennett. And in that moment, my feelings toward him softened just a touch.

"Why don't you set the table while I get it ready?" Mam said.

We only had a few things that matched, but there was enough for all three of us to at least have a knife and fork.

"I hear you've become quite the rabbit catcher," Mr. Bennett said as I moved around the table.

"Mm," I said, without looking up.

"Your mother says you've brought a few home. Some good ones."

"Not that good, like. Mostly they're little 'uns."

"I suppose we're all hungry these days." He smiled. "Even the rabbits."

"Aye."

He sat right back and laced his fingers behind his head. "So where's the best place, then — or is it a trade secret?"

I glanced up at him. "Back o' the woods. There's not as many as there used to be, but . . ." I stopped, almost annoyed with myself for being drawn into the conversation. I didn't want to like Mr. Bennett, but I just couldn't help it.

He smiled and nodded, like he knew what I meant. "A few years ago, we'd have been pleased there were no rabbits. These days, though, we wish there were more. Everything's upside down and topsy-turvy."

"That's what I keep thinkin'," I said. "Nowt's right anymore."

Mam came through carrying the chicken on a board, and she put it on the table in front of Mr. Bennett. "I told him to keep away from there, since that crash, but he never listens," she said. "Will you carve?"

"Boy's got to have some fun," Mr. Bennett said, sitting up and taking the knife. He whisked it against the edge of his fork to sharpen it, just like Dad always did. "And if he brings back something to eat, then why stop him?" He winked at me, then sliced into the chicken, separating the leg from the rest of the bird.

Juices oozed out onto the board and the meat came away easily, the white and dark both visible beneath the crispy skin. It couldn't have been more perfect.

"I haven't been over that way for a while," he said, cutting away the other leg. "Maybe I'll go with you one day."

"What for?" I spoke without taking my eyes off the chicken.

"Just to have a look."

"Nowt to look at." I watched him cut away the wings.

"I haven't checked on the pens for a while."

"They're fine," I said.

Mr. Bennett looked up.

"I mean, *I've* checked," I said, trying not to sound too defensive. "I *always* check."

Mr. Bennett nodded. "Well, then. That's good." He put the knife against the chicken breast and started to slice.

"I'm keepin' it all ready for when me da' gets back," I said, looking at Mam and then back at Mr. Bennett. "For when you need pheasants again."

"I think it might be a while before we have birds in there again," he said. "But, you know, it's not a bad idea. You could be my helper. Keep an eye on the pens for me, in return for the things I bring for you and your mother."

"Eh?"

Mr. Bennett stopped carving and looked at me. "I know you're not keen on me trying to help you and your mother . . ."

"Well, I . . ."

". . . so you can do some work in return for it."

"Like what?"

"Like looking after the pens, keeping them in good condition, and if I've a job that needs doing, I'll call on you — how about that?"

I shrugged.

"That way you'll be earning these things for you and your mother. The real man of the house."

"What kind of jobs?" I asked.

"I'll let you know."

I looked at Mr. Bennett, halfway through carving the chicken, and I looked at Mam standing by the table. She was waiting for me to answer him and I knew what she wanted me to say.

"All right, then," I said. "Aye."

"It's a deal." Mr. Bennett put down the knife and reached out his hand. I put out my own and we shook. I squeezed his hand tight so he'd know I *was* the real man of the house. Just like he'd said.

*   *   *

Mam brought potatoes that had been roasted along with the chicken, and there were boiled carrots. She'd even made a thin gravy with the stock.

"I think it must be more than a year since I had gravy," Mam said when she sat down and looked at her plate. "I don't know that I'll be able to eat all this."

"We'll give it a try, though, eh?" Mr. Bennett smiled at her and then turned to me. "I reckon Peter could eat half of it at least. He's got a hungry look about him."

That meal was the best meal I've ever eaten. Nothing I had eaten before tasted as good, and nothing has since. The only thing that would have made it better was if Dad had been there instead of Mr. Bennett. Although he wasn't so bad — he made lots of jokes and told stories, and I hadn't seen Mam so perky in ages. She looked glad that he was there and I enjoyed the way she seemed so . . . *lifted*.

As I ate, I found myself thinking about Erik, too, alone in the woods with no one. So, when Mam and Mr. Bennett were talking and looking at each other, I slipped a piece of chicken breast off my plate and into my pocket. I could feel it, wet and warm against my leg and, as soon as I could, I went upstairs and wrapped it in what was left of the already ripped page of my comic. I'd had to throw the last piece away because it was covered in egg. I wished I'd kept a piece of the scrap paper I'd found in the sideboard, because I knew that Mr. McPherson probably wouldn't give me anything for the comic with a whole page missing, but that didn't matter. I wanted to take something back for Erik.

Afterward, because it had been such a special meal, we didn't sit in the kitchen. Instead, we went into the front room —

somewhere we only ever went on very special occasions. I sat on the settee next to Mam while Mr. Bennett sat on the rocking chair by the window that looked out onto the village and across the sea.

"I was thinking about that German," Mr. Bennett said. "The one who came down on the parachute."

I looked up with a start. "Have you heard owt? Do they know where he might be?"

"No. All they have is the parachute — or what's left of it," he said. "Nothing else. It's as if he just vanished."

"Vanished?" Mam asked. "You mean he's still around?"

"Looks like he might be."

"I reckon he's long gone," I said.

"Or maybe he's just hiding." Mr. Bennett leaned forward and looked at me. "You haven't seen any sign of him, have you?"

"Me? No. Why would *I* have seen any sign of 'im?" I glanced sideways at Mam, who was looking at me with narrowed eyes.

"Have you seen somethin'?" she asked.

"No. Course not."

She stared at me as if she were trying to read my mind.

"Honest," I said.

"The reason I ask," said Mr. Bennett, "is that I thought you could be my spy."

"Spy?"

"Mm. It can be one of your jobs."

"Doin' what?"

"Well, you get out and about. You must see things. So, if you see anything suspicious, I want you to tell me or your mother straightaway. How about that?"

I nodded.

He sat back in his chair. "Seems to me those woods would be a good place to hide," he said, looking out the window.

"I don't like 'im playin' there," Mam said. "I've told 'im that before. He's not supposed to —"

"There's no one there," I said.

Then Mr. Bennett turned to me again. "There's a shed, isn't there? Maybe he could hole up in there."

"The soldiers looked," I said. "Just the other day. He's not there. Me and Kim play there sometimes and —"

"I told you not to play there and I know you don't take the blindest bit o' notice of me, but now . . ." Mam shook her head. "I don't know." She looked to Mr. Bennett for his opinion. "Should I keep 'im in, d'you think?"

Mr. Bennett kept his eyes on Mam as he thought about that, and there was a soft look about him. As if a contented smile was just at the corners of his eyes. Then he shrugged and said, "I think Peter's a sensible boy. He's the man of the house now, remember." He looked at me. "You'll be safe, won't you? If you see any Germans, you'll let us know, won't you?"

"Aye."

When Mr. Bennett was gone, Mam put a fire under the copper in the scullery to heat some water and we listened to the wireless while we waited. The copper was a sort of metal vat on four legs with a wooden lid and a space underneath for lighting a fire. It took a while to boil the water, but when it was ready, I went outside to get the tin bath. There was nowhere to keep it inside, so we kept it hung on the fence in the garden. I brought it in and put it in the kitchen, in front of the fireplace, then I pulled the curtains for privacy. Mam ran the hot water from a tap at the bottom of the copper into an enameled bucket and took it to the bath. It took a few journeys, but not many. Four inches was as deep as we were allowed, so it barely covered my backside when I got in. It wasn't too bad in the summer, but in the winter it was freezing, even in front of the fire. I was just glad I only had to have a bath once a week.

When I was in, Mam brought the knobbly lump of squashed-together bits of pink Lifebuoy and scrubbed my back while I stared down at the water. I was thinking about Erik, and how much he needed a bath and a change of clothes. Kim and I had mentioned trying to get him something else to wear, and I now thought it was time I tried to do something about that.

When Mam had rinsed the soap off me, she sat back on the hooky mat and looked at me. Her eyes were ringed red, almost like she'd been crying.

"I love you," she said.

"You look sad."

"I'm not sad," she replied. "I've got my Peter to make me happy."

"What about Mr. Bennett?" I asked. "He makes you happy, doesn't he?"

Mam made that sad face again. "I s'pose he does, in a way. It was nice of 'im to come round. He's nice, don't you think?"

I shrugged.

Mam sighed. "I understand why you try so hard to not like 'im, I really do, but Jack — Mr. Bennett — is a nice man. He's kind and funny and thoughtful and he's done a lot for us, Peter. He's done a lot for *me*. He's a good friend, that's all."

I ran the soap along my arm.

"He looks after us. Brings us things we need — things we can't get."

"He's always here," I said.

"He comes to check on us. Make sure we're all right. He does it for your da' as much as he does it for you and me. And I like the company."

"What about me?" I asked. "Am I not company?"

Mam raised her eyebrows and looked away to the window. "Not in the same way, Peter, no." When she looked back at me, she had that sad expression again. "Grown-ups sometimes need a different kind of company. You don't understand that now, but you will when you're older."

"I'm old enough," I said.

Mam shook her head. "Not yet, son."

"You like 'im, though."

"Aye. He's a good man, Peter. He's not your da', but he's a good man. And I think he's a bit lonely, like me, so it's good to have a friend, someone to talk to."

"Like me and Kim?" I said. "Someone your own age?" It made sense. I talked about things with Kim that I didn't talk about with Mam.

"Aye." Mam smiled. "Aye. A bit like that."

"And he's not your fancy man?"

"No, pet, he's not. Sometimes it's difficult, but I'm true to your da', I promise."

"What do you mean, 'it's difficult'?"

"I mean . . . well . . . I haven't seen him for such a long time and . . . I miss him, Peter. It's hard without him. I *need* him here."

"Aye," I said. "Me too."

After my bath, I went upstairs while Mam got in. I knew that after she'd had a bath, she'd put our clothes in the water to soak, so she'd be downstairs for a while yet. I had at least a few minutes to do what I needed to do. So I went to my bedroom, quickly put on my pajamas, and then slipped across the landing into Mam's bedroom.

There was a dark-framed double bed against the far wall, close to the window, and I tried not to imagine Dad pushing himself up on one elbow in bed to ask what was wrong. I stood there, as if rooted to the spot, staring at his side of the bed. I hardly ever went into that room. Even now, I almost never went in. But I remembered times, before the war, when nightmares or a full bladder woke me and I went into their room. It was always Dad who would wake up first, as if he'd been waiting for me.

I wished he were there right now.

Hearing a scrape from downstairs, I shook myself and reminded myself why I was here.

There was a dresser on the right-hand side, made of a different-colored wood, with a mirror over the top of it. On my left was the wardrobe, and that's what I went to, opening it up and looking in at the clothes. There wasn't much to look at. A handful of Mam's dresses hanging on one side, and a handful of Dad's shirts on the other. There were a few pairs of Dad's trousers on a small shelf at the top.

Movement downstairs again. The sound of water sloshing about in the metal tub, as if Mam was getting out.

I stood on tiptoes to take a pair of trousers, but when I pulled at them, the other pairs followed, the whole pile falling out into a heap on the floor.

A door closed downstairs and suddenly everything was happening in a rush. I knew Mam's routine and I knew I had to be quick. I didn't have much time. Mam had just been into the scullery to get the washing powder. She'd poured some into the tub, taken it back, and closed the door. Any moment now she'd be coming up the stairs. She'd walk right in and find me taking clothes and then . . .

I got down on my knees and grabbed at the trousers, folding them carefully but as quickly as I could. My hands were trembling, my fingers not moving fast enough, but I managed to get the trousers into a neat pile and I stretched up to slide them back onto the shelf, just as I heard the kitchen door open.

A creak. Loud and clear. The first floorboard in the hallway.

Mam was on her way. Any second now she'd come in and catch me.

I snatched a shirt from the rail and moved the other ones about to fill the space where one was missing. I closed the wardrobe and turned around, hurrying to the bedroom door. I slipped out of Mam's room and darted across to my own, just as Mam put her foot on the bottom stair.

"Peter?" she called. "What you up to?"

"Eh?" I put my head around the door.

"You up to something?" she asked, coming up the stairs.

"No," I said, showing her my most innocent face.

"Hm. I thought I saw you coming across from my room."

"No," I said. "Not me."

When Mam got to the top of the stairs, she looked at me. Then she turned to go to her room. She pushed the door open and stopped, turning around. "Stay out of trouble," she said. And then she went in and closed the door.

That night I lay in bed looking at the ceiling for a long time, thinking about everything that had happened over the last few days and beyond. I tried to remember what it had been like before the war had started, but I couldn't.

I thought about Erik in the woods and I thought about Kim stuck with her Aunt Hillary and I thought about Mam and whether or not she was happy. I thought about a hundred things — a *thousand* things. And muddled into all those things as I fell asleep, I wondered if I might have heard the sound of the kitchen door opening, the low murmur of voices. But my mind told me it was only the beginnings of a dream, and I sank deeper until sleep took me away from everything.

It was feet on the stairs and the horrifying wail of sirens that brought me back.

DUNKIRK

My whole world was in a panic again. The dual-tone rise and fall of the village sirens blanketed the night, and the hurried fall of feet rushed upstairs.

Mam came into my bedroom in a whirlwind, shouting "Get up!" and I scrambled from under the blanket. I shoved my feet into my slippers and Mam threw my robe around me, bustling me out before I had the chance to put it on properly.

"Mask!" she said, and I snatched my army bag from the peg by the door.

We raced downstairs and turned along the dark hallway, heading for the kitchen — and I stopped dead.

There was a figure standing in the doorway. Silhouetted against the lamp that burned on the table.

Mam bumped right into me, shoving me toward the figure.

"Don't stop," she said as she steadied herself. "Go!"

"Come on, you." Arms reached out to stop me from falling, and I looked up into Mr. Bennett's face. "Let's get you to the shelter," he said.

My first thought was to wonder why on earth Mr. Bennett was in our house, but I didn't have time to say anything because he grabbed my arm with a tight grip and pulled me through so I was in front. He pushed me toward the kitchen door and ushered Mam behind me.

I was the first into the night. I couldn't hear any planes yet, but the sirens were still blasting, so that meant they must be coming. I stopped to wait for Mam, who hurried out, tripping on the step. I reached out and grabbed her arm with both hands, keeping her on her feet. Mam steadied herself again and took my hand, and we set off across the garden toward the shelter. Mr. Bennett emerged behind us, putting out the lamp and closing the door before following. He overtook us easily and reached the shelter, yanking open the door and stepping aside to let us in.

He held out a hand to help me, but I ignored it and backed into the shelter, stepping down the short ladder into the dark. Mam came next, accepting Mr. Bennett's hand as she found her footing, and when she stepped down, Mr. Bennett came in. He pulled the door shut, muffling the sirens and leaving us in complete darkness.

"That was exciting, eh?" he said, coming down the ladder. "Persistent buggers, aren't they?"

Then I felt his presence beside me in the dark, and despite the musty, damp odor of soil in the metal tube, I could smell him. Something about that smell reminded me of Dad. It was the smell of sweat and soap and aftershave and the outdoors. And, for a moment, I thought it could almost have been Dad standing beside me. It made me feel strangely comfortable and secure.

"Got a candle or something?" he said, and then I heard the scraping of matches and light flared in the gloom. Mam stuck the candle on the shelf at the back and the flame on the wick grew, casting its orange circle of light.

"Phew," said Mr. Bennett. "That was quite a rush."

Mam moved me to the bunk and sat down beside me, putting her arm around my shoulders.

Mr. Bennett went to the chair opposite me and Mam, and sat with his forearms resting on his thighs. "Not exactly cozy in here, is it?" He looked around as if inspecting the inside. "Wouldn't be my first choice of where to spend the night, but it's better than getting blown up. And that Mr. Anderson knew what he was doing when he had them build these things. Safe as houses. So to speak." He smiled at Mam, but she didn't smile back. She looked frightened.

"Really," he said. "They're very sturdy."

"What if a bomb landed right on top of us?" I asked.

"Oh, that won't happen. Not here."

Outside, somewhere behind the wall of sound from the sirens, I heard the drone of engines break through.

"They're comin'," I said.

Mam's arm tightened around my shoulders.

"They won't come over us," Mr. Bennett said.

And then we heard the first distant whistle. The high-pitched squeal, like a kettle boiling on the range. It was joined by more, the bombs singing as they fell. In a few moments came the crump and thud, the dull, flat sound of impact.

Mr. Bennett watched us both with a serious expression.

"That's close," Mam said, squeezing harder still.

"Quite an unusual sound, that whistling. Almost tuneful," he said, but there was nothing tuneful about the sound at all. It was a terrifying sound — the sound of death falling from the sky. Some people even said the Nazis made their bombs especially to make that noise so that people would be scared.

"We should whistle with it," Mr. Bennett said. "Try." He put his lips together and blew, whistling a note that blocked out the sound of falling bombs.

I looked at Mam and tried to whistle, but my lips were too dry.

Outside, more bombs thumped into the ground, the explosions chased by more and more in quick succession. The ground shuddered and Mam's breath caught in her chest. She squeezed me tight and I felt her body shaking. It was a moment before I realized I too was trembling with fear.

"Everyone all right?" Mr. Bennett asked.

"I think so." Mam nodded and squeezed me again.

"I'm fine," I said, flinching as another series of explosions boomed in the night. The whole shelter shook, as if a giant were jumping up and down just outside. The shelf at the back rocked from side to side and the candle was snuffed out.

"I'll get it," Mr. Bennett said, and the shelter was filled with the dim light once more.

Outside, there was a lull in the explosions, but we could still hear the sirens and the monotonous drone of the airplane engines.

"Maybe that's the last of it," Mr. Bennett said.

"Why here?" Mam said. Her voice was tired and afraid. "Why here?"

"Maybe they're lost. They're terrible navigators." He sat back down again. "Trying to get the airfield at Acklington, or the listening post. I don't suppose they came all this way just to blow up some farms."

"Well, they're doing a canny good job of it," Mam said.

Mr. Bennett watched Mam with a look I hadn't seen before. It was like he was worried and happy and afraid all at the same time.

"Maybe they're just . . . getting rid of bombs," I said, swallowing against a dry throat. "They do that, don't they?"

"They do, yes." He glanced at me. "You're a clever boy. Brave, too."

I didn't say anything.

"And quick. I saw the way you caught your mam like that. She's lucky to have you to look after her."

"You were there, too, though," I said. "What —"

I stopped speaking when I heard the high-pitched whistle sing out in the night again. The sound of a falling bomb. And it sounded close. So close.

"Hell's bells," Mam said.

I tensed and squeezed my eyes shut, waiting for the blast. Waiting for the bomb to fall right on top of us. Waiting to be blown into a million pieces. This was it; we were going to die. Squashed into a metal shell, half buried under the ground, we were going to die.

The whistling stopped with the dull thump of something hard hitting the ground, and a split second later a tremendous explosion rang in our ears. The bunk shook, soil rained down from the ceiling, and the candle went out again.

My ears rang in the silence that followed and we sat in the darkness without speaking. My head felt numb, like it had done the day the plane crashed, and my body tingled.

"Are we alive?" I said.

"Hell's bells," Mam said again.

Once more, it was Mr. Bennett who lit the candle. And when there was light, he came to the bunk and sat beside Mam. He put his arm around her shoulder as hers was around mine. And when I looked down, I saw Mam reach out with her free hand and take his. She gripped it so hard her knuckles turned white.

"Not as close as it sounded," he said.

"Close enough," Mam replied. Her voice quivered and I felt her whole body shaking.

We all stared at one another for a while, knowing how lucky we must have been, and then we heard a sound like a hundred pattering feet on the roof of the shelter.

Mam's eyes widened. "What was that?"

"Incendiaries," Mr. Bennett said, getting to his feet. "Stay here." He went to the short ladder and stepped up, pushing open the door.

"What are you doing?" Mam stood up. "You can't go out."

Mr. Bennett didn't reply. Instead, he pushed the door wider and climbed up.

"Where are you going?" Mam took a step toward the ladder and I followed her.

Outside, he turned and looked down at us, standing there.

"It's not safe!" Mam shouted.

"Stay where you are," he replied. Then he shoved the door shut and sealed us back in.

"What the hell is he doing?" Mam said, going right to the bottom of the ladder. "He's going to get himself killed. I can't lose two . . ."

But I wasn't listening. I knew what Mr. Bennett was doing. If the Nazis were dropping incendiaries on us, and we'd heard them falling on top of the Anderson shelter, there'd be fires starting up all around our house. Maybe even some on the roof.

The Nazis dropped all kinds of things. They dropped mines that lay hidden on the ground and only exploded when you stood on them. High-explosive bombs were made to blow up buildings, destroy everything, but some people thought incendiaries were worse. They were much smaller, weighing no more than a handful of potatoes, but they were dropped in a big bomb that opened in the sky and let out clusters of them. When they hit the ground they ignited and started fires that were meant to spread and burn everything and show the other planes where to drop their bombs.

And I knew what I had to do — what I *wanted* to do. Like the moment I had hit out and punched Trevor Ridley, I decided enough was enough. I was sick of being scared. I didn't have to sit in the dark, afraid. I could do something. I could push away the crippling fear and I could actually do something.

"I have to help him," I said, going to the ladder.

"What?"

"I have to help," I repeated as I squeezed past Mam and began to climb up. "I'm the man of the house now."

"Get back here, Peter Dixon!" Mam grabbed the back of my bathrobe. "You can't go out there!"

"I have to," I said, turning to look back at her.

"There's nothing you can do."

"At least let me see what's happening," I begged. "If they're dropping incendiaries, everything could be on fire. Mr. Bennett can't save it on his own."

"Then let it burn."

"No!" I took her hand and tried to pull her fingers away. "I won't. We'll have nothing left."

"Peter Dixon, you're not —"

"And what if Mr. Bennett's in trouble?"

Mam's words trailed away and she stared at me.

"Please," I said.

Then she sighed and nodded. "All right." She let go of me. "All right. Just a look. But be careful."

I scuttled up the short ladder, and when I reached the top, I pushed hard on the door, almost falling back. Another good shove and the door swung open and I climbed out into the night.

The rise and fall of the sirens' moaning was louder outside, but the engines were fading. I looked up and saw the planes, at least five or six of them, maybe a mile away now, turning out to sea. Farther along the coast, searchlights pointed up into the sky, and the dull pounding of the ack-ack guns thumped in the distance. The sky lit up with explosions popping in the air around the planes.

But what was happening right there in our garden was much more frightening.

Over by the kitchen door, Mr. Bennett was trying to kick a burning incendiary away from the house. There were four or five other devices on fire, dotted around the garden. Metal tubes, finned at one end and flat-nosed at the other, bursting into flames, burning brightly, sputtering sparks and thick white smoke that billowed around us, filling the night.

None had landed near the henhouse, but I could hear the hens making a fuss, squawking like a whole skulk of foxes had got among them. They were terrified, and their noise mingled with the smoke to make the stuff of nightmares. And, close by, there was smoke coming from inside the netty, curling under the door and pouring out into the garden.

"Get back inside," Mr. Bennett shouted, waving a hand at me, but I ignored him. Instead, I called back to Mam, telling her to pass me up the shovel.

"What?"

"The shovel!" I said, and I thought Mam was going to say no — that she was going to make me come back inside. "There's fires everywhere!" I shouted.

"The house?" Mam asked.

"No!"

"Hens?"

"No!"

Mam hesitated just a second longer before she jumped into action, taking the shovel and passing it up to me by the handle. Then she snatched the stiff broom and followed me up.

I went for the fires close to the house first. We were lucky that none had landed on the roof, because I knew they could smash through and start fires inside, and that would have been the end of our house, for sure.

Mr. Bennett managed to kick his incendiary right out to the front gate. It arced up into the air, trailing smoke, and landed with a thump and a spatter of sparks. Before Mr. Bennett could follow it, I went as close as I dared and began digging dirt and throwing it over the burning tube. Smoke plumed around me, the smell of fireworks and petrol filling the air. Mr. Bennett came over, making sure I was all right, but the fire was out now, and I was banging the dirt down hard on the incendiary to make sure it was out for good.

Mr. Bennett nodded at me, then turned to Mam, who came to his side clutching the broom. "Stirrup pump?" he said, taking it from her.

"No."

"Use the bucket, then." He pointed.

While Mam went to the pump and began filling the bucket with water, Mr. Bennett took the broom and started flicking the other incendiaries away from the house, and I chased after them, throwing soil over them. Mam followed that up with a good dousing from the bucket.

By now, the netty had started to burn, flames licking under the door, the smoke thickening.

"Must be inside," I said. "Gone through the roof."

"Stay back," Mr. Bennett said as he approached it, hand in front of his face as the heat increased. He kept low and pulled open the door. Immediately, the flames leaped up and thick black smoke belched out, pushing Mr. Bennett back.

Mam stood wide-eyed, staring as the netty went up in flames.

Mr. Bennett pulled the bucket from her grasp and rushed to the water pump, frantically working the handle. I ran into the house, through the kitchen, and into the scullery. I snatched up the biggest pan at hand and hurried back outside.

Mam was working the pump now, so Mr. Bennett and I took turns to fill up, and we ran backward and forward, throwing water onto the fire. Coming back for my third refill, though, I heard Mam shout, "Peter!"

I looked up in surprise.

"You're on fire!"

I glanced down and realized that in all the excitement, I hadn't noticed that my bathrobe belt had come unfastened. It had worked itself loose and was trailing on the ground behind me — at least, it *had* been trailing on the ground. Now it was almost all gone, burning like a fuse, the flame working its way right up to the tail of my robe, and that had now started to burn.

Before I could react, before Mam could even react, Mr. Bennett took one step toward me and threw his bucket of water at my legs. The cold water hit me like a shockwave, soaking everything below my waist, and I stood for a moment looking down at myself, then up at Mam and Mr. Bennett.

And then Mr. Bennett began to laugh. He laughed loud, throwing back his head, and I couldn't help joining in, but Mam didn't find it too funny. She came over and hugged me tight and I could feel her shaking, so I stopped laughing and hugged her back.

"I'm fine," I said. "Let's get this fire put out."

Then Mam went back to the pump as Mr. Bennett and I returned to our fire duties.

By the time all the fires were out, the sirens were sounding the all clear in the village.

"Better check right round," Mr. Bennett said, striding off into the darkness.

"Well, you're comin' inside to get changed," Mam said to me. "You'll catch your death otherwise." She put her hand on my back and marched me inside, taking me upstairs and fishing out some dry pajamas.

"Eee, look at the state of us," she said, putting the fresh pajamas on the end of the bed. "Black and covered in soot. We both prob'ly stink, too. And right after bath day." She looked at me for a long time, like she was thinking about something, then she smiled and kissed me on the forehead. "We're safe, though," she said. "That's what matters."

She left me to get changed, and when I went downstairs, Mr. Bennett was just coming in the kitchen door.

"All clear, I reckon," he said. "I've checked right round the house and nothing's burning."

"I can't see any fires in the village," Mam said, going to the door and looking out in the direction of the coast. "D'you think we should go and see if anyone needs any help?"

"We definitely should," I said, thinking about Kim. "We should go now and —"

"I think you've done enough for one night," said Mr. Bennett.

"But I want to make sure Kim's all right." I looked at Mam.

"She'll be fine," she said. "The village is safe."

I stood at the door and looked out toward the village, wishing I could see right to Kim's house. I put my hand to my brow as if it would help me look into the dark better. Then I scrunched up my eyes and peered in the direction of the woods, wondering how Erik was feeling right now.

"There's no fires," Mam said. "It's all right. You can check first thing in the mornin'." She led me back inside and closed the door.

Mam made tea for her and Mr. Bennett, and I had hot milk. We'd drunk all the fresh, so it was powdered and didn't taste right. I sipped it, though, not wanting to waste it.

We all sat quietly, thinking about everything that had just happened. I watched them, seeing how they sat side by side, close, but not too close. They kept looking at each other as if there was something they wanted to say.

"Lucky you were here," Mam said eventually, looking at Mr. Bennett. "Dunno what we'd have done otherwise. Prob'ly the house would've burnt to the ground."

"Wasn't all me," he said. "Peter did a good job, too. You should be proud of him."

"I am," she replied.

Watching Mr. Bennett across the table now, I couldn't remember all the reasons I'd disliked him so much. Instead, I could think of a lot of new reasons to like him. He made Mam feel safe and he did so much to look after her and me. Most of all, though, I thought he was very brave. And I believed he had saved my life with that bucket of water.

"Mr. Bennett?" I said, forcing him to look away from Mam.

"I think you've earned the right to call me Jack," he said. "Anyone who can stand beside me and fight fires like that can call me by my first name." He leaned forward. "You'd make a fine soldier."

I felt myself swell with pride.

"I'd rather he didn't," Mam said.

"Is it true you were in Dunkirk?" I asked.

"Peter." Mam stopped me, but Mr. Bennett held up a hand.

"It's all right," he said. "Yes, I was there."

"What was it like?"

He took a deep breath and didn't say anything for quite a while. I was beginning to think he wasn't going to answer when he said, "It was bad, Peter. Very bad. I wouldn't wish it on my worst enemy."

"Not even on a Nazi?"

He thought about that, staring down at the tabletop, then he shook his head. "No, maybe not even on them . . ."

"Me da' was there," I said.

"I know."

"But he went back to war."

"And you think that isn't fair, don't you?" said Mr. Bennett.

I shrugged.

Mr. Bennett got up from the seat next to Mam and came to sit beside me. "This is very difficult to explain," he said. "Part of me wishes I'd gone back. A *big* part of me. I wanted to fight, see? And when I think about all those men who went back, lots of them my friends, I often wish I was with them. I wonder why it is that *I* came home. But on the other hand, I know I'm lucky, and I'm glad to be here."

"Did you get wounded?"

"Peter, I think that's enough," Mam said, but Mr. Bennett ignored her.

"Yes, I did, Peter. I *was* wounded. And now I'm not fit for active service."

"Where did you get wounded? Is that why you got a scar?"

"Lots of places," he said. "It was bomb shrapnel."

"So what happened?"

"Well, we were in a bit of a sorry state. Tired, hungry, beaten, and trying to get away from the Germans. We just wanted to get home. I was with a group of soldiers heading back to the beach when we heard the Stuka dive-bombers coming. You can imagine a little bit what that's like, right?"

I thought about the noises we'd just heard that night. The whistles and thumps, the explosions. I nodded. "Aye."

"Well, there wasn't a shelter like there is here, so we jumped into a ditch. Just a muddy ditch at the side of the road that didn't protect us much from the blast. I was luckier than the others."

He didn't need to explain that to me. I imagined him lying in the muddy ditch, surrounded by dead soldiers.

"I had shrapnel in my face, my legs. A very big piece in my ankle." He gave me a smile; the kind grown-ups make when they're not really happy and nothing is really funny. "And now I'm home."

"Did you kill any Nazis?" I asked. "When you were in France?"

"Yes, I did."

"But not all Germans are Nazis, are they?"

"Hm?"

"Not all Germans are Nazis," I said again. "They don't *all* want to fight us, do they? At least, that's what Kim says."

"Well, Kim might be right," he said.

I nodded and looked over at the thick curtains covering the window and I thought about Erik, my German friend.

A DIFFERENT KIND
OF DESTRUCTION

The next morning, I was anxious to get out and make sure Kim was all right. Putting out the fires and talking to Mr. Bennett had distracted me for a while, but as soon as there was nothing else to think about, she'd popped back into my mind and stayed there all night.

When I got to the top of the hill, I could see her jogging across the field. And way beyond that, near the village, but on this side of the road, a crowd had gathered on the edge of the field. The people were staring across in the direction of the Black Bull pub, just along the inlet where the burn trickled out into the sea. There were soldiers there — some busying about, others standing in front of the crowd, as if trying to keep them back.

On the other side, there was only one soldier guarding the wrecked plane. It wasn't one of the soldiers I'd spoken to yesterday.

Kim was out of breath when she reached me, as if she'd been running as hard as she could. She was in shorts, as usual, and she had a bandage wrapped around her leg where the bayonet had scraped her.

"We got a letter," she said between breaths.

"What?"

"From Josh. We got a letter saying he's all right."

"When?"

"Yesterday. Well, the letter was from my mum, but *they* got a letter a few days ago."

"That's brilliant," I said, but I couldn't help feeling a twinge of jealousy.

"See. I told you they'd be all right if we looked after Erik. I told you."

"Aye, you did." I was happy for Kim, but her getting a letter just made me think of Dad.

"He's still in Africa — we don't know where exactly — but he's fine. Isn't that good?"

"Aye," I said. "It really is."

Kim stopped and looked at me as her breath came back. The happy expression fell from her face. "You'll get one soon," she said. "I just know you will."

I forced a smile and nodded, and we sat down to stare out at the village, not speaking.

"That was quite something last night, wasn't it?" she said after a while.

"We got firebombed." I was glad for the change of subject.

"There were some in the village, too. Bombs coming really close."

"We had to put 'em out," I told her. "And the netty caught fire."

"Burn your bum?" she asked.

"Nearly. Me robe was on fire. Jack had to put it out and —"

"Jack?"

"Mr. Bennett," I said. "He was in the shelter with us 'n' everything."

"He was at your house?"

"Aye." The way she said it reminded me I never did find out why he was there. But somehow it didn't seem to matter so much anymore. I felt closer to him now. He looked after Mam. He'd asked me to call him Jack. We'd put fires out together. And he'd even told me his war story.

"So what's going on over there?" I asked. "Why's everyone standing about?"

"Unexploded bomb from last night."

"There was one that close to the village?"

"Right next to the pub," she said. "Lucky it didn't go off." She shook her head. "Were you scared?"

"Last night? No."

"Me neither," she said, and we looked at each other for a long moment, both of us knowing the truth.

"Well," I admitted. "Maybe a bit."

Kim tightened her lips and nodded. "Yeah. Me too."

Everyone was afraid when the sky was filled with the screams of falling bombs and the terrifying thud of their explosions. Any one of us could be killed, and anybody who said they weren't scared was pretending.

"I tried to get a look at it but they're keeping everyone away," Kim said. "I heard someone say all the houses are going to be evacuated."

"*All* of 'em?"

She nodded and we were quiet for a while, watching the silent crowd in the distance.

"Erik showed me a photo yesterday," I said. "Of his mam and da' and his brother, Konrad."

"Konrad?"

"Aye. He's fourteen. And Erik's nineteen. He wrote it on some paper I took."

Kim turned to look at me. "I never thought much about him having a family . . . I bet they're worried sick."

"Like we are. Well, like *I* am."

"I'm still worried about Josh," Kim said. "He's still away. And the letter was from a few weeks ago; they take ages to get here, you know."

"I know."

"You're not cross, are you?"

"About what?"

"I don't know. About me not being here yesterday. About me getting a letter."

I thought for a moment, then shook my head. "Not really. Just jealous, I s'pose. I'm sorry if —"

"That's all right," Kim said, putting an arm around my shoulder. It was the kind of thing any good friend might do, but it felt different when Kim did it. Special and comforting.   .

"I'm really glad for you," I said. "Really I am."

And then she did something that took me by surprise as much as it had done the first time she did it; she leaned over and kissed me on the cheek. Except this time I didn't wipe it away.

"What was that for?" I asked, my heart beating just a little bit faster.

"For . . . I don't know. For being my best friend. For being glad for me." She shrugged. "And for being Peter Dixon," she said as she stood up. "Come on, let's go see Erik."

On our way down to the woods, I remembered that Kim hadn't heard all my news. "They came into the woods again yesterday," I said.

"Who?"

"Soldiers. That Sergeant Wilkes." I told her about what had happened and she listened with her mouth falling open.

"Sounds like you've been having much more fun than me," she said. "Hiding from soldiers, putting out firebombs. Aunt Hillary was trying to teach me to knit, which was absolutely ghastly. She made such a fuss when I got in."

"What did you tell 'er?"

"That I caught my leg on some barbed wire."

"And she believed it?"

"She said what on earth was I doing climbing over barbed wire in the first place? Barbed wire was there to keep things out, not for children to climb over."

"Oh."

"And she said Mum and Dad sent me here to keep me safe from bombs, not so I could go around cutting myself on rusty old pieces of barbed wire."

"What did you say?" I asked.

"I told her it wasn't rusty."

"She didn't stop you from comin' out again, though?"

"Obviously not." She spread out her hands.

I looked at her leg. "Does it hurt?"

"Nope. I could've killed my aunt, though. She made me wear a dress while she washed my shorts. I'm glad you didn't have to see that."

"So am I."

It was good to have Kim back by my side when we sneaked into the woods. She'd only been away for one afternoon, but it hadn't felt right without her. And so much had happened yesterday, it felt like it had been days ago.

When we were safe among the trees, I found us each a good stick and together we swiped the heads off the nettles.

"Take that, Trevor Ridley," Kim said, crashing her stick into a thicket of thistles. "Have that, you smelly pig."

I laughed, careful to keep it quiet, and joined in. "And you, Bob Cummings: Outta my way."

We hacked our way through a thousand bullies, swirling and twirling as we sent ripped pieces of leaves flying into the air. We swiped and chopped so that our sticks dripped green, and we giggled to each other until Kim said she might even wet herself, which made us giggle even louder despite the fear that the soldiers might come.

By the time we came across the burn, we were high with excitement. Kim was lifted by news of her brother, the thrill of the bombing raid, and I was glad we were together again, but all the exhilaration fell away when we came to the place where Dad's shed stood. Because there we saw a very different kind of destruction.

The pheasant runs were all smashed. There had been six of them, all in neat rows, and even though they were overgrown with weeds, the cages had been fine apart from the one we'd used. But now they were all broken. All Dad's work smashed to pieces. Someone had pulled off the wire, throwing it into the banks of nettles, and the wooden frames had been snapped as if they'd been stamped on and then cracked against the trees. I'd felt rotten when I broke the one we used for Erik's splint, but this was horrible. It was as if someone had come into my house and broken all my belongings.

"What happened?" Kim stood and stared.

It was bad enough that the runs had been destroyed, but the worst thing was what they had done to Dad's shed. The door was open and the inside had been ransacked. There were tools all over the floor where someone had tipped the toolbox upside down, and there were some outside in the dirt. The paraffin heater was on its side, and the stool had been thrown into the nettles where the runs were. It looked almost as if a German bomb had landed on the area and blown Dad's things all over the place. But there was no scorching here. There wasn't the smell of explosives.

"What happened?" Kim said again.

"Trevor Ridley," I said, feeling hot tears in my eyes. "I just know it." They'd been near here yesterday, and must have come inside for a closer look after I'd gone. I couldn't think of anyone else who would do something like this. So he'd come back for his revenge after all.

"Fat lot of good it did hittin' 'im," I said, fighting back the tears. I didn't want Kim to see them. "Just got 'im more angry."

But even though they had destroyed all those things that meant so much to me, that quickly went from my mind. The shed could be tidied, the runs could be rebuilt. Even the thought that they might have found the gun seemed unimportant, because what I was most worried about was Erik. Our friend Erik. He'd been here the whole time. First with this, then with the bombs falling.

I ran to the place behind the shed, dropping to the ground and crawling through the small gap in the undergrowth.

"Erik?"

Erik was sitting with his back to the sycamore trunk, pressed to it as hard as he could, holding his arm straight out in front of him. And in his hand, he was holding a gun. The gun I had found at the plane crash.

I stopped suddenly and Kim bumped into me as she scurried into the den right behind me.

"What?" she said. "What's wrong?"

For a long moment, Erik stared at me, holding the gun straight out so the barrel was pointing directly at my face.

The gun was no longer dirty and clogged with mud. The barrel was dark and hollow and ready for a bullet to be fired along it. Somehow I just knew it would work. He must have found where I'd hidden it, and spent his time making it ready in case he needed it.

I looked up from the end of the barrel and saw Erik's face. I saw the way he twitched because he was afraid, and I imagined how he must have felt, cowering in hiding, listening to the noise of the boys wrecking the pens. He would have pictured them as soldiers, just a few feet away, ready to kill him.

"It's all right," I said, moving farther in, giving Kim room to come alongside me. "It's all right."

Erik swallowed hard and lowered the gun. He nodded and put it on the ground in front of him, placing it carefully. He held both hands out to show me he meant no harm.

"It's all right," I said again.

Erik said something in German, and I was frustrated that I couldn't understand what he was saying and that he couldn't understand me. All we could do was look at each other and show that we meant no harm.

Erik's breathing was heavy as he calmed down. He sucked great swooshes of air through his nose and blew them out in a rush, so we sat and waited for him to relax. And when his breathing was normal again, he showed me the palms of his hands.

"Erik," he said. "Peter. Kim. Friend."

"Aye," I said. "Friends."

"He must've been terrified," Kim said. "He must've heard them out there and wondered what was going on."

"Trevor Ridley," I said. "I'll kill 'im."

Erik took out a piece of scrap paper and the pencil. We waited while he drew a picture of a plane. His hands were still trembling and it wasn't a very good picture; he wasn't much of an artist and the lines were shaky. Then he drew some boxlike houses underneath and made lines come down from the airplane. He drew an explosion of gray lines over one of the houses and put a question mark beside it.

"He wants to know if anything got blown up," Kim said.

We both shook our heads and Erik sighed deeply, closing his eyes. Then he nodded and put up his thumb. *"Gut."*

"I got you some clothes," I said, opening my satchel. It was bulging and I'd had to fasten the strap on the very last hole. "There's a bit of chicken, too. From last night."

"You had chicken?" Kim asked.

"Mr. Bennett brought it."

"Lucky you. Make sure you invite me next time."

I passed everything to Erik.

"We'll have to take off the splint if he's going to get changed," Kim said.

It would have been easier to cut the binding, but we didn't want to waste good rope, so we picked at the tight knots until we could slip them loose. The pieces of wood fell and Erik waggled his ankle.

"Looks like it's just about better," Kim said. "Come on; let's leave him to get dressed."

We went outside, walking into the woods in different directions, but there was no sign of anyone, so we encouraged Erik to come out of the den. He was still having a bit of trouble walking, but he was much better. He could walk quite well without holding on to anything. Kim had done a good job.

I thought I might feel bad seeing him in Dad's clothes but, really, it was just strange. They were a bit big on him, but they made him look completely different. He wasn't a Nazi airman anymore.

"He just looks normal now," I said.

"Well, of course he does," Kim replied.

"No, I mean —"

"I know *exactly* what you mean. He looks like everybody else."

"Aye."

Kim and I collected together all the broken wood and piled it close to the shed. I had already decided I was going to fix everything, make it just like it was before, so we divided it into two piles — broken beyond repair, and reusable — and when we were finished, I saw that I'd need to find a lot more to rebuild the runs.

"Don't worry, we'll get what we need," Kim said. "We'll make it as good as new, I promise."

And while we collected the wood, Erik went into the shed and gathered the tools from the floor, laying them out on the bench. One or two were lost in the nettles, but Kim and I found most of the ones that had been thrown out.

"I was thinking," I said. "He can't stay here forever. Mam said the war's going to last much longer, and Erik can't live in the woods all that time."

"Why not? Maybe that's *exactly* what he'll have to do."

"But he can't. It's too dangerous. Think what would've happened if Ridley had found him."

"He has a gun; maybe he'd kill them."

I looked across at Erik, sitting in the shed, laying out tools. "He wouldn't."

"How do you know?"

"I just know."

Kim sighed. "You're probably right. We'll have to think of something."

"Like what, though?"

"I don't know, Peter."

And right then, in that moment, I had the awful feeling that while we had meant the best, we had actually done the wrong thing for Erik; that we had taken this all too far and that it was going to end badly for all of us.

I looked from Kim to Erik and back again, scared for my two friends, then I shook the dark thought from my mind, and carried on with the cleanup.

When we'd collected and sorted the wood, we set up a production line in the shed. Erik removed any dirt from the tools and passed them to me one at a time, I oiled and rubbed them, Kim put them away in the toolbox.

"There. That didn't take too long, did it?" Kim said when the final tool was in its box and the shed was tidy again.

"Not too long," I agreed. "Thank you."

Erik put out his hand like Mr. Bennett had done last night. "Friend," he said.

I looked down at it and then at his face. I put my hand in his and we shook. "Friends," I agreed. Then he and Kim did the same.

We risked going to the burn, where Erik put his foot in the cold water.

"They're not really any different from us, are they?" I said, watching Erik lean back and look up at the sky. "Germans."

Kim turned to look at Erik. "No," she said. "They're just the same."

"I wish it was all over, don't you? That we could all go back to normal."

"Mostly," she said. "But then I'd have to go back to Newcastle."

"Don't you want to? Don't you miss your mam and da'?"

"Of course I miss them, but then I'd miss you, wouldn't I?"

"Would you?"

"Well, I wouldn't miss your silly remarks, but, yes . . . I'd miss you. Wouldn't you miss me?"

"Yes," I said. "I would."

Just then there was a sudden loud boom from somewhere in the distance. Erik stiffened and jerked his head round. The birds stopped singing. The sound echoed, faded, and was gone.

"What was that?" I whispered.

"Sounded like a bomb," Kim said. "In the village."

"We should go and see."

Kim nodded and turned to Erik, who was watching us. She held up her hands, palms out. "Stay here," she said. "Don't move."

THE PHANTOM
AIRMAN

We saw that a lot had happened while we'd been in the woods that morning. Just as Kim had said, the whole village had been evacuated, and when we crested the hill, we could see that the crowd standing on this side of the road had grown. They were a long way off, two fields from where we were, and they all had their backs to us. All eyes were turned to the coast.

No one had thought to come this far away, but from where we were, we had a clear view all the way to the Black Bull, and it was a bright day, so we could see the soldiers busying around. One side of the pub was in pieces, the wall completely blown away, and a steady burn of black smoke rose to the sky, much like it had done the day Erik's plane crashed.

"Wonder what happened," I said. "Looks like they blew up the pub."

"Let's go and find out."

So we crossed the fields and came to where the whole village had gathered. The men had congregated in one place, where they smoked cigarettes and pipes, nodding and rubbing their chins. The women were shaking their heads and standing with their hands on their hips, wanting to get back to whatever they'd been doing. The children just wanted to find out what was going on.

We melted into the crowd, sticking together, listening to what people were saying.

"Is it the invasion? Are they coming?"

"It's just a bomb from last night. Had to do something with it."

"They blew it up?"

"Mr. Charlton was trying to get them to move it, the daft old so-and-so."

"You'd think he'd know better, bein' the warden and everythin'."

"No, it's the German. The one that escaped."

I felt a hand grab my shirt and I turned to see Mam standing behind me. I must have pushed past without realizing it was her.

"I might've known you'd be right in the thick of it."

"Hello, Mrs. Dixon," Kim said.

"Hello." She smiled. "So where do you two think you're goin', eh?"

"We want to see what happened," Kim said.

"Plannin' on sneakin' through, eh? I don't think so. Come on back home, I think we've seen enough."

"But Mam, I . . ."

Mam shook her head at me and held out a finger. I knew what it meant. It meant "do as you're told." So I dropped my shoulders and looked at the floor.

"See you later," I said to Kim.

"Don't you want to come, too, pet?" Mam said, bending

down to speak quietly. "I've made some delicious biscuits, but there's far too many of them. We might need some help."

"Biscuits?" Kim pretended to be unimpressed. "Oh well, then, I suppose I could help."

We left the rest of the village to stand outside wondering what was going on, and made our way back to Hawthorn Lodge. "D'you know what happened?" I asked as we walked.

Mam pursed her lips as if in serious thought. "Well, people are talking, but they all say different things."

"Like what?"

"Well, now, let's see. Mrs. Dudley thinks the Germans are invadin'. She thought she saw a ship out at sea and now there's a whole fleet of German ships comin' to blow us up."

"That can't be right," Kim said.

"Mrs. Howard, on the other hand, thinks it's the Phantom Airman. She says he's sabotaged the village pub."

"*Phantom* Airman?" I asked.

"That parachutist. They've been searchin' all over, but there's no sign of 'im. No one ever found 'im, did they?" She looked at me. "So that's what they're callin' 'im in the village."

"The Phantom Airman." I looked at Kim. "I like that."

"And then Mr. Shaw said there was an unexploded bomb from last night and the soldiers evacuated the village and blew up the bomb to keep everyone safe. Now which one of those do you think is true?" Mam asked.

"Erm . . ." I pretended to think about it.

"I like the one about the Phantom Airman," Kim said, glancing at me. "I like that one a *lot*."

Mam was right about the biscuits; they were delicious. We sat at the table, with a plate because Mam wouldn't allow crumbs, and we had two biscuits each. Mam had a cup of tea, while Kim and I had a glass of milk.

"I wish my aunt made biscuits like these," Kim said. "Actually, I wish she made any kind of biscuits."

Mam laughed and told Kim she could come to our house and eat biscuits any time she wanted.

And when there was a knock at the door, Mam hardly even flinched. She took a sip of her tea and she went to the door and pulled it open.

There was a boy standing on the step. He was dressed in navy blue and his bike was leaning on the fence. I knew who he was. He was the telegram boy.

He couldn't look Mam in the eye as he held out the telegram.

Mam took a step back and shook her head. "No." She retreated a few paces into the kitchen and put her hand out to steady herself on the table. She wobbled a little, and sat down in her chair, staring ahead.

The boy waited on the step. He looked at me and Kim sitting at the table, then he bent down and put the telegram on the mat.

"I'm sorry," he said. "Sorry." Then he turned, climbed onto his bike, and rode away.

THE TELEGRAM

Mam stared at nothing. It was as if she had turned to stone. She sat for a very long time, facing the window. I stared at the telegram that lay on the mat. Beside me, Kim put her hand on mine.

Outside, the birds continued to sing. The sun continued to shine. The telegram boy made his way to his next delivery. The villagers waited to be allowed back to their homes. But in our kitchen, no one moved. No one spoke.

And after many minutes, Mam took a deep breath and pushed herself from her chair. She moved as if her legs had no strength, then she forced herself to stand straight, gathering her thoughts, composing herself. And when she was ready, she took two firm steps over to the mat and bent down to pick up the telegram.

When she straightened up, she held the telegram out but didn't look at it. She turned to me and forced a smile and said, "Will you excuse me a moment?" Then she went to sit on the settee opposite the sideboard.

I didn't turn round to look at her, I was almost too afraid, but I heard her tear open the telegram.

261

Kim and I sat at the table with our half-eaten biscuits, and we listened to Mam sobbing.

Kim kept her hand on mine, and when she spoke, she said, "You should go and see your mam."

Mam was sitting on the settee, looking up at the place where the wireless was on the sideboard. Dad's letters leaned against it, all tied up with twine. Above them, his shotgun rested on the rack, as if he were going to walk in right now to get it. He would come into the kitchen, wearing his boots, and Mam would tell him off for bringing in the dirt. She'd tell him he was getting mud on her nice, clean floor, and he would smile at me and wink, coming in anyway and reaching up for his gun.

"You comin'?" he would say.

But he wouldn't say that anymore. He wouldn't come into this room ever again and he wouldn't ever reach up for that gun again.

The telegram was lying on the settee, so I sat down next to Mam and picked it up. A piece of clean white paper with the Post Office heading at the top. Strips of slightly different colored paper had been stuck to it, and on those strips were the words we had feared so much:

DEEPLY REGRET TO REPORT THE DEATH OF YOUR
HUSBAND D. DIXON ON WAR SERVICE. LETTER FOLLOWS.

Dad's ID number was on there, too, as if to confirm they had the right D. Dixon.

"What did they do to him?" Mam said without looking at me. "What did they do to your poor da'?"

I couldn't have answered even if I'd wanted to. I felt so much sadness and anger inside me. Much more than I'd ever felt toward Trevor Ridley. So much more. My chest felt so tight, I thought I might choke to death right there on the settee. My throat seemed to narrow, my whole body was tingling with fear and confusion and every other bad and terrible emotion I had ever felt. I wanted to do something. I wanted to blame someone. I wanted someone to pay for what they had done to my dad.

And when I looked up at his letters on the sideboard once more, I knew exactly what I was going to do.

I jumped up from the settee and ran from the room. I didn't look at Kim as I left the kitchen. I went straight to the door and threw it open, running onto the path, through the gate, and across the lane. I ran and ran and ran. It was as if I had unlimited breath. I had become something other than me. I was outside of me, looking down at this small boy running like a madman, climbing the hill. I slipped over and over, always getting up again, always running. My eyes burned and my chest burned but I kept on.

I didn't see the villagers waiting by the road for their homes to be safe again. I didn't see the group of boys who watched me race across the crest of the hill, and I didn't hear Kim's calls from behind as she gave chase. All that existed was me, running.

I went over the hill and down the other side, my legs moving too quickly for me as I went down. The slope was too steep to be taken at speed, so I fell forward, tumbling on the grass, bumping on the rabbit holes, but I hardly noticed. When I stopped rolling, I picked myself up and started running again.

By the time I came to the barbed-wire fence, I had started to slow. I jogged to the wire and climbed through the section I'd cut away, not caring that the soldier at the crash site might see me. I had no thought for anything.

Coming from the sunshine into the woods, where everything was darker and cooler, I started to run again, heading through the place where Kim and I had used sticks to hack the nettles. The leaves that remained brushed the exposed skin of my legs and arms, leaving stings that would swell into tiny bumps. Thistles scratched at me, and branches came out from nowhere to whip across my legs. One branch even caught the side of my face, running a ragged scratch, but I ignored it. I kept on going. Through the woods. Through the nettles. Through the burn.

Until I came to the den.

Erik reeled with surprise when I burst in. He lifted the pistol to point it, but lowered it when he saw me. He started to smile, but I came in without a word. There was only turmoil in my mind, I had no time for smiling or speaking, I had something to do. I was here for a reason. I had to repay them for what they had done to Dad.

As Erik put the gun on the ground, I snatched it from him. I fumbled with it, turned it around, and I pointed it right at his chest.

My breath was coming in sharp hitches.

"Your fault," I said between breaths. "Your fault. Bloody, *bloody* Germans. Your fault."

Erik shook his head, held out his hands, and spoke quickly. I don't know what he was saying. Perhaps he was pleading for his life, begging me not to kill him. Perhaps he was telling me he wanted me to do it. I don't know.

"It's your fault," I said, putting the barrel of the gun against his chest, pushing hard, as if I was trying to force it right through him. "You killed me da'."

"No," Kim said from behind me. "Erik didn't do it. Not Erik."

"Might as well have been!" I shouted without taking my eyes off him. "They're all the same! They're killers! Murderers!" I pushed the gun harder.

"That's not true, Peter, and you know it. It's just not true." She came right in so that she was behind me and she put her arms round my waist, pressing her face against my back. "Not true," she whispered.

I squeezed my eyes shut, forcing the tears out onto my cheeks.

"You're scaring him."

I opened my eyes again and looked at Erik, seeing how afraid he was.

"Oh, Kim," I said. "What am I going to do now?"

"You're going to be all right," she said. "We're all going to be all right. I promise."

I felt myself relax. I took the gun away from Erik's chest.

"Put it down," Kim said. "Please. Put it down. He's our friend."

I lowered it, letting it fall from my hand.

"That's better," Kim said, and I turned to her and put my arms around her and held her tightly and I cried and I cried, and Erik and Kim sat with me, neither of them saying a word.

When I finally stopped and looked down, I saw I was still holding the telegram in my left hand.

Erik took the corner of it between his fingers and waited for me to release it. When I did, he held it out in both hands as if he could read it. But he didn't need to be able to read the words to understand the message it brought. His eyes scanned the paper, his face without expression. He tipped back his head against the trunk of the sycamore and closed his eyes. He allowed his hands to drop to his lap, the telegram still held fast.

"We should get you cleaned up," Kim said.

I must have looked a state. I'd fallen so many times. My knees and elbows were bleeding, as was the scratch on my face. I put my fingers to it and felt the rough edges of the place where the branch had raked my skin when I ran past. I didn't care what I looked like, though. In that instant, nothing mattered.

"You don't want your mam seeing you like that," Kim said. "She needs you now. She needs you to be extra strong. Come on," she said, gently encouraging me to leave the den.

She led me outside and together we went to the burn. I stood by the water and Kim crouched to wet her hands and rub the dirt and blood from my knees. The clear water tinkled against the rocks.

"We need to get you home to your mam. She'll be worried sick about you, running off like that."

I pictured Mam sitting at home, still on the settee, looking up at the letters leaning against the wireless.

"You'll be fine," Kim said, dipping her hand to scoop more water. "You'll see. Everything will be —"

"What's goin' on here?"

Kim snatched her hand from the burn and turned around.

"I thought we might find 'em here," Ridley snorted to his friends. "I *told* you they'd come back. Little runts."

"Get lost," Kim said. "Leave us alone."

I tore my eyes away from the clear water. I'd been almost mesmerized by it, watching the bubbles form and disappear, seeing the vague reflection of the treetops swirling in its eddies.

Trevor Ridley was right there. He was standing in my woods. His friends were there, too. Adam Thornhill and Bob Cummings. They were walking in the places where I had walked with my dad, places they wouldn't have dared come to if he'd been here. They had destroyed all my dad's hard work, smashed the pens and made a mess of his shed, and now they had come back.

I wasn't going to allow it.

"I see you've tidied up." Ridley made a show of glancing around. "I told you I was gonna get you." He pointed a finger at me.

I ran at him.

"What the —" Ridley took a step back, tripping on a tree root that rose from the soil. He fell backward, losing his balance, and I threw myself at him, pushing him right down onto the ground. I sat on his stomach and I balled my hands into fists and I hit him. I hit him as hard as I could as many times as I could before he twisted, grabbed my hands. Adam Thornhill was slow to react, but when he did, he took hold of my shoulders and dragged me from his friend. He pushed me onto my back, and then Trevor Ridley saw his moment.

He leaped on me, as I had done to him. He was much bigger than I was, much stronger. He was heavy, too, his weight crushing down on my chest. He sat there, pinning my arms and looking down at me, then he hit me square on the nose.

Pain shot through my head. It started at the tip of my nose and spread out like clay, smothering my whole face and wrapping itself around me. I shouted out and struggled, writhing under him as he raised his hand to hit me again.

"Get off him!" I heard Kim shout, and she threw herself at Ridley, knocking him right off me. I scuttled away, getting to my feet in time to see Ridley stand and face Kim. Thornhill and Cummings grabbed my arms and waited for their leader's instructions.

"I'm not scared to punch a lass," Ridley said, advancing on Kim.

"Go on, then." She didn't step back. Instead, she raised her hands like a boxer.

I was afraid for her. *So* afraid.

"You think you're going to hit *me*?" Ridley said.

Kim answered by stepping forward and throwing a punch at Ridley's stomach, but he dodged her attack and came back with a counterpunch, hitting her hard in the chest, knocking her back with great force. She stumbled, reeling, twisting, putting out her hands to break her fall. She seemed to move in slow motion.

And as she fell, a gunshot cracked.

I turned to see Erik standing a few feet away, pointing his pistol at the sky. A trail of smoke wisped from the gun, snaking up into the air as Kim went down.

Her hands were on either side of her body when she hit the rock at the edge of the burn. She made no sound at all as her forehead thumped into the dark, wet stone. She just stopped moving.

Her whole body went limp and she slipped sideways to lie facedown in the water.

Ridley froze, looking across at Erik, who was shouting at them in German. Yelling like a maniac.

Kim lay with her legs on the bank, her face and shoulders in the water. Erik stood where he was, pistol raised.

I opened my mouth to shout her name, but nothing came out.

Cummings and Thornhill maintained their hold on me for a fraction of a second before I tore my hands away from them and ran to the burn, splashing into the water. I took hold of Kim's shoulders and turned her over. There was a cut on the right side of her forehead, swollen and angry, and there was blood. Her black hair floated in the water like wet feathers. Her eyes were closed.

I struggled to pull her from the burn, looking up at Trevor Ridley, but his focus was on Erik, and he was backing away, hands out. When Erik came forward again, still speaking in German, lowering the pistol to point it at them, Ridley and his friends turned and ran back into the woods.

OVER

Kim was too heavy for me. I tried and failed to lift her, angry with myself for being so weak. I sobbed and called her name, falling back in the burn as I lost my footing, getting up and trying again. And then Erik came and gently moved me to one side.

He picked Kim up from the water, grimacing from the pain in his foot, and carried her to the bank, where he laid her on her back. He put his hands on her chest and pushed down, repeating the movement a few times before Kim opened her eyes wide and took a deep breath. She stared, looking around in surprise, as if she didn't have any idea where she was.

Erik stroked her head and smiled.

"It's all right," I said.

"What happened?" she asked. Her voice was hoarse, as if she had a sore throat.

"You fell over," I said. "Dunched your head."

"Trevor . . ." she said.

"He's gone."

She closed her eyes.

"You're freezin'," I said, touching her face.

"Did they see Erik?" She spoke with her eyes closed and she sounded woozy, as if she was falling asleep.

"Aye. They saw 'im."

"Do they know who he is?"

"Prob'ly, aye."

"Then he needs to get away." Her words were quiet now, almost a whisper.

"What I need to do is get you somewhere warm. You need help. Come on."

I shook her and she opened her eyes, just a crack, but she didn't focus on me. Her eyes were rolling and when she closed them again, I could see the movement under her eyelids.

"She needs help," I said to Erik. "Help. Doctor."

Erik nodded. "Doctor."

He handed me his pistol, then put his hands under Kim's body and lifted her as if she were a princess. Her arms hung by her sides, her legs dangled as if all her muscles had relaxed.

"You need to get away," Kim said to Erik. "Get away." But we ignored her, and I crossed the burn and began walking through the woods. Erik limped behind me, carrying Kim in his arms.

Our progress was slow despite the urgency. Erik was weak from everything that had happened to him, and I tried to help as much as I could, but Kim was too heavy for me to carry. We struggled to take her under the fence without hurting her, and together we climbed the hill.

Every few seconds I looked at Kim's face, putting my hand to her chest to check she was still breathing. Erik hobbled and twisted his face in pain as he carried her, but not once did he put her down or stop to rest. He breathed heavily as we climbed the hill, and there was sweat on his forehead, running down into his eyes.

A gentle breeze slipped over the crest of the hill, cooling me as I looked down at Hawthorn Lodge.

It hadn't been more than ten minutes since Erik fired the gun, but already an army truck had stopped in the lane and soldiers were heading across the field in our direction. Five or six of them, with their rifles pointed toward us. There were others by the vehicle, one of them leaning on the hood, sighting along the barrel of his rifle, but still Erik didn't hesitate. He limped on, holding Kim in his arms.

Behind the truck, Mr. Bennett was standing one pace ahead of Mam, holding his hand back to stop her from coming to us. Trevor Ridley and his gang were there, too, looking on with excitement.

Above, the sun shone in a blue sky peppered with only a few wisps of cloud.

The soldiers advanced, calling out when they were close to us, telling us to halt. But we ignored them and kept on, coming closer and closer, stopping only when we were just a few feet from them. It was Lieutenant Whatshisname, the one who had come into our kitchen that day. Sergeant Wilkes was beside him, rifle raised.

"We got 'im," he was saying. "We should shoot 'im now. They're sneaky, these Jerries."

The lieutenant held up his left hand to silence Sergeant Wilkes. In his right, he clutched a revolver, pointed at Erik.

"You all right, young man?" he asked me. "We heard shooting. Did *he* do this? Is this the German?"

"Course it was 'im," said the sergeant, still aiming his rifle at Erik. "He's dangerous. Don't trust 'im. Look, he's hurt that lass." Beside and behind him, the other soldiers bristled like dogs expecting a fight.

"That's 'im!" Trevor Ridley shouted. "That's the German! He tried to shoot us! *He* did it! Get 'im! Shoot 'im!"

"No," I said, coming forward. "No. It wasn't 'im. He's just tryin' to help."

The lieutenant narrowed his eyes. "Trying to *help*?"

"It was them lads," I said, pointing. "They're the ones what pushed her in the burn. She banged her head and now she needs help. It was *them* what did this. Erik's tryin' to help."

"Erik?"

"That's his name."

"The German?" He lowered his pistol a little.

"Aye," I said. "He's a good man. He's our friend."

And Erik stepped forward, lifting out his arms. His face was contorted with the strain of holding Kim, but he stayed like that until the lieutenant lowered his pistol completely and spoke again.

"Wilkes, take the girl."

"But, sir —"

"Take the girl."

"What about the Jerry? Do you want me to secure 'im or —"

"Take the girl, man; do it quickly. That's an *order*."

"Sir." Sergeant Wilkes came forward, slinging his rifle over his shoulder. He took Kim from Erik and stepped back.

"Get her down to the doctor, right away."

"Maybe one of the others should —"

"*Now*, Sergeant."

"Sir." Sergeant Wilkes turned and hurried back to the truck.

Then it was my turn to step forward. I took Erik's pistol from my waistband and held it out to the lieutenant. "He's surrenderin'," I said. "You can't shoot 'im."

"Shoot him?"

"I know you want to, but I won't let you," I said. "You can't. He's not so different from us, you know."

The lieutenant took the pistol from me. "No one's shooting anyone, son. We don't shoot prisoners who come quietly. Not in this king's army."

I looked over at Sergeant Wilkes laying Kim on the grass and Doctor Jacobs coming to her side. "Not even him?" I said. "The sergeant?"

"Not anyone. We're not barbarians, son."

"Promise? On your life?"

He saluted. "I promise." Then he turned and gestured to the other soldiers, and two of them came forward to take their prisoner. But when the first of them reached out to grab Erik's arm, the German airman pulled away and took a step toward me.

"Halt!" shouted the lieutenant as he raised his pistol and, behind him, rifles rattled as the soldiers bristled and weapons were pointed.

But Erik ignored them as he stood straight, looked me in the eye, and extended his hand.

"Stand down," the lieutenant said to his men. "It's all right."

I reached out with my own and let Erik close his fingers around mine in a handshake.

"Freund," he said. "Friend."

"Friend." I nodded.

And then the soldiers took his arms and pulled him away, breaking his grip, unbalancing him and dragging him on his heels until he found his footing. They walked him to the back of the truck and ushered him inside.

As he stepped up, my friend Erik looked back at me. He nodded once and smiled. Then the soldiers closed the door, and he was gone.

KIM

Kim and I didn't get into trouble for what we'd done. I think people were too concerned for Kim's well-being, and felt too sorry for me and Mam. Everybody knew about the telegram.

In the village, a few days after Erik was taken away from us, I saw the lieutenant — the one who promised me Erik wouldn't be shot — and I asked him what had happened to my friend. All he said was that he was in safe hands. They'd taken him to a camp where he would stay until the end of the war. I wanted to believe him, I really did, but he refused to tell me where the camp was and I couldn't help thinking they'd done something to him. All the talk I'd heard had been about what they were going to do when they caught the German soldier, so it was no wonder I thought the worst.

After that day, Kim had to stay in bed for almost a week and I wasn't allowed to visit her even once. I went to her aunt's house every day until she called the police and they sent a bobby round to Hawthorn Lodge to warn me off. Mam gave him a cup of tea and a biscuit and listened to what he had to say, then she went round to Kim's aunt and told her she was a silly woman and that if she had any care for her niece she would let me see her. But even that didn't work.

When Kim was better, though, she used to sneak out and come to see me. Mam would always make a fuss over her, telling her what a good friend she was, and I think she even grew to love Kim as much as I did. She made Mam smile and, in her own way, she helped us both to deal with the news brought by the telegram.

Kim and I spent many afternoons in the woods that summer, repairing the damage Ridley and his friends had done to the pens. They were never used again, as far as I know, but I'm glad we fixed them all up just as if they were new. It would have made Dad proud, and I wished he'd had the chance to meet Kim. I'm sure he would have loved her, too.

Kim remained my best friend for the next few years. When her aunt found out about our continuing friendship, she threatened to send her back to Newcastle, but she didn't ever carry out that threat. Eventually she settled to the idea of us being friends, and by the last years of the war, she even allowed me to set foot in her home once or twice.

We were both sixteen years old when Kim moved back to Newcastle, and I remember it as clearly as I remember the day she fell into the burn and almost died. She had changed a lot by then. She was still tough, and she was still an adventuress, but she was no longer afraid to put on a dress from time to time — something that pleased her aunt to no end.

She was wearing a dress the day she left. It was blue, and light because it was late summer and the day was warm. Her hair was longer then, almost to her shoulders, but it was still so black it was almost blue, and the sun shone on it so that when I hugged her, she felt warm and I pressed my cheek against hers and wished I never had to let go.

When she waved from the window of the bus, I stood at the roadside and wondered what I was going to do without her.

Kim had once told me that she was going to be a nurse, like her mother, and knowing she was in Newcastle was always a small comfort to me, but when I heard the news that Kim had gone on to university at Oxford to become a doctor, I knew she was lost to me forever as life went on in our little village.

Mr. Bennett offered to marry Mam, and she turned him down a number of times, before finally agreeing. They were married after the war, and Mr. Bennett made for a thoughtful husband who was always good to Mam. He never replaced Dad, and I don't think he ever tried to, but I think Dad would have been pleased to know that Mam had someone to look after her.

I kept on at school, finding a love for stories and writing, which is what I do now. I write. Perhaps it was all those adventures.

I sold my first story to a magazine when I was eighteen, and after my first book was published, there were others — stories that went on to be popular enough that people in our village still say, "He used to live here, you know — up at Hawthorn Lodge."

It was those stories that brought Kim back to me.

I never enjoy parties very much, there are always too many people and too much noise, but I had promised some friends I would go along. They knew someone who had read my books and wanted to meet me. So it was that I found myself surrounded by people I didn't know, with a glass of champagne in my hand, wishing I were somewhere else.

But when she cleared her throat and spoke my name, it was as if there was no one else in the room. Everything in the world had stopped except for us.

"Peter," she said.

"Kim."

When I turned around to meet her, she looked exactly as I'd imagined she would. And when she smiled, I knew I'd never lose her again.

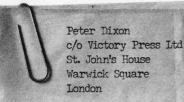

Peter Dixon
c/o Victory Press Ltd
St. John's House
Warwick Square
London

3rd November 1954

Dear Peter,

I have tried many times to write this letter, but it is
hard to know what to say. Maybe I can only say thank you for
being my friend when I was alone and afraid. It is many years
ago, but as if it happened yesterday.

I wanted to write to you for long time but when the
soldiers took me, they would not tell me what was the place
where you live called. They kept me in a camp that was not
far away I think. It was a place where I could smell the sea.
I was allowed to write letters to my family and after one
year, they let me work on a farm that I liked very much. The
people were kind to me like you and I learned to talk and
write some English (forgive me if it is not so good, but I try
hard). I should not have been afraid to be caught and I think
it was better for me in the camp than up in the air. When the
war was finished, I was sent home and now I am married and
living in Hamburg with my wife and baby boy Peter.

I think about you and Kim many times and wanted to write
a letter but did not know your address until someone sent me
your book called The Souvenir. I told them about you and they
remembered your name and our story that you tell in your book,
so I write to your publisher and hope you get this letter.

I hope you forgive me for the trouble I made for you and I
hope that Kim was all right after that day at the water. I am
very sad for what happen to your papa also. If he was like
you, he must have been a very brave man.

I have written my address so you can write to me if you get
this letter and I cross my fingers and wait to hear your news.

Thank you for everything.

Your very good friend,

Erik Friedmann

Erik Friedmann

ACKNOWLEDGMENTS

I'm not sure exactly where the seed of this book came from, but I do know that a lot of hard work and support from a great number of people has helped it to grow and put it in your hands. So thanks must go to my agent, Carolyn, who always tells me the truth, no matter how painful it might be. Thanks also to Barry, both Rachels, and all the fantastic staff at Chicken House who have welcomed me into the coop and worked so hard to make this book what it is. A nod and a knowing smile go to my wife and children, who are not only my first readers but have to put up with all my distant looks and forgetfulness. I really couldn't do it without them and I'm always thankful for their encouragement and understanding.

I'd also like to acknowledge all those who suffered in those dark years between 1939 and 1945.